This is a work of fiction and any resemblance to any person, living or dead, any place, events or occurrences, is purely coincidental. The characters and story lines are created from the author's imagination or are used fictitiously.

Wake To Dream: Copyright © 2016 by Lily White

Cover: Cover Me Darling

lily@lilywhitebooks.com
http://www.facebook.com/authorlilywhite
www.lilywhitebooks.com

I0634078

WAKE TO DREAM

A psychological thriller by Lily White

If you are interested in reading additional books by Lily White or would like to know when new books are being released, Lily White can be found on:

Facebook and

Twitter

Join the Mailing List!!!

If you are interested in receiving email updates regarding additional books by Lily White or would like to know when new books are announced or being released, join the mailing list via my website: Lilywhitebooks.com

Join the Facebook Fan Group!!!

If you are interested in receiving exclusive previews for upcoming novels, or to participate in giveaways, join the fan group for Lily White Books via my website: Lilywhitebooks.com.

Other Books by Lily White

Her Master's Courtesan
(Book 1 of the Masters Series)

Her Master's Teacher
(Book 2 of the Masters Series)

Target This

Hard Roads

Asylum

Author Note and Disclaimer:

This book is intended for entertainmen purposes solely. I have taken many liberties with the subject matter mentioned in the story and this book does not represent a clinical view or realistic interpretation of the psychological disorders mentioned and described.

TABLE OF CONTENTS

ONE

12:30 p.m.

Gray walls.

Black table.

Plastic, fake red roses.

Everything in place, the dust on the tables untouched by human fingers.

Nothing can change because if anything changes, the room is no longer real.

...drip...

"Alice? ... Ms. Beaumont? ... Alice Beaumont ..."

Fast enough to wrench the muscles in her neck, Alice's delicate and emaciated face shot up to lock eyes with Dr. Chance, fingers of anxious dread tracing along her spine. She found him to be sensitive and sweet, if not for his insistence to return her to places she'd rather remain buried.

"Is it my time, doctor?"

He nodded.

Gray walls.

White door.

Dark wood desk.

White and beige striped couch.

Still the same. Still safe.

...*drip*...

"How are you today, Alice? You appear...stressed." His voice was discordant, bits and pieces understandable, but the rest filtered by the white noise of air rushing from the vents in the ceiling.

"Are you taking your medications?"

"Yes," she nodded, her lips forming the word, but her voice so weak she wasn't certain she'd spoken.

"Good," he answered, his assured tone a bare whisper in her thoughts. "Please, sit down."

Five steps across the room, three steps over the soft, patterned carpet. Four cushions. A white throw draped loosely over the armrest.

Her jaw clenched, her head ticked sharply to the side. Her body had a mind of its own.

"I'm having the dreams again. They don't stop." Terror softened her voice before breaking it apart entirely. "They're relentless."

With a soothing voice to coddle the fragility of Alice's psyche, Dr. Chance asked, "Are the medications helping you sleep?"

Her head shook, a wild movement that felt impossibly fast. "I sleep too much."

Thick silence fell, only broken apart by the doctor's gentle voice. "You've never told me about the beginning, you know? All I have to help you are the dreams." Another suffocating moment of silence. "Tell me what happened in the beginning."

"Can it matter?"

Seconds passed, the clock ticking oddly from the wall. Why hadn't he answered?

Had she actually spoken?

A grumble sounded, her throat clearing away the lump of festering fear that clogged it. "Will the beginning help, doctor?"

"Yes."

Violent tremors shook her, the nightmare of *the beginning* a wash of pure horror across her thoughts. "She was taken."

"Who...was taken?"

"My sister. They took her. Those bastards took her." It was as if a finger had pressed the volume button, Alice's voice increasing until it was a feral screech on her lips. "They are hurting her! Don't you understand? We have to find her. I have to find her."

"I don't want to talk about the dreams today, Alice." Annoyance in the doctor's voice, determination to make her discuss the topic he wanted. "We're going to start from the beginning."

Hair slapped her face when she shook her head again. Alice's arms were a tight band wrapping her torso, her feet tapping out a rhythm too fast for any sane person. "I don't know if I can."

Suddenly soothing, the doctor's voice changed as fast as Alice's emotions, his patience vying against her insanity to wrestle her behavior under control. "Let's go back to the beginning, Alice, to before the day Delilah was taken. Maybe remembering where you came from will tell me more about where you are now."

"It's not pretty."

...drip...

"It's never pretty."

"Take me there," he insisted.

"You'll scream, Doc."

Silence. He always let silence hang there, a thick and obscene shroud that promised death. "I won't scream."

Hers was a smile that could only be achieved by the insane.

"They all scream."

TWO

It's often said that dreams are what you make of them. Alice believed the saying; she held onto that belief even as she approached the monstrosity of an old Victorian home covered and crumbling beneath the weight of a rampant, bright green vine.

Windows that filled the three-story height were dirty and broken. The double doors that had once been a grand entry were barely clinging on to their hinges. For fear she would tumble through the loose and decaying boards of the front steps, she tested her weight first before beginning the climb.

Gripping the tattered and worn handle of the briefcase her mother had bought her on the day she graduated college, she squared her shoulders and tilted her chin in feigned strength of mind.

I can do this, she thought to herself, a lie she'd adopted as her daily mantra, a lie that pushed away the nagging whispers that she'd been delegated the worst of the lot.

Her career, thus far, had never panned out. She kept pushing forward, changing directions as often as an impatient person changed lanes in heavy traffic. Regardless of the career type, she always ended up in the same place: a layperson learning the ropes while being assigned the impossible and daunting task.

Pulling her phone from her pocket, she dialed a number she hadn't yet memorized, checking the number twice before punching in the last few digits.

"What's wrong?" Her boss, Sarah, never had time for pleasantries.

"I think I have the wrong house," Alice explained. "You can't possibly expect me to sell this."

"Three story Victorian on the corner of Woods Boulevard and First Street?"

"Yes, that's where I am."

"Then you have the right one and you will sell it." An intelligent person would understand the veiled threat in Sarah's response. Silence ticked between them before, "I have faith in you. I couldn't put my finger on it when I first hired you, but I knew something was there. Impress me."

The door shoved open with a screech, a cloud of dust rolling through the fractured sunlight from within the house. Alice grimaced to find that the interior was as dilapidated as the exterior...if not more so.

"Oh, and one last thing," Sarah added, her voice more chipper now that Alice hadn't complained further, "there might be squatters, so be careful going in. Call me with your thoughts after you've performed a full evaluation."

The line went dead, along with Alice's dream of a new and successful career.

Wrinkling her nose against the thick stench of mildew and mold, the distinct sliver of something that had died but not yet fully rotted away, Alice placed a hesitant foot inside the structure.

"Hello?"

Her voice echoed back at her, a haunting repetition of her fear in the one single word.

Scrabbling feet of a rodent against wooden floors could be heard in response, but nothing indicating that a person was inside.

Muttering to herself, Alice gingerly moved about the entry room, her body angled oddly in order to peek into what was technically a formal dining room, if not for the tree that was growing up through the floor.

"There's no way," she muttered to herself, "unless the buyer has a bulldozer to take to the place."

Vibration from her purse pulled her attention to her phone, but she ignored it, opting instead to keep an open eye on the shadows of the house. Just because she received no response when she called out didn't necessarily mean no person was inside.

Creeping forward, she cringed each time the floor creaked beneath her feet, the sickening crunch of rotted wood threatening to drop her into the crawl space of the home with each step she took forward.

And to think she had two more floors to go.

Quitting this job would leave her in dire straights, but if this is what she had to look forward to, her life and wellbeing was worth more than the possibility of a commission from a sale.

Another vibration reminded her that someone had called or sent a message, but she ignored it again.

"Damn it, Alice. Get it together, woman."

Fishing around in the giant purse she wore crossed over her body, she fingered the can of mace she kept on her after leaving home and living alone. Never before had she used the aerosol weapon, but the peace of mind it afforded her helped her stumble a few more steps into the interior of the antique kitchen.

Definitely a tear down, she thought, somewhat dismayed that the owner of the house had allowed it to fall into poor shape. Glancing up, she admired the vaulted ceilings and carved wood crown molding. Such a shame that neglect had ruined what would have been valuable features.

Winding stairs took her up to the next level, bedrooms spaced out evenly through the dimly lit halls where light from the windows could barely penetrate. The floors groaned to take her weight, her fingers clenched tighter to the strap of her purse as she peeked into each room that she passed. Not as worn as the first floor, but still desiccated to the point where it couldn't be salvaged.

A service stairwell was hidden behind a door at the end of the hall, the hinges falling away from the frame entirely when Alice yanked it open. Laying the heavy partition on the floor, she spit out the dust that had covered her mouth and tongue. Her clothes were smeared with the same dust, patches of spider webs woven into the ancient brown dirt.

The third floor was nothing more than an attic converted into a spacious room. Possibly a bedroom at the time it was inhabitable, the vaulted roof arched down on the sides, and a small closet door was set off to the right.

Blankets and trash littered the floor, the smell of human excrement a thick irritation in her nose. Coughing in response to the abysmal state of the space, Alice was thankful that large windows allowed in enough light to let her know she was alone.

The only task left to do was investigate the closet. In old homes such as this one, doors led to peculiar places, and Alice was unable to ignore her curiosity as to where the three foot doorway led.

A secret passage wouldn't make the house more valuable, but it would lend a touch of mystery when the potential buyers arrived to inspect the property. If only she could block their view of everything except for the odd, small door.

Hunched over and dragging the weight of her briefcase and purse, Alice reached out with a trembling hand to pull at the knob, hopeful that the door would open and reveal something she could use to sell the place.

A gentle tug wasn't enough to loosen the door from the frame and she feared ripping it off entirely if she pulled much harder. Twisting the knob again, she pushed back her fear and...

"That door tends to stick when it hasn't been opened in a while."

She was a pile on the floor before the man who'd spoken could catch her fall. His strong hands wrapped her biceps, dragging her to her feet before she could flinch away from his touch.

"I didn't mean to startle you," he said, "I thought my presence would be helpful. You're the realtor, correct?"

Alice's suspicious eyes narrowed, her gaze settling on the sharp lines of the stranger's face. "How did you get up here without me hearing you? The entire floor is practically falling apart. You're not supposed to be here. This is private property."

Inching away from the frightened woman, the stranger held up his hands in placation. "My name is Maximilian Frost."

Recognition of the name pulled Alice from the terror she felt. "Your family owns the house."

His lip twitched in response to some unknown thought. "I find it hard to believe my family owns anything, especially when considering they're all six feet beneath the ground."

Her eyes narrowed more, and he smiled. "May they all rest in peace."

Shaking off the remnants of her shock, she kept her eyes trained on the man while her hands moved quickly to brush the dust and debris from her clothes. "My name is Alice Beaumont. And yes, I'm the realtor."

"It's a pleasure to meet you, Ms. Beaumont. Have you had an opportunity to walk the entire house?"

Unable to dislodge all of the filth from her white shirt, she sighed in resignation. It wouldn't please Sarah to know the buyer's first impression of the realty firm was a wet behind the ears agent with dirt covering her clothes. Perhaps the decrepit state of the home they were touring would distract them from Alice's state of dress. "Everything except for this closet. The door appears to be jammed tight."

Taking the time to study the man's face, Alice first noticed his strong jaw and cutting cheekbones that cast sharp lines of shadow across his cheek. Five o'clock shadow dusted his skin, the hue matching his obsidian hair. A straight nose sat above full lips.

But that was only half his face. The other half was hidden behind a tragic and disfiguring scar. Mottled and misshapen, his skin was obviously burned, bearing the evidence of attempted skin grafts that failed to completely cover the damage done. Even with the scar, he was a handsome man, character and the need to survive written into the imperfection of his skin.

Most startling of all were the clear blue eyes that stared back as observant of her as she was of him.

"I apologize for my reaction, Mr. Frost..."

"Max," he interrupted, not surprised in any way at the manner in which she studied his face. "I prefer to be called Max."

Stepping forward, he moved into the sunlight that barely broke through the filth laden windows. Alice sucked in a sharp breath, the scant bits of light illuminating the depth of the color of the man's eyes, the shock to her system a palpable thing.

"Max," she corrected herself, "are you able to open the door?"

Not fully a smile, the corners of his lips pulled up in amusement. "I am. Although, I have to ask: Are you sure you want it open?"

It was an odd question fitting of the odd house in which they were located. Nothing about this experience set Alice's heart at ease. "Of course, I'm sure," she lied, her determination to stay employed vying with the strong urge inside her to run from the house and never look back.

He smiled, "It's just that the closet is, most likely, filthy. Just like the rest of the house."

It wasn't until that moment that she noticed the clothes the strange man wore. They weren't shabby or out of style, just peculiar in their formality. Perhaps he was a businessman, so conditioned to dressing in a suit and tie that, even on the weekends, he couldn't find it in himself to dress in a simple t-shirt and jeans.

A black button down shirt stretched over his broad shoulders and chest, the wrinkle free material tucked into the trim waistband of his slate gray, linen pants. A black leather belt held the pants loose over his hips, a crimson tie tight around his neck. Not a speck of dust could be found on his clothes. Alice wasn't sure how, in this environment, the lack of dust was even possible.

She felt a nagging sense of inferiority in comparison to Max. Her income wasn't enough for her to dress well, and the white shirt and navy blue skirt she wore were sale items purchased at the local bargain store. At the time, she'd found them nice enough for the beginning of her new career, but not now that she stood in the presence of a man of obvious wealth and sophistication.

Her phone vibrated from her purse, the man's eyes dragged to the bag by the noise. "Do you need to answer that?"

Her lips fell apart on an answer that she couldn't easily voice. Shaking her head after a few awkward seconds, she forced the answer from her tongue. "No. I'll get to it when I'm done here."

He grinned in response. "Very well. If you'll allow me to squeeze around you, I'll happily open the door."

Due to the slope of the roof, two people couldn't stand next to the door at the same time unless one was willing to be on hands and knees. Not willing to stoop in front of a man she barely knew, Alice politely moved aside to allow him closer to the jammed partition.

The antique handle gave out a deafening clang when Max finally dislodged the door. Dust wafted out, just like every other room in the house. Shadows and cobwebs filled the interior, a single bulb hanging down, swinging slowly as if caught in some imaginary breeze.

"Can you turn on the light?" Fear laced her voice.

Reaching inside, he pulled the switch. The bulb failed to fire to life. "I'm afraid not," he said, moving away from the door so that he could stand upright and brush the dust from his clothes. His eyes locked to hers. "You're welcome to take a look."

Caught in his hypnotic gaze, she fought to find her voice within the thick blanket of attraction that wrapped her. Barely a whisper, she finally responded, "Yes. Thank you."

Bending down, she inched forward beneath the slope of the ceiling, her head moving inside to look at the closet, when she felt the soft touch of Max' hand to her back, the contact startling in its familiarity.

Her phone vibrated again.

THREE

Gray walls.

Black table.

Plastic, fake red roses.

Still the same.

"Are you ready, Alice? As usual, you're right on time."

"Yes, doctor."

White door.

Dark wood desk.

White and beige striped couch.

Still safe.

"Take a seat," the doctor requested, "I'd like to begin the session discussing what you told me last time we met."

Although her body felt more under control than it had the last time she'd met with Dr. Chance, time still moved sluggishly, every small movement, or the slightest sound, stretched out far too long. Alice felt like she was working against some invisible force, a tension pushing against her uncomfortably as she lowered herself onto the couch.

"You look better," the doctor observed. "Your movements aren't as fitful as the last time we met." He waited for her to look up at him before commenting, "The medications must be working."

Shaking her head slightly, she tried to remember the last time she took the medications, but the past day was hidden beneath an opaque blanket, her pain and stress too much for her to remember events with any clarity. If he said the medications were working, she'd believe him, even though she couldn't recall anything before sitting in his waiting room.

"What did we talk about the last time I was here?" Even to her own ears, her voice sounded far off and broken.

A soothing balm against the chaos in her head, his words broke through the fog. "We discussed the beginning as I'd requested. Although, I'm somewhat confused by what you told me."

Alice forced her eyes to his, opening her mouth to answer, but then deciding against speaking at all.

Realizing she wouldn't respond, Doctor Chance added, "You told me about a house you were trying to sell. Do you remember?"

Blinking her eyes, she brought herself back to the present, shaking away dreams that still held her in their grasp. The visions would stop when she woke, but the terror and pain always followed, no matter what she did to escape.

...drip...

"I remember the house," she admitted.

"Why did you take me there? That house had nothing to do with your sister. Did it?"

Her head fell forward into her hands. "I don't know, exactly. It was the phone calls, I think."

"What about the phone calls, Alice?"

...drip...

Shaking her head, she attempted to dispel the thick clouds that lingered after she dreamed. The present was never so elusive as that moment, her struggle a losing fight to remain on track with the conversation.

"I think...I can't be sure because I don't specifically remember checking the phone, but I must have. They were telling me something, most likely that she was gone. I don't believe I needed the calls to tell me that. I already knew something was terribly wrong."

He was quiet for a moment, contemplative. "Explain it to me."

The last thing Alice wanted was to go back there...to that day. But if it would help her heal, if it would leave them with nothing but the dreams left to discuss, she'd indulge him.

"I felt scared the second I stepped foot into that house. It was a slithering thing at first, a tendril wrapping my spine."

She shivered, forcing herself to walk back into the run down house on the corner of First and Woods. "There was no reason to fear the house. It was only a neglected structure."

"But yet it terrified you?"

"It did," she recalled. "Looking back, it wasn't the house that frightened me, it was a feeling that something was amiss. Maybe it was a link I shared with my sister, the blood in her veins calling to mine. Maybe that's why the dreams began when they did."

A resigned sigh filtered into her thoughts, the doctor's voice finally pulling her attention back to him. "Your sister wasn't in the house."

"No. But she was taken when I was there. She had to be. Those calls..."

...drip...

The sound was beginning to irritate her. With cold, dead eyes she scanned the room, her head slowly twisting over her neck. A door was set off to the right that she'd not noticed before, closed so that she could only guess what lay beyond it. "Is that a bathroom?"

The doctor nodded. "Do you need to use it?"

...drip...

"No," she answered, "but you should fix the faucet."

Narrowed eyes studied her, questions obvious in his unspoken thoughts. "I'll take a look once your session is over."

Silence passed again, the reprieve from conversation a comforting thing. She knew it wouldn't last long.

"Before we discuss the dreams, I'd like to understand why you find them important. When did they start?"

"After." She waved her hand out in front of her, the movement jumpy and uncoordinated. It was as if she were trying to abbreviate everything that occurred between the phone calls and the dreams with the one vague answer.

"After what? Did you see your family after the phone calls? Did you go home?"

Agitation was rough against her skin. Anger built in her veins, an unsettling and inescapable pressure. "Does it matter?" She could only remember bits and pieces, fractured memories and images coming to her on the winds of a tempest storm.

"Do you really need to ask? What would you like to know about first? My mother screaming? My father drowning himself in a bottle of whiskey? Or about my younger brother rocking himself slowly on his bed? Will any of that help me find my sister?"

"No," was his curt, steadfast answer, "but it could help me find you. Isn't that the point of all of this? To help you?"

She glared at him, a feminine snort blowing from her before she declared, "You can't help me until I find her. It's that simple."

Without dignifying the statement, or acknowledging it so that it settled in her head as truth, he asked, "When did you see your family like that? So torn apart? When did you go home, Alice?"

"I don't know. Yesterday, today, back then. It could have been any of those times. If you want a specific date, I can't give it to you. It's all a jumble of chaos in my head, memories and thoughts scattered together with no order or reason."

She was crying, embarrassment rolling down her cheek on a single salty tear. Slapping at it, she knew the doctor saw the physical sign of her lack of control, but she hoped he wouldn't see it again.

"I'm not crazy, you know? I'm not. I just know things, dark things, sick things...really bad things. I know them, and I need your help to understand how to use them to save Delilah."

His eyes stared at her from behind thin, metal-framed glasses. His shoulders covered with the white jacket typical of doctors. In his lap was a clipboard and folder, the papers of which he flipped through after he released her from his inquisitive gaze.

"You told me you went to college. Was it for real estate?"

She laughed. "I thought you had a medical degree, Doc. You should know that you don't need traditional college for a real estate license."

"What did you study in college?"

Her head flinched to the left, a tic that she couldn't control when she was forced to remember information that was fleeting. "Neurology," she answered, the details springing back now that she'd forced herself to return to the past. "Cognitive neurology, specializing in sleep medicine."

Dropping the papers into his lap, the doctor sat back and studied Alice, more questions brewing behind his eyes. "And yet, you sold houses for a living?"

"Do you have a cigarette, Doc? I feel like I need one."

"Do you smoke?"

"No."

A shallow nod of his head, some decision made that he hadn't voiced. "You're looking for a distraction. I won't give it to you. Tell me about your education, Alice."

Glancing around the room, Alice spotted a box of tissues on the table by the couch. She hadn't noticed them before, but still took the opportunity to pull one from the box, her fingers working quickly to shred it.

In silence, the doctor watched her hands move over her lap, the thin sheet of tissue becoming confetti where she sat.

"Shred as many tissues as you like if it helps you relieve what you're feeling, but talk while doing so. Why did you go into neurology?"

"I had problems sleeping as a child. Night terrors. Sleepwalking." Her voice fell to a whisper, nightmares creeping back to her when she remembered those horrible nights.

Logically, she knew they were in the past, so far away that she shouldn't worry they'd return. "I wanted to understand."

"Understand the cause or -"

"I wanted to understand the nightmares, Doc. There has to be a reason for them, right? Like now?"

Scratching his chin, the doctor scribbled notes. "What you're talking about sounds more like the realm of psychology."

A burst of laughter escaped her throat, a chortle that surprised her as much as it made her cringe. Politics and polite behavior be damned.

"Psychologists are nothing more than glorified psychics."

Slamming a hand to her mouth, she attempted to catch words that flowed through her fingers like water. She wished to take them back, her eyes peering up at the man she'd just insulted and condemned.

An easy smile creased his lips despite the insult. "Explain."

Embarrassment was an acrid taste on her tongue. She hadn't meant to belittle his profession. Perhaps logic would ease the sting.

"Psychology, for the most part, is subjective. You ask me a question. I answer the question and explain what it makes me feel. Based on those answers, and my behavior, you calculate possible causes, and determine likely physical stressors that influence my behavior. And after that, you determine a treatment plan."

His eyes widened. "That's a thorough and well thought out response, Alice. I'm surprised."

Her head jerked to the side, her body reeling against her attempt to follow the logic of the conversation. Reality was no longer simple. Not when dreams continued to taunt her from within.

"Why?"

"Your response was linear and logical. That's atypical for you. But I'm confused as to your statement. You laid out a formula for my profession that is clinical in nature, yet you mock it as a psychic, and thus non-clinical, profession."

The tic in her neck was fierce, her hands working over the tissues she pulled from the box, one after the other, until they were nothing but scraps in her lap. Aggravation fought her ability to think clearly.

"Because it's subjective. You missed that part. The answers I give you could be lies. You base your diagnosis on lies."

Tapping the tip of his pen against the paper, he studied her. "But behavior doesn't lie, does it, Alice? Like you said, it's a factor in what I do."

Reality fragmented around her, the frustrating conversation slipping from her hold until she could no longer stay on topic.

The scraps of tissue fell to the floor when she answered, "I want to talk about the dreams."

A beat of silence, the clock ticking from the wall, the intervals of sound unevenly spaced. Had her mind shattered so much that even normal rhythm had been lost to her?

...drip...

"Fine. Let's talk about the dreams. We can come back to other topics at our next session."

He sighed.

"Tell me about the first dream, Alice. What do you remember?"

FOUR

It was disorienting, the ephemeral glow of fractured light, filthy windows lining the top of a room, her exposed skin practically frozen against a floor as cold as ice. Blinking open her eyes, she watched the barren walls morph and bend around her, the ability to focus on any one thing stolen by her confusion.

Where am I? Alice thought, metal links clanging together as she lifted an arm to push the hair from her face; bracelets slapping against each other over her wrists.

Damp and dirty, the room was unfamiliar. A destitute place with crumbling plaster walls and a sickening stench of mildew and filth. Everything was out of focus, not one object settling within its own perimeter lines.

Pure panic flooding her heart, she opened her mouth to scream. The sound tore at her ears as much as her throat, an echo of her fear encompassing her in a room she'd never seen before.

"Scream all you want. Nobody will hear you. Although, I prefer that you stop." Calm, cool, collected. Not a worry in the world. Not a trace of the visceral terror that flooded Alice's veins.

Flinching in response to the deep timbered voice that responded, her eyes searched the myriad of shadows, but saw nothing that would explain the presence of another breathing body in the room. She screamed again, her mind reverting to primal instincts, a victim made helpless by chains.

Her throat was hoarse and raw, the sound of her voice dying off into a ragged burst of uncontrolled breath.

"Are you done? Or will you continue going until you pass out?"

He was amused, the humor evident in his eerily calm voice.

"Who -"

"Stop talking," he demanded, cutting off her question before she could ask it.

"Please," she begged, "let me go. I won't -"

He laughed, the sound soft before he answered, "You know, it's always the same - in real life as well as in entertainment. It never ceases to amaze me how the same lines are used in movies: *Please let me go. I won't tell. I'll keep this a secret. They* never change the script, and even when it actually happens, people follow the same typical path. What do the victims expect to happen when they beg? That they'll be let go?

That the person who took them will respond: Oh sure, here, let me loosen those ties, and would you also like my name to take to the police? Perhaps a copy of my driver's license would be helpful?"

He paused, a resigned sigh filling the dark room. "I'm sorry, Alice, but that won't be happening this time. Save your breath."

He knew her, the use of her name a jarring realization. Changing course after gathering her wits and an odd bit of bravery, she said, "I can't see you. Where are you? At least show your face."

No response, no noise, nothing.

He stepped into view after a minute, but only so much that Alice could see his silhouette, a dark shadow in contrast to broken and dirt-filtered light.

"Is that what you want? To know your monster?"

Seeing him, knowing he was real and not an illusion cast by a frightened and disorganized mind, didn't help her in the slightest.

Unable to peel her eyes from the form of his body, she watched silently as he sat down in a chair she hadn't noticed before, the wood feet scraping against the cold, concrete floor.

"Where do we go from here, Alice?"

She didn't know. Her mouth opened again on her screams.

FIVE

12:30 p.m.

Gray walls.

Black table.

Plastic red roses.

"Good afternoon, Alice."

Still safe.

"Hello, doctor."

"Follow me into my office. We'll start where we left off last time."

Five steps across the room, three steps over the soft, patterned carpet. Four cushions. A white throw draped loosely over the armrest.

Still the same.

"We spoke of the first dream you had last time. Do you remember?"

Alice sat back against the cushions of the couch, her mind unsettled by the doctor's determination to start in again without giving her the breathing room that came with conversational pleasantries. "You just jumped right in there, didn't you, Doc? No *how are you*? No questions regarding my medications?"

He chuckled, although the smile on his lips didn't quite reach his blue eyes. "Would you remember taking them if I asked? Has your memory improved so much that you recall anything beyond my office walls?"

"There's nothing wrong with my memory." Spoken on a frustrated sigh, she couldn't hide the resentment in her words. "I remember every little sordid detail..."

"Of a dream?"

"Several," she quipped. A chill ran along her spine, exhaustion gripping at her heart and thoughts, every bone in her body sore for some unknown reason. Stress was the most likely culprit. No matter how hard she concentrated, she couldn't pinpoint any one certain trigger, it all blended together into a shapeless, filthy mass of memories and pain.

He studied her, his eyes taking in every detail, his mind recording every minuscule symptom in her behavior. "Have you had any restful sleep?"

Chortling at the ridiculous question, she gave him an answer that meant nothing. "Yes. No. Maybe a little. I don't know." Her eyes clenched shut, her voice dropping to barely a whisper. "I'm not sure it even really matters. I'll just wake up and discover that nothing has changed. She's still lost."

"And may always be." It was a quiet reminder.

As an afterthought, and perhaps to soften the blow, he added, "but I hope that isn't the case."

The tip of his pen tapped against his notepad. "You've studied neurology. You should know how important sleep is for the brain."

"I know..." Her mind went blank before she could finish the sentence. What, exactly, did she know? When it came to this? To the dreams? To the past and present that seemed to endlessly slide together into a mush of chaos and jumbled images?

There wasn't much she knew beyond the fact that reality was no longer a definite and tangible thing.

"Sleep is something I'm afraid of. It's something that is intended to refresh, but instead leaves me screaming in my head."

A single tap of his pen. "We should discuss something else. Your waking life, for instance. You told me you went home after your sister disappeared. What do you remember of that?"

Shaking the terror from her thoughts, she bunched up in her seat, her bent legs pulled tightly to her chest, caged by arms that were trembling. "Not much. I can't seem to settle my thoughts on anything, any one event. It's as if the memories have been shaken up and scattered, bits and pieces that come through the haze to slowly reveal themselves."

"Give me one. I don't need specifics such as date or time. Maybe if we record them all, we can put them in some proper order."

Thinking back, she pushed through the horrifying myriad of emotions and images, tugging at strands that led to specific thoughts until one in particular came to mind.

"The media is a bastard. Do you realize that? They glutton themselves on the cruelty of monsters; feed on the same fear and pain as the ones who directly cause it." She laughed, the sound more cynical than humorous. "And nine times out of ten, they're wrong."

Anger escaping her on a staggered breath, she lowered her forehead to her knees.

...drip...

"Tell me what you remember."

"I was forced to watch the news broadcasts about the abduction -"

"Forced?"

Looking at him, her eyes traced the worried line of his brow. "It's everywhere, you know? On every station. You can flip through the channels and get a different set of facts - all of them theories - none of them correct. Not really."

Ignoring the misdirection of her rambling, he led her back to the topic he wanted to discuss. "Who forced you?"

Swallowing past the knot of fear that clogged her throat proved difficult. For all the attempts, she gained nothing but aching fire in the sensitive, parched flesh. There was nothing left to do but give up and let the knot choke her, give up like she'd done so many times already in her life.

"Who, Alice?"

Their eyes met when she glanced at him from behind a tangled curtain of unwashed hair.

"Everybody."

SIX

"Would you like something to drink?"

Calm, collected, even kind, the voice broke through the sticky film of darkness across Alice's senses.

A dream. It was just a dream.

She wanted to refuse, but her throat was as gritty as coarse sandpaper. "Depends on what you're offering."

Her candor took the stranger by surprise, if his silence was any true indication of his reaction.

"Water," he answered after a span of silent seconds. There was no inflection in his voice, no anger or loss of control in response to Alice's behavior.

Nodding her head in acceptance of the water proved difficult. Alice was sluggish and uncoordinated. But the jostled movement had been enough.

Chair legs scraped against the floor, the rhythmic thud of shoes against the ground announcing the man's approach. The joints in his knees clicked when he knelt down in front of her, betraying either his age or the length of time he'd been sitting motionless in the chair.

With a face masked in shadow thick enough to conceal his features, he held a plastic bottle of water between them.

Alice's efforts of accepting the bottle were thwarted by a weakness in her arms, a remnant of whatever drug she'd been given.

"I would have sworn it would only take a few hours for you to recover." His head angled to the side, the length of his dark hair brushing his shoulder. "Apparently not."

"Max," she muttered.

His face was still concealed behind shadow, but she recognized the hair. She'd admired it when they met, but lost track until now.

How had she gotten here? Where was here? And why was he with her?

Reality crashed into the nightmare. Worlds colliding for no understood reason.

Maybe it wasn't a dream, after all.

"Are we in the Vic-" Her words felt scrambled, but she forced the question. "The Vic-" Shaking her head slowly, she had to get the question out. "The house I'm selling?"

"No," was his simple answer.

"Then where?" Her throat closed on the question, her body coming to life as the drugs eased off, but still revolting into spasms, the muscles learning how to function as they once had.

"You walked through a door, Alice."

Settling himself on the concrete at her feet, he studied her silently before adding, "and now you're here."

After uncapping the bottle, he grabbed her chin, sliding his thumb along her bottom lip before pulling her mouth open. The lip of the bottle met her mouth, tilting up to pour cool water over her tongue as he said, "Swallow."

Alice didn't trust the contents of the bottle, but the liquid slid down her throat anyway, a soothing balm against the burning flesh, and she swallowed fervently, greedily, until only a few drops were left.

Pulling it from her lips, Max recapped it and tossed it to the side, the plastic ricocheting off a wall that only existed in Alice's peripheral vision.

Her head fell back against a wall, a thick blanket of silence sliding between them until his smooth, deep voice broke it apart completely.

"I have something I'm going to show you." He paused, looking Alice over with a critical eye. "You can't walk. I'm going to carry you."

Terror should have filled her, but familiarity had bred acceptance. She knew this man. He'd presented as someone she'd easily converse with in a public setting. One that, despite the disfiguring scar, would be pulled into the fold of the respectable and admired.

This was not the type of monster that lurked in the shadowy realm of her dreams.

"Did I fall?"

It wasn't until her words echoed back to her from the walls of the empty, desolate room that she knew she'd spoken them aloud.

"No." A grunt escaped his lips, his strong body lifting her from the floor. Heat was thick across his skin, uncomfortably so.

Caged against what felt like cushioned steel, Alice's heart jackhammered beneath her ribs. Fear crept in, the threat of death seducing her into compliance despite her desire to fight his hold.

It's wrong...it's all wrong.

His steps were labored over the cement floor, his thick leather boots creaking with every small movement of his ankle; the sounds amplified by the pervasive moments of silence that came between.

Reaching a second level, Alice clenched her eyes shut against the onslaught of bright, white light that bathed the room. She opened her mouth to question him about where they were, but speech failed her, the words thick on the tip of her tongue.

As if sensing her struggle to fill the deafening silence, Max spoke, relieving her of that small part of her anxiety.

"I'll give you time to regain your strength. We'll need to discuss why you're here."

Kneeling down by a couch, Max dropped her weight on the cushions, keeping his eyes on her while busying his hands with something outside of Alice's field of view.

He stepped away after climbing back to his feet and crossed through into another room, disappearing from sight.

Widening her eyes and narrowing them again in a futile attempt to focus her vision, Alice curled up on the couch, her movements slow and delayed, but becoming stronger as time wore on. Minutes passed, each one returning to her some portion of her senses, some better functioning of her arms, head or legs.

The room was the same style as the Victorian she was selling, but rather than the state of decay of that house, this room was meticulously cared for, the wood gleaming in the light cast by ornate, overhead chandeliers. A warm glow bathed the room, a rainbow of muted colors glimmering from the sunlight shining through stained glass windows.

Elegant furniture was placed about the room, the types and colors of the textiles used blurring in her vision so much so that she couldn't quite make out the luxury of the interior design.

Eventually, Alice regained the ability to sit up. The room stopped spinning. Sound was no longer muffled and disjointed.

Panic set in when her mind cleared. Alice didn't recognize the room in which she was sitting, and there was a noticeable heaviness on her ankle. Logically, she knew better than to look down at that cold heaviness on her skin. Once she saw what she expected to see, she couldn't return to the belief that anything about this strange situation was normal.

However, every instinct in her, every knee jerk reaction, forced her head down and her eyes wide, terror coursing through her veins at the sight of light flashing off the dull, silver metal of the leg iron locked above her foot.

She screamed, her voice hoarse as a result of the drugs from which she was still recovering. Max entered the room, his footsteps measured, his expression horrifyingly neutral; he wasn't affected at all by her fear.

Her screams died off and he grinned.

"Welcome home, Alice."

SEVEN

12:30 p.m.

Gray walls.

Black table.

Plastic, fake red roses.

Everything in place.

"Alice? ... Ms. Beaumont? ... Alice Beaumont ..."

"Yes, Doctor."

Five steps across the room, three steps over the soft, patterned carpet. Four cushions. A white throw draped loosely over the armrest.

"That was quite a story you told me in our last session, Alice. What would you like to talk to me about today?"

She didn't remember sitting down, couldn't recall when the weight came off her feet, or when she crossed one leg over the other, tucking both beneath her.

"What?"

Her eyes sought out the doctor, his face concealed in shadow cast by the direction of the soft, ambient lighting in the room.

"You shared with me the dream you had about the owner of the house you were selling." He paused, tapping his pen against the pad of paper in his lap. Glancing up, he shook his head just barely.

"I have to admit I'm somewhat confused how the dream has anything to do with your sister...or your current *emotional* state."

Alice laughed. "Is that a nice way of calling me crazy?"

"No," he answered, his tone serious and devoid of the humor she'd attempted to interject into the conversation. "Are you feeling okay, Alice? You're more scattered than normal. I thought you were improving with the medication."

Alice was scattered, her thoughts like puzzle pieces tossed haphazardly about that would never again fit together. "The dream had everything to do with my sister," she argued, ignoring his attempt to draw the subject of their discussion away from the dreams. "Don't you see it, Doc? The phone call, and then -"

"Then what? The imagination is a finicky thing, Alice. I believe every mental process is tied together, conscious and subconscious. Perhaps if we can construct the pieces of your real life - if we can improve your waking memory - we can understand why your subconscious is flooding you with these images and ideas."

Twirling a strand of hair around her finger, her eyes locked on the skin turning white from lack of blood flow. "I like to think it's a psychic connection. Delilah is communicating with me. She's telling me what's happening to her."

With another tap of his pen, the doctor straightened his posture where he sat. His movement was sharp, dignified, but quiet so it wouldn't startle her. He leaned forward until she looked at him, but somehow still managed to keep his face obscured by shadow. "Like twin communication? Is Delilah your twin?"

A simple shrug was followed by Alice's weak voice. "Might as well have been, we look just alike."

"Are you Delilah? Are you making up this sibling in your head to protect yourself from something that frightens you?"

Her eyes shot to his face, tracing the cut of his jaw before moving up in an effort to see the features concealed by the lack of bright light. "That's ridiculous."

"You've never told me about your family. Nothing substantive, at least. I have theories about what is most likely occurring with you. Tell me about your family, about events that happened before the day your sister disappeared."

Ignoring his request, she laughed. "Theories." The word fell from her lips with disbelief weaved into the two syllables. "I have theories, too. You just don't want to hear about them."

"You have dreams."

Her body tensed, the movement a full shudder that ran through her bones. "What makes your theories more important than my dreams?"

He paused, the silence between them birthing other sounds in the room. The ticking of a clock. The sound of dripping water from that damn bathroom faucet.

"My theories are based in science. Your dreams -"

Mimicking his earlier words, Alice argued, "Science is a finicky thing, Doc." When he didn't respond, she admitted, "and if I were Delilah, I wouldn't be here."

"Where would you be?"

"Trapped in that damn house. Where else?"

His voice was no longer soft or soothing when he asked, "Are you saying you believe the owner of the house you were selling has taken your sister? Do you honestly believe that your dreams are so accurate that you know where she can be found?"

"No," she confessed. Shaking her head, she slapped away the strands of hair that fell in front of her eyes. "That's not what I'm saying." Her voice trailed off, reality shifting again to a point where she didn't know how much time had passed since she'd last spoken.

Breathing out a sigh, she acknowledged his accusations. "If you don't believe I have a sister, you can check the news. Her name was everywhere at one point in time."

"At what time?"

"I don't know," she admitted.

Two more taps of his pen and he relaxed against his seat, his attention fixed on her.

The tick of the clock filled the silence. The faucet continued to drip.

"If I listen to your dream this afternoon, do I have your agreement that you'll listen to my theories during our next session?"

She wasn't sure she could make that agreement. She never knew when the fog of confusion would swallow her whole. But what other choice did she have? She needed to understand the dreams, and the doctor was her only hope.

"I agree," she managed to lie.

A simple nod of his head. With his pen poised over paper to record and dissect the lurid details, the doctor gave her his rapt attention, waiting to explore her hidden and prophetic world.

EIGHT

A thin, black shirt did very little to disguise the fit body beneath. Shadows traced lines of corded muscle, the cloth stretched over shoulders too broad for such delicate fabric.

Dark linen pants wrapped around thin hips, traveling lower to bulge out over thick, solid thighs. Max's booted feet were set at shoulder width where he stood motionless and silent.

When he cocked his head to the side, the thick wave of his black hair dusted his shoulders, the obsidian depth of color drawing the eye to his face half marred by scarring that could only have been left by fire.

Even with the disfigurement, his features were captivating and haunted.

"I'm sorry it had to come to this."

Alice swallowed, the lump thick and sticky, barely sliding down her throat enough for her to speak through parched and cracked lips. "To what?"

Taking one step forward, he braced himself from moving closer, his eyes darting around the room before settling back on her face. Alice's thoughts were cloudy, perhaps lending to the odd feeling that he was fighting his desire to approach.

"The use of drugs is unfair and barbaric. I realize that. Technically, it's just as bad as a caveman knocking a woman over the head with a club." He paused, his facial features tightening as he winced as some unspoken thought. "But you wouldn't stop screaming. I just wanted it to be quiet, you know? Homes should be quiet."

The room came into focus, but light played in through the windows casting an ethereal glow. Dust motes sparkled in the diffuse streams of morning, amber illumination lending a hazy quality to the room.

I'm dreaming, she thought. *It's nothing more than my imagination.*

The thought helped ease the quivering fear in her heart. What was more: it gave her strength and a touch of bravery she believed impossible had this scene been true reality.

"You can't hurt me," she said, the statement matter of fact and without question.

Eyes narrowed in response to her words, he answered, "That's not my intent, but accidents happen." His tone was regretful. It piqued her curiosity, but not enough to question him.

"You're not real," she insisted. Attempting to sit up, she felt sluggish, but it wasn't the crippling boneless feeling from before. Her body ached, her tongue swollen and thick, but despite that, she found the ability to speak. "How can you hurt me when you don't exist?"

His head cocked to the side, his features focused in such a way that Alice wondered if he'd understood what she'd said. Were her words more garbled than she thought?

She didn't have to wonder long.

"I'm not a ghost, Alice. Not yet, at least." His steps were loud against the wood floor, his hand warm where it caressed her tear stained cheek. "Do you feel me? Am I cold?"

"Just a dream," she insisted.

He smiled. "In a way, yes. But not in this way."

Silence fell between them, the susurration of his skin sliding down her face as loud as a jet engine in her head.

"You're so beautiful. Just as I knew you would be. We'll get you dressed...get you ready for your new life. You'll shine, Alice. It'll be what you always wanted. An escape from the life that has done nothing but hurt you. Even in dreams, you could never escape."

But this was a dream. Was her conscious thought bleeding into her nightmares? Was she waking up while still remaining asleep?

Her brows pulled together, confusion saddling her until the air was ice against her skin. Glancing down, she ignored the way he stroked her hair, her breath hitching in her chest to find her body unclothed.

"You didn't suffer," he whispered. "Quite the opposite, in fact."

Tears burned her eyes, understanding weighing her down even more than the lasting effects of the drugs he claimed he'd used. "Did you...?" Sobs choked her voice, rendering her silent.

As if the explanation would excuse the abuse, he spoke to her softly. "You were so cold. I was trying to keep you warm. There was so much vomit that I couldn't clean it up, and then you were cold. If it means anything, I fought to resist. But you begged. As soon as I saw the mess you made of yourself, you begged."

An acrid smell hit her nose, stains on the cushion of the couch outlining where her upper body had once been. Vomit. It had to be. The scent of bile was distinct.

"You'll beg again," he promised. "But not now." His eyes found hers, the light sparkling in the depths of frozen blue. "Let's get you ready. I don't want you to be cold anymore."

Lifting her from the couch, he swung her towards an open door, the metallic clang of a falling leg iron slapping the wood at his feet. Alice faintly remembered the biting cold of the restraint circling her ankle, but the memory was distant and fading. He must have released her when she'd been unconscious.

Where was her fear? As a child, she woke drenched in sweat when the monsters came to toy with her. She'd screamed until her throat was torn, her limbs flailing even as her parents attempted to soothe her panic.

Nothing had consoled her in her youth, but perhaps experience, age, maturity, or exhaustion consoled her now. Was she screaming in the darkness of her bedroom without even knowing it?

"How do you know about my childhood?" It occurred to her finally that this man was intimately aware of her nightmares, but there was no reason for the knowledge. She hadn't told him since she'd woken, she didn't believe it was possible for her to have spoken while drugged.

His hands were warm against the skin of her thighs, the flesh of his palms callused and rough. When she'd first met him, she wouldn't have believed him the type for manual labor. But initial impressions can be wrong.

"I know a lot of things about you. Does the source really matter?"

As she pulled further from the effects of the drug she'd been given, her awareness of her nudity came more into focus. Beneath her ribs, her heart sped, the muscles of her body tightening with each lumbering step Max made through the maze like halls of an ornate and beautiful home. Queen Anne, she guessed, if the woodwork and other details she remembered of the style were accurate.

The walls were painted in brilliant jewel tones: emerald green morphing into sapphire blue, the intensity of purple emphasized by the stark white fabric of the furniture sporadically placed throughout.

Her eyes peeked inside the rooms they passed, her mind drifting aimlessly until led back to the conversation they were having. "The source matters," she muttered.

"Even if this is just a dream?" There was a teasing quality to his tone.

A dream. Yes. It was an explanation she could accept. The circumstances shed light on the details. Her capture, the trancelike state that refused to release her...her nudity, especially.

How many times had she found herself naked in some public setting? The dreamscapes breathed life into her anxieties and fears; into the insecurity she felt when reality snuck back to remind her that she was never good enough for the world.

It made sense that a figment of her imagination would share the same memories that made her who she was. He was tapped into her subconscious simply because he was created by it.

After climbing a flight of winding stairs, Max carried her into a spacious bedroom. Her eyes traced the lines of the arched ceilings, the rigid lines of heavy wood beams that seemingly supported the room.

Despite having carried Alice through the large house and up a flight of stairs that would have winded her had she climbed them herself, Max's heart rate wasn't racing against Alice's cheek where it was pressed tightly to his chest. His rate of breathing was even and unstrained. His strong arms didn't tremble in response to the weight of her body. He was unaffected, his physical prowess made more evident by his steady hold.

Placing her in a seat, he knelt down beside her, his hand reaching out to balance her against the high back chair.

"Are you ready?" he asked, his eyes alight with some emotion Alice couldn't name.

"For what?"

"Your new life. The life you've dreamed of having."

Shaking her head, she stared at him, confusion evident in her expression. "Never dreams. Only nightmares."

"Until this moment," he promised.

Alice wanted to believe him, but she knew she'd wake up to find herself alone in the darkness of her room.

Pushing up to his full height, Max strode across the room, crossing the distance in a few long strides. He disappeared into a large walk in closet, leaving Alice alone to gaze about the room.

What at first seemed an innocuous space, one filled with luxury and fine furnishings, came into focus.

The devil was in the details, it seemed.

Her breath caught at the sight of the chains that hung above the bed, the glint of light against metal striking fear into her heart and mind. Forcing her view from the chains, Alice scanned the span of white, plush carpet across the floor, her attention becoming fixed on the odd stain that spread out from the bathroom door. It was obvious that water had crept into this space from the stone tile, the gray muck color stained pink at the edges.

Her focus became acute, her mind spinning with jumbled questions when another stimulus drew her attention.

Sound blasted from another room, the astute voice of a news anchor happily chirping away as she relayed the gruesome events of the world. Had the sound been there the entire time? How had Alice not noticed?

...body...Beaumont...missing woman...

Her eyes widened, as did the ice blue eyes of the man staring down at her from his position at the closet door.

Her lips parted. "My sister," she mused, more to herself than to Max. She recognized the news broadcast, understood that it was a memory come to life within a dream.

With a yellow, flowing garment held tight in his hands, Max smiled.

"Do you understand now?"

NINE

12:30 p.m.

Gray walls.

White door.

Dark wood desk.

White and beige striped couch.

Still the same. Still safe.

"How are you today, Alice?"

She hesitated by the couch, her focus caught by a red throw draped over the armrest. Her feet fidgeted over the rug, her hands wringing over themselves as she pondered the atypical item.

"Alice? Please take a seat." A beat of silence before the doctor's voice became tinged with concern. "Alice? What's wrong?"

"It's red," she muttered, her eyes darting about the room to study the other details. Nothing else had changed, but the throw...it wasn't right.

It wasn't safe.

Panic blossomed in her chest, her breathing tight and arrhythmic. The edges of her vision blurred as the doctor moved around her to pick up and inspect the throw.

"Another patient was ill," he explained. "I grabbed this one from the closet and sent the other out to be laundered." From behind her, he asked, "It's just a blanket, Alice. Is this what has you so distressed?"

"Not the same. Not safe. Not..." She breathed in deeply when the splash of red was gone, her body jolting when the doctor's hands touched her shoulders.

"Sit down. Place your head between your knees and breathe."

Guiding her into the position he wanted, the doctor knelt by her side, his knees cracking as he bent his legs. "I didn't know the features of the room were so important to you, Alice. I apologize for the change. I wouldn't have done it if I'd known."

Tears streamed down her cheeks, the warm liquid cooling as it traced the path of her jaw. The salt taste on her lips made her cringe. The loss of control was startling, like falling back and losing whatever progress she'd made, if she'd made any at all.

"It's the only thing I remember. The room. The furniture. I can't recall anything beyond that, but I know it's where I'm supposed to be."

Sitting up, she locked her eyes to his. "I don't know why."

"Nothing. You remember nothing." Not exactly a question, but a statement of disbelief. "Do you know why you're here?"

Moving to his chair, the doctor took his usual place within shadow, the ambient light in the room highlighting the pad of paper he pulled from a side table to his lap. Cerulean blue plastic flashed beneath the light, the movement of his pen drawing Alice's focus until she became fixated.

"Alice?"

Pulled from her fascination, she lifted her head. "To remember the dreams. To find my sister."

"Do you remember the agreement we made at our last session?"

"He keeps asking me if I understand," she answered, evading his question. "I'm sure that means something. I know he's hinting that I'm on the right track."

The doctor breathed out heavily. "That wasn't my question."

Frustrated by the disappointment in his tone, Alice blurted out every excuse she knew for her behavior. "I only remember the room. I know I'm supposed to be here. It's the only way I can save her. But the walls, the door, the couch - that damn faucet - it's all I have, it lets me know where I'm supposed to -"

"Alice, stop." His voice was stern, his words shushing her as quickly as if he'd clapped his hand over her mouth. She paused, her breath hitching in her chest.

"I need you to focus when you're in this room. I need you to listen intently to the questions I ask." It was a verbal slap softened by a delicate and neutral voice.

Nodding her head, Alice dragged in a steadying breath. "I can focus," she promised more to herself than to him. "Losing control won't save Delilah, will it?"

He didn't answer immediately, instead he allowed the ticking clock in the room to count down the seconds before he would eventually break the silence. "No, Alice. Losing control won't help you save anybody."

Another beat of silence passed.

"The agreement we made at our last session was that I would listen to your dream if you would listen to my theories regarding your dreams at this session."

Alice looked up and sought his eyes within the shadows. "Theories. Yes, Doctor. I'll listen to your theories."

"Except, that's not what I want to discuss today. I hope you don't mind."

His sheepish tone pulled a smile from Alice's lips. "What would you like to discuss?"

"Your dream," he chuckled. "Specifically, the last one. We'll save my theories for our next session, but for now, I want to clarify some of the details you've given me."

All she could do was nod her head once.

"You've insisted that these dreams are a means of communication, that your sister is somehow telling you what's happening to her. And yet, the symbols, the characters and events, seem oddly out of place."

"How so?"

Tapping his pen against the pad of paper in his lap, the doctor didn't answer immediately. Alice knew he was in his head, searching and examining whatever information he'd determined wasn't in keeping with the purpose she knew her dreams carried.

A single tap more and his head snapped up, his eyes hidden behind the typical veil of shadow that consumed them. "Let's start with Max. From what you've told me, he was a man you met while selling your first house. He's been the main character, or symbol, in your dreams, yet you don't believe he is the same person who abducted your sister or contributed in some other way to her disappearance."

Alice retreated inward, searching and scrounging until she'd found the bleak memories he questioned. His recitation confused her. He'd blended her waking life with dreams. "I think that's correct. Yes. That must be what I told you."

"Why him? What significance does he have that ties him so intimately to your dreams?"

The tic in her neck returned, her body curling in on itself, tucking her tightly against the cushions as if the soft cage might protect her from her fears. Time passed slowly, or quickly, she wasn't sure which.

The wall clock ticked. The faucet dripped from an adjacent room.

Conflicting images flashed in her mind, a jumpy film reel that hadn't been tended so that the movement skipped from one scene to the next. When the answers came to her, she stilled in her seat, the explanation revealing itself and momentarily easing her confusion.

"He was there when I got the phone call. Perhaps I somehow linked the two? If dreams are a way for the mind to record memory, and if those two events - the call and my meeting Max - occurred at the same time, is it possible that the details became intertwined as my mind processed them in sleep?"

"Anything is possible," he replied, his tone distant, yet thoughtful.

With his observant gaze fixed on her, he smiled. "Good focus, by the way. Your response was more in line with your education. It's what I would expect of a person trained in neurology. Are you feeling better?"

"I'm more comfortable, yes."

Nodding his head, he answered, "That's excellent. We can't get to the bottom of these dreams unless you're following the conversations."

A brief pause before, "By your reasoning, Max has been introduced into these dreams because he was present for the phone calls you believe were the first notification that your sister was missing, correct?"

Struggling against the return of confusion that always clouded her mind in a thick fog, she gave one succinct nod of her head. "Yes."

Without missing a beat, he asked, "But how would you know that the call was the first time you learned of your sister's disappearance if you never answered the phone?"

Alice stared blankly at him, not sure how to respond or if she even knew the answer to what he'd asked.

Prodding her along, he explained, "From what I have in my notes, you kept dismissing the ringing phone, refusing to answer even once while you were in the house. What occurred after you left that day? Did you eventually answer that phone call?"

I must have, she thought, her mind dragging her back to moments she wished to have never witnessed. The violent moments, the volatile emotions raging within the house as her family fought.

Her father screamed and tore apart Alice and Delilah's bedroom, panic turning his skin red as he searched for something that Alice couldn't remember clearly.

But even worse than the screaming was the incessant whispers from her mother, the tormenting words that floated through the house reminding Alice to remain out of sight, to hide until her father's rage had calmed down.

The memories blurred and twisted together, her mind so confused she couldn't separate the past from the present, the present from a future that may or may not be.

How does a woman disappear?

Alice had asked the question so often that it became an anthem shifting reality into something insidious and shallow. Humans didn't just disappear. Objects went missing, pets and cars, but humans? It didn't make sense, not when the person gone had been a constant in her life.

Did she answer that phone call? She didn't remember. But logic told her she must have because she remembered being in her childhood home, tears streaming over her cheeks, her mind begging for a moment of peace amidst the screams and terrifying whispers.

Delilah's absence was the only thing Alice could remember that would have caused such horrible things.

"Yes. I think so," she responded, her tone sure even though her mind was anything but.

The doctor gave her a moment to reconsider before continuing forward in the conversation. When she didn't speak again, he leaned forward, the light still not penetrating the cloak of shadow that concealed his observant eyes.

"For now, we'll consider Max a character associated with the discovery of your sister's disappearance. I'm not convinced it makes sense, but lingering on that question isn't in our best interests at this time. Not if we intend to delve further."

Scanning the pages, he dragged a long, elegant finger down the length of his notepad, his head angling ever so slightly when some thought caught his attention. The movement drew Alice's eyes, something familiar causing her heart to beat harder.

Before she could pinpoint exactly what it was about his movement that captivated her, he glanced up. "I noticed, also, that Max' behavior is a little odd."

Alice chuckled, a single burst of laughter escaping her lips. "Besides the fact that he chained me up and stripped me naked? That's not standard for men, is it?"

He didn't laugh with her. "Actually, those acts are what I consider normal about the dreams."

Her lips parted as her jaw dropped. Pulling away from her shock at his statement, she said, "Explain."

He tapped his pen, a sound that used to annoy her, but was now as intrinsic to these sessions as the ticking clock or the incessant dripping of the bathroom faucet. Even now those drops of water announced the passage of time, loud and rhythmic against the silence of the softly illuminated room.

"Your sister has disappeared. She's been assumed abducted. Because she's a woman, the natural inclination is to believe that she's been imprisoned in some way, stripped naked for nefarious purposes. Perhaps rape, or perhaps the simple degradation of being forced to expose herself to a stranger." He paused, giving Alice time to interpret his words and contain the anger she was feeling in response to them.

"In truth, even men who are abducted can endure those forms of physical and psychological torture, but we, as a society, don't always jump to that conclusion as quickly as we would with a missing woman."

Finally understanding the intent of his statement, Alice leaned forward, the subtle movement allowing her to focus on his observations and thoughts.

"With that in mind, I find it odd that Max seemingly cares for you in the dreams. He apologizes for his actions, he admits what he's doing is wrong. Even more bizarre, he promises to improve your life, thus stripping you from issues you've suffered since you were a child."

"My sleep disorders," Alice agreed. "The nightmares that have always been with me."

The doctor nodded. "Precisely. And yet, in a previous session you claimed that the *bastards* that took your sister were in some way hurting her. How would you know? Surely, not by Max' behavior. So how?"

Alice pondered the question, the answer easily revealing itself. "Because I haven't told you all the dreams. You have to hear the entire story in order to understand."

"Then we'll continue to explore the story. Tell me your next dream, Alice, and I'll save my theories for another session."

TEN

Standing before the full-length mirror, Alice surveyed the garment she'd been instructed to wear. It wasn't her normal style, definitely not a color she considered flattering for her pale pinkish skin tone.

Canary yellow cotton covered her body, a simple dress that was fitted in the chest and waist, blossoming at the hips to flow over her legs. The material was tucked at the waist in such a way as to make the skirt appear full, as if crinoline pushed the skirt out, not fully belled, but close.

A demure neckline was adorned by a scalloped white collar, a set of pearls circling her neck threatening to choke her.

On her feet were a pair of modest white pumps, the heels only an inch off the ground, her legs covered by nude nylons.

From behind her, Max approached, his eyes surveying her clothed body, approval and satisfaction obvious behind the light blue color. His feet were heavy against the ground, his chest pressed up against Alice's back as his gaze met hers in the mirror.

Rubbing his large hands over her shoulders and down her arms, he leaned in to brush his lips across the shell of her ear, those same lips moving softly over her skin as he whispered.

"You look beautiful, Alice. So much more appropriate than what you were wearing before."

She shuddered beneath the heat of his breath. "I was naked before," she argued, rebellion a subtle note in her tone.

A soft kiss against her cheek, his chest vibrating with soft laughter against her back. "I meant before you sullied yourself. Such a dirty woman, Alice."

Anger crept through her veins, steeling her spine as the glint of metal chains hanging from a beam above the bed flashed within the mirror. "Who the fuck are you? What are you doing to me?"

Even she was surprised by the burst of sharp rage. The drugs no longer numbed her, and willful independence rushed back to the surface with such intensity it stilled her body after the words escaped her lips.

His fingers dug into the soft flesh of her shoulders, the edges of his nails cutting half moon circles into her skin from above the thin cotton sleeves. Max spun her towards him, the force of the movement throwing her off balance in both body and mind.

In a placid tone, one entirely devoid of the anger she herself was feeling, Max warned, "Don't curse at me, Alice. *Ladies* don't use such foul language."

His hand slid up her shoulder, the pressure from his fingers lingering on her skin as he traced the line of her jaw. He wrapped his hand over her mouth before squeezing. Her lips pushed out, her cheeks concaved and burning beneath the strength of his grip.

Alice tried to pull away, but his grip was too tight, too strong for her to do anything more than shake her head as helpless as a horse attempting to escape its bridle. Tears stung her eyes as Max pressed her against the cool surface of the mirror, her neck angling awkwardly until the back of her head rested against the reflective glass.

Leering down at her with calm precision in his gaze, Max allowed the silence between them to become deafening, dangerous, devoid of emotion or censure. Alice would have preferred his anger or rage - anything beyond the terrifying silence - because it was the lack of emotion within him that made his thoughts completely imperceptible, his next move completely unknown.

Trapped between Max' body and the mirror, Alice was reduced to a timid creature by nothing more than the vice-like grip of Max' steady hand. His grip wasn't so painful that it forced her to scream, but it wasn't gentle either. Rough, uncomfortably tight, forcing the tender skin of her inside cheek to grate against get her teeth: his hold was a warning.

"I don't want to harm you," he explained, a hushed tone to his voice that hinted at regret - or possibly, a veiled confession. "I won't harm you. But I will make you hurt."

A grimace broke Max' placid and controlled expression. His brows pulled together, but were relaxed again within the same breath. His eyes had darkened as well, but that, too, dissipated with such speed that Alice wondered if she'd only imagined the shadow that fell across his gaze.

"Listen to me. Obey me," he paused, the ice cold of his blue eyes fixed to her wide, terrified stare, "and I will give you the life you deserve."

His words repeated in Alice's head, defiance blossoming inside her at the softly spoken commands. What life could he give that she didn't already have?

Sure, her career hadn't always brought her satisfaction, and she couldn't sleep even one night without screaming, but there wasn't anything she wanted or needed that could be provided by another person. All her issues were within herself, problems and puzzles she alone would have to navigate and repair.

Fear had kept her from retreating inward to solve the problems she had; fear, and the paralyzing pain of having lost her only sister. Unless Max could return Delilah to her, unless he could piece together her family that had been shattered on the day Delilah disappeared, there was nothing this man could do for her that would improve the life she'd been given.

Their eyes remained locked as Max released his grip over her mouth, his gaze searching her face, his knuckles softly brushing over the red, raw marks across her cheeks. A nagging thought whispered along Alice's senses, a theory that begged to be spoken.

"You have my sister," Alice guessed, her voice gritty with panic, but hopeful that she'd discovered the answer to a question that had plagued her for so long. "You have Delilah."

His head cocked to the right, his eyes flashing with hidden knowledge and obvious amusement. "No, Alice, I have you."

Terror flooded her veins, a loss of control overtaking her and forcing a violent tremor through her body. Tears stung her eyes and reality spun around her. "Let me go," she begged.

"I'm afraid I can't do that," he answered, his body leaning down until his mouth brushed her ear, his breath a blanket of heat against her neck. "I'll never let you go."

Straightening his posture so that he towered over her trembling and terrified form, he added, "And you won't want to go. Not after I've transformed you."

Casting his eyes towards the hallway, he instructed, "Come with me downstairs. I've much to show you."

Struck by the antiquated phrasing he'd used, Alice stared at him wide eyed. The tone of his voice had been so dignified, his cadence regal. He was a man who had come from wealth and privilege, every facet about him made that one fact painfully obvious.

Max' hand slid down her arm, his fingers finding and entangling with hers. She didn't bother struggling to break free, she already knew the crippling strength of his grip. If he were to squeeze her fingers as tight as he had her cheeks, it was likely the bones would be broken.

Crossing through the bedroom door, Alice again noticed the sound of the television in another room. The announcer had moved on from the morbid news broadcast regarding the disappearance of her sister and was now introducing another person to discuss the mundane details of the weather. The easy change in topic, and the cheerful quality to the anchor's voice, sickened Alice because it took away from the reverence that should have been paid to the news that a woman was missing.

After being led through a maze of dimly lit halls, she squinted against the harsh light of the grand stairwell. Small crystal chandeliers were hung so that they followed the gentle curve of the stairs. The crystal above her head shimmered in a soft breeze, the same oddly cold breeze that ruffled Alice's hair and kissed goosebumps across her skin.

Shivering in response to the change in temperature as they descended the stairs, Alice crossed one arm over her chest for warmth, but didn't dare attempt to wrench her other hand from Max' grasp.

They reached the downstairs landing, her foot barely on the floor before Max jerked her in the direction of the kitchen. Sharp pain burst through Alice's tailbone and across her hips when Max forced her down onto a seat at the small breakfast table.

Lowering himself until he could glare at her at eye level, he grinned. More feral than friendly, the expression was alarming, especially for the way it deepened the lines of the scarring across Max' left cheek.

Slowly, methodically, his tone that of a patient adult speaking to a child, he said, "We're married, you and I. You are now my wife."

Stunned and confused by the odd statement, Alice narrowed her eyes, her brows pulled tightly together. "What?" she stammered. "What do you mean by that?" How she was able to get the words out, she wasn't sure. Her entire body was locked up, all except for the frantic hammering of her heart.

His placid expression never waivered, his calm demeanor and cool temperament at odds with the panic rising in Alice's throat. "Events have been set in motion," he explained, "lives merging and becoming dependent upon each other."

He paused, the breath of air he blew out between his lips ruffling the errant strands of wavy black hair that framed his face. "It's like I said upstairs, Alice: you will listen to me, you will obey me, and you will honor me."

"And if I don't?" she dared to ask, a note of barely contained rage hidden within her question.

Sculpted lips pulled apart into a feral grin, the expression not reaching his eyes except for a few faint lines that creased his cheeks. "Then I'll have to train you to do better."

Pushing up onto his feet, he broke their stare, his hands folding over themselves where he tucked them behind his back.

His booted steps ticked off his instructions as he paced in front of her, his tone calm and collected, a man who expected to be given everything he demanded.

"You will serve the functions of my wife while living in my house. You will cook. You will clean. You will greet me when I return from my errands outside of our home."

His heavy steps stopped, his body twisting in her direction while he delivered his last demand. "You will eventually perform other duties of a wife -"

Alice's gorge rose, a strangled cry falling from her lips at the implication of what would be expected - or forced - from her. Her thoughts went to the chains that hung above the upstairs bed, the strange stain on the otherwise pristine white carpet. Panic ratcheted inside her, each beat of her heart hard and swift as adrenaline poured into her veins.

"But, we are not there, yet."

His codicil statement did nothing to calm her heart. All she wanted was to go home, even if that home was forever locked in depressive chaos. She didn't want to be this man's wife. She didn't cook or clean - she wasn't willing to submit to whatever perverted *duties* he had planned for the time when they were *there*.

Her eyes searched the large chef's kitchen, her attention skimming past the gleam of stainless steel that contrasted sharply against the intricate woodwork of the Queen Anne home.

Under any other circumstance, she would have taken the time to admire the luxury of the skillful blending of modern and antique. She would have longed to live in a house such as this - if it wasn't for the psychopath who called it home. Under this circumstance, however, a situation so utterly strange that she questioned whether it could be real, she chose to forgo her admiration of the interior design in order to map in her head every exit she could possibly use to escape.

Following the line of her gaze, Max tilted his head and smiled. The gesture was becoming commonplace to him, a curious behavior that made him uniquely bizarre.

"If you're looking for a way out, you won't find one." Inching closer to her, he explained, "Every window is barred and there is only one door that leads outside, a door to which only I have the key." His smile stretched over his cheeks, the scarring on one side becoming more pronounced as amusement shone in his eyes.

"Although it would have been entertaining watching you run about trying to free yourself, I thought it only fair that I warn you and save you the trouble." Darkness flashed in his eyes, his expression softening until it was neutral.

"You are now here, Alice. There is no other choice. There is no other place where you can exist any longer."

ELEVEN

12:30 p.m.

"Alice? ... Ms. Beaumont? ... Alice Beaumont ..."

"Yes, Doctor."

Five steps across the room, three steps over the soft, patterned carpet. Four cushions. A white throw draped loosely over the armrest.

Alice lowered herself to sit on the couch, clutched a pillow to her chest, and raised her eyes to look at the doctor.

The glint of his metal eyeglass frames perfectly outlined the shadowed space of his eyes. Another shadow cut across his cheeks, a hollow space formed beneath the perfect and high cheekbones. His skin appeared rough with stubble, his full lips smiled kindly.

"How are you today, Alice? I hope the change in medications has helped you remember your day to day activities better."

Her head ticked to the side, a muscle spasm aching beneath the space where her neck met her shoulder. "You changed the medications?"

The kind smile dropped into a frown. "That answers my question," he mumbled.

Thought held him silent for five rhythmic ticks of the wall clock before he continued with the discussion. "You know, your condition is rather unusual. It makes me want to consult with you due to your expertise as a neurologist. That is, if you think you still have the ability to recall your training in that field."

At the mention of her education - a subject that was safe because it took her back to *before,* Alice's concentration perked up. Her mind suddenly sharp and without the confusing numbness that clouded her thoughts, she asked, "What would you like to know?"

"If I told you I had a patient who experienced bouts of probable amnesia that weren't particular to a specific past time period, to a specific event, or ongoing anterograde, what would you suspect was the likely cause?"

Pouring over the knowledge she'd gained in school, her hospital residency and later rotations, she pieced together the objective facts any neurologist would want to know before answering such a question.

"I would first wonder if there was a head trauma of some sort: an accident maybe, some type of impact or fall. If there was none, I would consider medical emergencies, a stroke perhaps, some type of bleeding or swelling in the brain, possibly a tumor. Beyond those causes there could be an illness, dementia, the beginning stages of Alzheimer's, or maybe even infection."

"And if none of those existed? If the patient were completely healthy and unharmed?"

She laughed, "Then I would defer to your expertise as a psychologist."

He grinned, the low light in the room touching the soft tilted corners of his full mouth. "Why are you here, Alice?"

Her breath caught in her chest, uncertainty creeping along her spine, her nerves tingling cold where it touched. "To talk about the dreams. To save Delilah." She hated that her response sounded more like a question, a query sent out in search of some meaningful confirmation and agreement.

Drawing her legs up onto the cushion of the couch, Alice curled over herself, shrinking into a tight ball that she knew couldn't protect her from wherever the doctor was going with this conversation. Even knowing the position she held wouldn't soften the blow of whatever truth he thought he knew, it comforted her still.

"Can you think of any other possible reason you might be here, Alice? Anything that can explain the memory loss, the fact that you remember nothing outside this office? Is your reality hazy even now?"

She didn't like the soft quality of his voice. He was walking on eggshells while asking the question, attempting to awaken something inside her while being careful not to push her over the edge.

"I remember other things," she argued, indignation a sharp note to her tone.

His pen tapped against his pad, the papers rustling as he flipped through seeking out the bits and pieces he'd recorded of their conversations. "Let's discuss your memory. In a clinical context. Perhaps your past and your education can help clue me in to facets and symptoms - causes - I may have missed."

Shaking her head, she retreated into a haze of emotional numbness. She didn't want to discuss her memory, it had nothing to do with why she was there. "We're wasting time, Doc. We're running out of time." The clock ticked twice before she added, "Delilah is running out of time."

"Time is of the essence, Alice, you have made no truer a statement than that. But I must admit, I don't believe Delilah exists."

Alice looked up, her eyes locking on the doctor, narrowing with the vehemence running through her blood in response to his statement.

How dare he question the existence of the one person he was supposed to help her find?

"And if she does exist, I don't believe she has anything to do with these dreams."

Anger became her strength, wrenching her from a comfortable, numbing haze and focusing her on the object of her outrage. The doctor had no right to question whether her sister ever lived. Alice knew she'd lived. She'd been held by Delilah. She'd laughed with her. She'd shared Delilah's elation during their highs in life, and during their lows, she'd shared her tears.

"You haven't let me finish," she argued, her muscles shaking as she straightened her posture on the couch. Swinging her legs down so that her feet slapped against the floor, she bent forward, her eyes locked to the doctor's face, her finger pointing at his chest. "You haven't heard all the dreams. How can you make such ridiculous accusations when you haven't heard the entire story?"

Satisfaction was in the subtle rise of the doctor's brow, amusement playing at the corners of his lips as he leaned forward to accept Alice's challenge.

"I was wondering what it would take to breath some life into you." His posture mimicked hers, his body settling back against his chair as she relaxed against the couch.

The faucet dripped. The clock ticked.

His voice distracted her from both when he finally said, "Prove to me she's real, Alice. Tell me how Delilah has anything to do with these dreams."

TWELVE

"Come back to me, my beautiful girl. Come back."

A low voice, silk over grit, broke into the blackness, the warmth of a single finger slid down the skin of Alice's cheek to run along the line of her jaw.

Blinking open her eyes, she brought her vision into focus, the scuffed, rounded tips of worn leather boots the first thing she saw.

Hands pressed against her shoulders, her body pushed against the uncomfortable wooden backrest of a chair.

"What happened?" she managed to ask, her tongue thick and her mouth parched dry. "Where am I?"

A deep toned laughed answered her, not boisterous and loud, but quiet and cruel. "You're home," the man said, his name slowly returning to her thoughts. "You hyperventilated and passed out."

Her eyes shot up to lock with his.

"Don't worry, my love, you were only out for a few seconds. I caught you before you fell forward out of the chair."

Max. The name came back to her. Understanding of the situation returned. A tremor ran through her bones, her empty stomach cramping as the rush of blood thundered in her aching skull.

Either oblivious to her crushing fear or apathetic of it, Max settled himself at her feet, his hands reaching out to grip around her ankles. "We were discussing your new life. I hadn't gotten far before you panicked."

His fingers slid up her calves, a delicate touch for a man that was twice her size.

"You have no reason to panic. You should be happy with what I have planned for you. There will be no struggle, no worries or concerns. Life will become magic as it should."

Releasing one leg, he reached up, his knuckles barely rubbing against her cheek before she flinched away from his touch. She couldn't move far before he extracted his hand. Rotating his clenched fist up, he released his fingers. Light flashed against a coin held in his palm, her eyes widening as a slight grin pulled at his lips.

"You had something behind your ear," he teased. "A simple trick, but only the beginning of all you can discover."

Alice wanted to retch. "I don't like tricks. I don't like magic. I want to go home."

His fist clenched over the coin. "You are home." His arm flew out, the coin a torpedo across the open room, pinging off the wall before tumbling over the tile floor. Alice watched as that coin seemingly spun over itself, seconds passing before it fell unceremoniously to its side.

By the time she drew her attention back to Max, he'd pushed himself up to his feet, glowering down at her from his full height of six foot four.

It was unknown to Alice why she chose that moment in particular to act out. Perhaps it was an instinct to survive, or anger towards this man for making decisions for her life without soliciting her permission or opinion. It could have been something as simple as a remnant of her teenage rebellion, still alive inside her despite the years she managed to grow and mature.

For whatever reason it was, her next actions came without clear thought, without logical analysis of what could, or could not, be accomplished with violence.

Shooting up from her chair, she took Max by surprise, easily running past him, struggling not to trip over heavy feet. Her balance was precarious, the movement of her legs and arms uncoordinated, but she kept going, refusing to stop for even a second to look back.

Noticeably absent was the sound of heavy steps behind her.

Ignoring the lack of pursuit, she ran to a window, jewel toned sunlight flooding her determined features as she cast aside the curtains to find the shadow of bars beyond the stained glass. Closely spaced and thick as her arm, even if Alice were to break the glass, those bars would prevent her escape.

Her gaze shot to a thick wood door. She didn't need to approach to understand that even if it led outside, it wouldn't be her path to freedom. Seated on the wood was a heavy deadbolt lock, the key missing, leaving an empty hole that mocked her captivity. Above the lock was a modern numerical keypad, a red light flashing that was at odds with the antique details of the house.

Spinning in place, she felt feral, an animal caged as it awaited slaughter. Her pulse pounded a frantic beat, sweat slipping down sticky skin as her eyes swept the room for anything that could be used as a weapon.

A lamp sat on a side table next to a white, tufted chaise lounge, the shade a beautiful and intricate piece of stained glass sitting atop a heavy iron base. Lunging for the lamp, she ripped the power cord from the wall before raising the weight of the lamp above her head and turning to find that Max was nowhere within view.

The house was deafening in its silence, her rushing blood a pulsing beat that flooded her ears as she took a tentative step towards the kitchen.

Where had he gone, and how had he moved without her being aware he'd left the room?

Alice's body stilled, her breath sputtering from her lips as she attempted to focus. Her gaze traveled the length of the room, peeking into the kitchen as she spun in place desperate to find the man who had dragged her into this nightmare.

Time ticked past, a grandfather clock chiming from a distant room, the cheerful melody taunting her with a sense of home and normalcy. After the clock struck noon, the house was returned to a sickening silence.

"Are you done yet?"

She spun on her heels at the sound of his voice, the lamp yanked from her trembling fingers before she could react. The shade shattered against the ground where it was tossed, Max' fingers gripping into her thick hair before she was ripped off her feet.

Her body crashed to the floor beside the shattered lamp, her palm cut open by the broken glass. The deep, dark crimson shade of blood caught her gaze just before her body was pulled up, turned and slapped back against the ground like a slab of meat. The trace amount of breath remaining in her lungs was forced out by the weight of Max' body crushing down on her own.

Straddling her stomach, Max held her shoulders to the ground, a placid mask of indifference on his face, his shoulder length, obsidian hair a wild frame around his head.

Alice bucked against him despite her grim understanding that she was helpless beneath him.

"Stop fighting me, Alice. There is nowhere you can go. You're only making things worse."

His controlled voice was in perfect contrast to Alice's panic. It angered her that he controlled himself as much as he controlled her. She wanted him enraged, wanted him losing that terrifying control so that he would make a mistake, so that he would err and give her the upper hand.

"Fuck you!" she screamed, spittle spraying from her lips onto his cheeks, her teeth gnashing against each other as she bucked and twisted in a futile effort to escape his hold.

Anger flashed behind his blue eyes, only a momentary weakness before he wrenched back the control she hated more than anything. The glimmer of his loss wasn't enough to satisfy her. She wanted the rate of his heart to match hers, wanted his sunkissed and scarred skin to match the fierce red mask of anger she wore.

He wouldn't give her the reaction she sought, she knew that, yet she craved it regardless.

"I've already told you there is no way out. Why do you waste your time trying? It makes no sense."

After brushing away a hot tear from her cheek, he ran the tip of his thumb along her jaw, a smile playing at his lips, widening with every burst of her struggle. When her body stilled, exhausted from the fight she never had the chance to win, he closed his eyes, opening them slowly to stare down at her from beneath thick black lashes.

"I think it's time I tell you something." His eyes scanned down surveying slowly the way her chest rose with erratic breath, the cold blue orbs pausing to focus on the pulse point in her throat. "But not like this. Not in this position. Can I trust you to behave if I let you up?"

Her jaw ticked, her teeth throbbing from how tightly she held them clenched. Her thoughts drifted then to a memory that until that moment had been dormant:

She was eight years old, her sister nine. They'd gone with their father to a convenience store for ice cream on a hot and humid summer day. Upon entering the store, both their young eyes were drawn to a headline on the front page of the local paper in a bin displayed at the front of the store. It was an image of a young woman, her hair long and blonde, her eyes wide with the hope of a bright future.

Beside that photo was another: the same woman, her body broken and beaten, left hanging from raised train tracks that cut through the sky and ran across the four lane highway that led out of town.

Things were different back then. The topic of sex was buried like the devil's sinful secret, but shock and gore, the horror of man's violence was put on display, a warning to the young about the evil that lurked in every shadowed corner.

Her father kneeled down behind them, a hand on the shoulder of each of his girls. His eyes scanned the article, a low whistle escaping his lips. "Well, would you look there. The poor woman made the wrong choice, it seems."

Ripping her eyes from the disturbing image, Alice glanced back at her father, a question written into her raised brows.

Pulling his large hand from her shoulder, he pointed to the text. "If you read there, you'll see she had a choice." Lowering his voice to a bare whisper, he explained, "It says that the girl had a gun pointed to her head in a public setting. The man must have told her to go with him or he'd shoot. Pretty standard stuff with criminals: the warning. Had she fought then, she might have lived, or at least she would have died quickly with a bullet in her head."

Turning, he looked each girl in the eye before continuing forward.

"The woman chose to go with the man. Most likely she was raped and beaten, only the Lord knows how many days that poor woman suffered. And look where she ended up."

He sighed, his head heavy with the weight of the violence staring them in the face. "I'll give you this piece of advice now: if you ever find yourself in her situation, you fight, even if it means you take a bullet for the struggle. Because the quick death will be a hell of a lot easier than whatever that sick bastard will do to you when he gets you away from that crowd and alone."

Alice promised herself then that she would fight, no matter the circumstances, no matter the risk, she would fight. Little did her father know that his words on that humid summer day had been prophetic, spoken to two small girls who would one day become women faced with making that same choice.

Delilah disappeared when she chose to go with whatever monster had taken her from her family and her life.

And, Alice, who'd developed a significant fear of those types of stories after that day, refused to make the same mistake.

If it was her life or the life Max had decided she would live, she would choose a quick death over the endless torture the following days and weeks could deliver.

Her body went limp beneath him, her mind focused on breaking his aggravating self-control.

Locking her eyes with his, she steadied her voice, delivering each word with the strength of her conviction. "Fuck you."

Another flash of anger. Another fleeting moment in which she'd broken through his calm demeanor to reveal the monster inside.

She was expecting rage. She was expecting fire. She was expecting his fist to rain down on her in beating, bone breaking blows.

What she got instead was the taunting, cold touch of his sardonic grin. His lips tilted at the corners. Shadow touched his face, adding an edge to the sharp line of his cheekbones. A strong jaw ticked on one side drawing Alice's attention to the mottled scars.

Gripping one hand into her hair, he pulled her head down tight against the ground. His other hand wrapped over her face, his fingers tightening against her cheeks, irritating the previous injury he'd caused.

"You will learn, Alice."

Max' weight was barely off her before he wrenched her body off the floor. Pain shot through her skull, her neck having snapped back from the force of his pull.

Dragged through the room by her hair, she grabbed his wrist. Her nails dug into his skin, her mouth opened on a scream.

Unfazed, Max tossed her onto a couch, a leg iron locking around her ankle as she reached up to press her hands against the searing pain in her scalp.

Once Alice's feet were secured, Max cuffed her wrists, overpowering her easily.

"If you can't behave on your own, I'll have to correct your behavior. I'd like to show you how."

He shot up onto his feet, pacing for several seconds before turning back towards her.

His low baritone voice was matter of fact. His words more perplexing than his behavior.

"Between the fifteenth and seventeenth centuries, English monarchs had a slight problem. The young prince specifically. You see, no king should be spanked or punished by anyone except for another king. However, the reigning king was often away. So what then do you do with the troublesome boy who would one day inherit the crown?"

Confusion muddied Alice's thoughts, the topic too bizarre.

"Why are you telling me this?" She winced, the movement of her jaw pulling at the raw skin on her scalp.

"Because it has everything to do with why you're going to obey me." Pacing again, he was careful to place the back of his heel against the tip of the other shoe. One after the other: his steps tempered, measured, controlled.

"When the young prince misbehaved, and the king was away, the court attendants had to be creative. How do you punish someone when they were untouchable?"

He looked up, locking his ice cold gaze to hers.

When she didn't answer, he said, "You use a proxy, Alice, a whipping boy. You find and punish someone so close to the prince that he still feels the pain even when it isn't his own body being abused."

Alice's mouth went dry, her jaw tight, her thoughts flooded by the confusion elicited by his cryptic statement.

Without another word, Max left the room, taking Alice by surprise. A keypad beeped in the distance, the pneumatic hiss of a heavy door whispering to Alice from across the space of the room.

Able to sit, she pulled her body up, her wrists still cuffed in her lap, her ankles bound to the leg irons attached to the foot of the couch.

From her position, she was unable to see through the doorway out of which Max had left, but she was able to hear the first notes of a strangled cry.

Forcing her focus outward, she listened. Each heavy, booted step was accompanied by the sound of something being dragged over the floor. A whimper, a moan - whispered pleas that mimicked the fear she felt inside.

The sounds of the steps grew louder, more pronounced as Max approached the room, a woman's cries piercing the quiet stillness of the house.

Alice's eyes widened, her head shaking a silent plea that what she saw wasn't real.

Entering the room, Max dragged a body behind him, moving to the center of the space before pulling the struggling woman up to her knees.

Time slowed.

The room spun.

Alice felt dizzy staring down at the woman at her feet.

"Do you recognize her, Alice? Do you understand now?"

His words were laced with venom, evil creeping out with each syllable spoken. In his assured tone was the knowledge that he'd won whatever game he was playing.

Alice knew the game didn't end here. It couldn't be that simple, that merciful.

No. This game was just beginning.

"Do you recognize her?" His voice was demanding, cynical, disturbed. It was the voice of a predator, of a man on edge, bloated with a sense of determination and power.

Alice flinched at the booming sound, the echo of pure menace that buoyed throughout the room.

Her breath held in her lungs, she studied the woman in front of her, her eyes looking past the sack that covered the woman's head, down farther to where the ends of long, stringy blonde hair fell limp beneath the dirty brown sack. Trembling at the feet of a monster, the woman was dressed identical to Alice, her body a touch thicker, her curves more feminine.

It was a body that Alice knew well.

Tears burned at the back of Alice's eyes, understanding slipping into the confusion, recognition stealing what little breath remained in her lungs.

She looked up at Max, locking terrified eyes to his, her voice stolen by the realization of what he planned to do.

A sick smile creased his sculpted lips, his gaze burning with anticipation and pride.

"Do you know why the whipping boy worked so well to control the prince, Alice?" A menacing grin touched by a soft voice. "Do you?"

The tears she'd fought fell down her cheeks; thick and hot they were ice cold by the time they reached and rolled along her trembling jaw.

"The whipping boy worked because he'd been raised with the prince. Because of their shared love and affection, each injury the boy received hurt the prince as well. Just as each injury this woman receives will be yours."

The room grew quiet, the weight of the situation crushing the rebellion remaining in Alice.

"Fight me again, and I'll hurt you. Forget to obey, dishonor me in any way, and this woman will pay your price."

He smiled, the gleam of his white teeth bright beneath the lights of the room.

"I promised I wouldn't harm you, Alice. But never forget I warned you that I do have ways to make you hurt."

THIRTEEN

12:30 p.m.

Gray walls.

Black table.

Plastic, fake red roses.

Everything in place.

"Alice? ... Ms. Beaumont? ... Alice Beaumont ...'"

"Yes, Doctor."

"It's your time. Are you ready?"

Nodding her head, she rose from her chair in the waiting room, the soft notes of classical music drawing her attention to a speaker at the top of the wall. She'd not noticed it before, nor the paintings of different landscapes that sat at equally spaced intervals beneath it. Black frames, simple so as not to distract from the beauty of the paintings themselves.

Five steps across the room, three steps over the soft, patterned carpet. Four cushions. A white throw draped loosely over the armrest.

Alice sat down.

Crossing one leg over the other, the doctor pulled his notepad from the side table to his left, placing it in his lap before clicking his pen and scribbling out a note Alice couldn't see.

His gaze shot up, his eyes hidden behind the shadow of the low lit room, the metallic frames of his glasses flashing beneath the scant bit of light that touched them.

"How are you today?"

"I think I'm better," she answered, curling her legs up against her body, her arms wrapping around her bent knees. "I'm tired. I feel empty." As an afterthought, she said, "But I think that's good."

The doctor regarded her closely, the clock ticking off the seconds he waited before asking, "Why would being empty be good?"

"Because I'm not heavy. The weight I've been carrying, it's absent." She paused, fighting desperately to gather her thoughts to herself, to make sense of what she wanted to say. "Not entirely, but I feel lighter. Does that make sense?"

He nodded, his pen scraping softly across the pad in his lap as he jotted his notes. "Your last session was a bit traumatic. The dream you described for me was much more violent than the others. Much more disturbing. Perhaps a weight was lifted simply to get that particular dream off your chest."

Alice gave him a sad smile. She'd barely begun to tell him the sequence of dreams and, already, he was concerned by the images in her head. "Did you see her? Do you understand now how Delilah fits in? Had I gotten that far?"

The dripping sound of the faucet filled the silent space between them, each drop punctuating the anxious tension building inside her.

"There was another woman in the dream you described. Do you believe that woman is your sister?"

Flipping through pages, he reached up to resettle his glasses on his nose. "From what you told me, she had some type of sack covering her head. The features you described were only the ends of her hair, the body type and the fact that she was dressed similar to you."

"She was dressed identical to me. The dress, the shoes: it was the same. But it wasn't her features that made me realize it was her. It was what he told me."

"He? As in Max?"

Alice flinched at the sound of the man's name. Even knowing the dreams were nothing more than illusion, that Max was nothing more than a symbol for the true monster that took her sister, Alice still experienced a visceral reaction to his name.

"Yes," she answered, her voice a haunted whisper, "Max."

"Was it that dream, in particular, that led you to believe that all the dreams are a message from your sister?"

Alice nodded. "I think I'm being shown what's happening to her. How she's being held. How she's being treated."

"How do you know it's her?"

"Because of what Max told me. He said that the proxy only worked because he'd been raised with the prince. If I'm the prince in that scenario, then the only person the proxy could be is Delilah." She was practically shaking by the time she finished her response, so angry that she had to explain every miniscule detail to make him understand.

Taking a calming breath, she counted off the seconds in her head, forcing her hands to stop trembling in an effort to regain control. "The features that I could see fit Delilah: the color of her hair, her body type. It all fit. Who else would it be?"

Not looking up from his notepad, the doctor asked, "Do you believe there's another woman being held with Delilah? That you've somehow stepped into the shoes of another missing person? Another victim?"

"No." Her response was immediate, absolutely certain in its tone. The strength of her voice surprised her. It had been so long since she'd been sure of anything. But this? This she was sure of. It was the reason she was here. It was the message she couldn't ignore.

"I think my role in the dreams is a fabrication of my mind, a fabrication intended so that the story makes sense. I'm an observer. But, there's something I'm missing. Something right there in front of me that I can't figure out."

"I think you're right. I think you are missing something."

Her eyes studied the doctor, his easy posture, his demeanor, the way he toyed with the pen in his hand as he waited for her to acknowledge his words.

"You believe me?" Her heart pulsed harder, an uneasy feeling in her stomach that, perhaps, she'd misinterpreted what he'd said.

He sighed, his face cast down at the notes in his lap, his pen ticking with agitation in his hand. "We should discuss your memory, Alice."

It wasn't an answer to her question; it was a deflection.

"What about my memory?"

"I'd like to discuss what you do and do not remember in your waking life."

Alice turned to lean against the armrest of the couch, purposefully diverting her eyes. She wasn't interested in her waking life. It didn't matter if Delilah wasn't part of it. Until her sister was found, until Alice learned what happened to her, she was perfectly fine with forgetting every detail of such a cruel and unfair existence.

"My memory is fine. The dreams -"

"I'm not here to help your sister, Alice."

Her eyes shot to his, a sore muscle in her neck wrenched by how quickly she'd turned her head. Alice had never heard his tone so sharp. He was frustrated, possibly angry. The shift in his temperament sliced through her.

"I'm here to help you."

Struck by the firmness in his voice, Alice resigned herself to the topic he wished to discuss. "Fine. Let's talk about my memory."

He stared at her, his pen tapping against his notepad before he admitted, "You'll be happy to know some of this has to do with the dreams. At least, in part."

When she didn't respond, he continued, his tone that of a doctor ignoring the disinterested attitude of his patient. "Have you suffered any traumatic head injuries in your life?"

"No," she responded quickly.

"And your memory of your past is complete enough for you to know this for a fact?"

Guilt rode her for being obstinate. The doctor was only trying to do his job, but she felt like time was escaping her due to these silly questions. They wouldn't save Delilah, therefore they held no importance to her.

"Except for the nightmares, I had a normal childhood. I never suffered any accidents or illnesses that would explain significant memory loss. Beyond the night terrors and other sleep issues, I was a normal, healthy person. At least until -" Her voice trailed off leaving a weighted silence where her words had once been.

"Until what, Alice?"

"Until that phone call," she admitted.

"The call you received at the house you were selling? The one about your sister's disappearance?"

"Yes," she breathed out. "That one."

The sound of the doctor flipping through the pages of his notes wasn't loud enough to distract from the annoying drip of the leaky bathroom faucet. Alice counted the drips, reaching three before the doctor's voice drew her attention back to the conversation.

"You seem to have excellent recall of the dreams. The details you're able to give me are much more consecutive, much more intricate than anything you've given me about your day to day life. In fact, it appears to me that even within the dreams, you're aware of events that occurred in previous dreams. Does any of that make sense to you?"

Alice grinned, the expression mocking an odd truth she'd lived with her entire life.

"I've always remembered my dreams...my nightmares. It was a large part of my problem as a child. I'd wake up screaming, and even though I didn't remember them immediately upon waking, I'd always return to them when I next went to sleep. It was as if waking up did nothing to dispel them, they always returned, the details never lost to me while I was sleeping." She paused, her eyes studying her hands as they worried the frayed hem of her shirt. "Being awake meant nothing. Real life was simply an intermission."

"You remembered an occurrence with your father and sister in your last dream, a conversation you had when you were a child about a murdered woman. Can you recall that conversation now?"

"Clearly," she answered. "It's like I told you, Doc. Those memories are still with me. It's everything *after* that's fuzzy." She barked out a humorless laugh. "But trauma will do that to a person, won't it?"

Conceding to her point, he answered, "Yes. Trauma can do that to a person." He tapped his pen once. "You mentioned the word *after*. What does it mean to you?"

"My life has been bisected by an event. There was my life with Delilah in it, and my life when she was gone. Before and after."

He studied her behind shadow, the low light in the room concealing his expression - his thoughts.

...drip...

"You ever going to fix that faucet, Doc?"

Ignoring the off topic question, he commented, "You know, the information you're giving me now makes sense, at least as it relates to some theories I have regarding your sleep disorders. I think they may tie into the dreams you're telling me."

She barked out another laugh. "The nightmares I had as a child were the disorder rearing its ugly head."

"What makes them different from the dreams you're having now? Stress can trigger sleep disorders, especially in people who have had them before."

Determined to make him understand, she struggled to remain on topic, to keep up with the flow of logical conversation. "Because if the dreams in my youth were the same as they are now, then I don't need to be seeking the help of a psychologist."

"Who's help would you need?"

"I don't know. A priest? Whoever deals with prophecy? The dreams now are a connection to my sister. The dreams back then? Well, if they were connected to someone, I didn't know it."

Silence passed between them, the doctor's mind sifting through the same muck that kept Alice constantly clouded in confusion. Giving it a voice didn't help Alice, and she wasn't positive the doctor would be much help either.

His words spoken slowly, he answered, "I'm not sure I believe in prophecy, Alice. Psychic connections and all that. I'm not even sure a church could help you."

"Well, you know what they say: Where science ends, God begins. Anything is worth a shot if it saves my sister."

He didn't acknowledge the remark, his focus persistent. "I think you might be on to something. You hadn't mentioned before that the sleep disorders came back after your sister's disappearance. That falls in line with what I know about them. Most people have them as children, but grow out of them. Is that what happened in your case?"

"They never stopped. Not fully. But they weren't as bad when I was a teen, or when I was in college. They were following the pattern that most doctors assumed they would. That's what made me believe that studying neurology could help. There had to be an explanation. I thought that, because I experienced them myself, I would have more insight while studying them. There's a difference. People who haven't gone through it can't understand, and all the theories out there about the whys and hows of them don't make sense. It's all speculation and conjecture. Of course, when I explained my theories, I was laughed out of the profession. Which is why I turned to other types of work. Everybody thought I was insane."

"What disorders, specifically, did you experience?"

"Night terrors, sleep walking, sleep paralysis. Name it, Doc, and I probably had it at one point or another."

Frustration made her body tense. The conversation wasn't helping her with the problem she was here to solve. "We're wasting time talking about this. The key to all of this is in the dreams. My sister is telling me where she is and what's happening to her and we're wasting time going over the same tired bullshit."

Her eyes shot to the doctor's face. "I want to talk about the next dream."

She expected him to argue, to continue on the path he'd chosen to discuss. Surprising her, he relented.

"Fine, Alice. We'll pick this back up in another session. Tell me about the next dream."

FOURTEEN

"I'm not a monster, Alice. Not entirely."

A handsome face came into focus as Max entered the room, Alice's eyes blinking away tears that had turned the edges red and raw, that had streaked the porcelain skin of her cheeks.

There was an air of dignity about him. The way he spoke, the way he walked with assured strides - long and powerful - before settling down into a leather chair opposite where she remained tethered to the couch. Despite the scar that belied some distant tragedy he'd endured, he carried himself with strength and authority, untouched by the ravages of a cruel world.

"She won't suffer, not if you prevent it."

Her gaze drifted to the doorway that led from the room they occupied. Beyond that threshold was her sister, tethered and bound, a rough textured sack covering her head.

"Where are you keeping her?"

Alice's thoughts returned to the cold, dark basement where she woke, the frigid cement floor that pressed against her skin and chilled her to the bone. Enough time stuck in that environment would make any person sick, both physically and mentally.

"She has a room of her own," he explained, his body leaning forward to grab a remote from the coffee table between them. "I've made it comfortable for her. As long as you behave, she will be cared for."

"Why are you doing this?" she asked, refusing to look back at him and meet his eyes.

A grandfather clocked chimed in the distance. When the last bell had tolled, he answered, "Does the why really matter? It won't change things. A better question would be what you can do to prevent the situation from becoming worse."

She looked at him then, saw the glimmer of amusement in his eyes to know that he had her trapped, a mouse left to run the labyrinth he'd laid out for her.

There was no fight left in Alice. It wasn't her life alone that hung precariously on the line.

Twisting to face the left side of the room, Max hit a button on the remote, a television screen coming to life that Alice wouldn't have noticed unless he'd drawn her attention to it. Hung on a wall, the black screen blended seamlessly with the interior decor, a dark space concealed simply because the decor around it sparkled and drew the eye.

Hitting another button, Max said nothing while he watched Alice, studying her reaction as she first recognized what had been revealed on the screen.

A closed circuit camera view of a small, well lit room revealed a woman sitting on a bed, her head concealed by the hood that covered it. Curled over herself, her shoulders shook on a sob, but the sound didn't carry through the speakers of the television.

It was the room where he kept her sister, Alice realized, a room that was in stark contrast to the person it held.

Delilah had never been feminine. Momma always said that even as an infant, Delilah had cried when she was forced to wear the frilly dresses most mothers loved to clothe their little girls. She'd scream and complain until the frocks were removed, much happier in her skin than in satin and lace. She never liked pink, she wouldn't be caught dead playing with dolls.

She was a tomboy through and through, much more suited for sports, climbing trees and splashing in mud puddles than for playing dress up and tea parties.

Alice was the opposite, her attention always drawn to pastels and sparkles. If not for the nightmares, she would have been her mother's perfect living doll.

Growing up, Alice had been the poster child for lace dresses and patent leather shoes. She'd love to wear bows in her hair and would cry if even a speck of dirt marred her clean skin. She'd been everything Delilah was not, but still loved her older sister for humoring her and sitting at the tea table anyway.

With those memories locked tightly within her thoughts, she was thrown even more off balance by the room Max had prepared.

Pink paint covered the walls above white chair rails that ran the room. Posters with kittens and rainbows were hung on each wall, a day bed pushed off to the side with a gold frame and white, frilly bed sheets. The carpet was pink shag that matched the paint, and dolls were scattered throughout the room on shelves and perched to appear lifelike on a large, overstuffed chair.

Clothed in the same yellow dress that Alice wore, Delilah herself resembled a doll, if not for the hood covering her face.

Alice felt sick, the contrast of the innocence of youth against the sinister truth of their captivity - of the wicked game this man was playing - perverting every happy memory she had growing up.

Hot summer days spent lingering in sunlight, the sticky mess popsicles would make when they melted too soon, endless hours splashing in community pools or riding the rope swing into the large lake that sat in the center of her small town: all of those things were now scarred and made dirty by the image of a woman bound, a hood covering her head concealing the tears she shed for her captivity.

Alice hated that room, hated Max for the twisted life he'd forced upon Delilah.

"You'll be able to see her at all times. There are televisions in every room, each one tuned in to the camera monitoring her. You'll see that she is safe and unharmed, as long as you behave."

"Is that supposed to appease me?" she asked, anger dripping from every word. "You're holding her like a damn animal. Can she even breathe beneath that hood?"

He grinned, unfazed by the vehemence in her voice. "If she falls over dead, then I'll assume she couldn't." He paused, smiling more broadly in response to Alice's obvious distress. "However, since that hasn't happened yet, I believe it's safe to assume she can breathe just fine."

Forcing herself to calm down, Alice struggled to keep from staring at the television, from being a silent observer to her sister's pain and fear. "What happens if I don't behave? Will you kill us both?"

He chuckled, the sound cynical and cruel. "Death would be too easy, Alice. Killing you would mean I'd have to start all over. If you'd like to find out what happens with bad behavior, you're welcome to step out of line. I promise that you won't like the results. It'll only take one time to break you completely."

He was so confident in his statement that it elicited in her a need to rage, a heady desire to spit in his face and wipe the sadistic grin from his lips. Fear held no place inside her, only the scathing heat of her fury.

Had it been her alone, she would have given him every reason to punish her, would have taunted and pushed him to a point of no control in the hope that death would become her escape. But what could be gained from disobedience? Nothing except being an accessory and witness to her older sister's torture.

Left with no choice, Alice resigned herself to fate. Her voice weak with easy defeat, she asked, "What do I have to do?"

He studied her, his fingers steepled at his lips, a brow arrogantly lifted. "I'm pleased to hear you finally ask the proper question."

Self-loathing filled her, distaste for the submission she gave.

Standing from his chair, Max approached the couch to kneel down beside her, his shoulders shaking from soft laughter when Alice leaned away from his body. Meeting her gaze only for a moment, he turned his attention to her legs. His hands were hot against her skin as he unlocked the leg irons, the touch almost too much to bear on skin rubbed raw by chains.

Leaving her hands cuffed in front of her, Max grabbed Alice's arm to lift her to her feet. She wanted to shake away his touch, wanted to claw and bite like a rabid animal caged. The instinct to fight was a quivering beast inside her, only silenced and stilled when her eyes focused on the television screen.

Delilah. Weak, bound, and on display. How long had he kept her and how much had he broken her already?

There had to be another choice, a different avenue where they both could come out of this intact. They would never escape unscarred, but there was a chance they could escape with enough strength to survive.

Led back to the kitchen, Alice was directed to a barstool. "Sit. I'll cook tonight..."

Max leaned down, his warm breath rolled across her cheek on a cynical, mocking whisper. "...but only because you've already been through so much."

A gentle squeeze of her shoulder and he walked away, placing the center island between them.

Moving about the kitchen with the ease of a master chef, Max laid out ingredients on the counter. Unconcerned with what Alice might do, he placed a butcher's cleaver between them. She eyed the cleaver, her bound hands balling into fists in an attempt to resist reaching for it. It was so close and all she had to do was grab it.

"Tempting, isn't it?"

He glanced back at her, an arrogant tilt to his full lips. Wavy hair, black as a raven, hung loosely over one side of his face and concealed his scar. Alice swallowed down a knot in her throat, hating herself for thinking she'd be attracted to him in a different situation.

"The cleaver," he pointed out, tilting his chin in its direction. "It would be so easy to just grab it. To swing it in my direction."

He turned towards her fully and met her stare. "To kill me?"

Disgust rolled through her. "I wouldn't do that," she lied.

He grinned, a dimple indenting his cheek, the mark made darker by the shade of black stubble along his skin. "You're not that easy, Alice. Don't lie."

Wrapping his long, elegant fingers over the handle of the cleaver he picked it up off the counter, turning it in such a way that the light in the room flashed against the metallic blade. Spinning on his heel, he raised it shoulder height before bringing it down on the cutting board, embedding the blade into the wood.

The noise was a shock to Alice's already tense system, her entire body flinching as if that blade had been embedded into her body instead.

Max glanced at her from over his shoulder. "I hope you like your steak rare. Personally, I prefer when the meat is warm, but tender, easy to slice and chew, the blood running hot and thick against the tongue."

The color drained from Alice's face, her gorge rising until she had to fight to not heave onto the floor. Max grinned and returned his back to her as he grabbed a thick slab of beef to slap it down on the cutting board next to the cleaver.

Using the cleaver, Max chopped thick steaks from the slab of beef, the rhythmic sound disturbing Alice more than it should have. In an effort to distract herself, she asked, "Why did you say I'm not that easy?"

He glanced back at her from over his broad shoulder, a glimmer of some unspoken thought sparking in his eye. At first, he didn't respond beyond that momentary stare. His hand moved purposefully as he continued chopping, the veins in his forearm corded beneath his sunkissed skin.

"I knew the moment I saw you," he finally explained, refusing to look at her. Placing the cleaver down, he pulled a knife from a block to his right, vegetables from his left. The blade chopped as he spoke, adding an insidious warning to the tone of his voice.

"You're not a victim. Not entirely. The truth is in your eyes, your body language. One glance at you and I knew you've been fighting your entire life."

Captivated by the rhythmic chop, frozen in place as she watched his arm move with absolute precision, she asked, "How would you even know that?" Her voice dropped to a whisper, her gaze pulled from watching him to view the television screen seated in the corner of the room.

Max hadn't lied. Every television in every room was tuned to the cell where her sister was kept.

Delilah sat motionless on the bed where she was chained, her head fallen forward as helplessness weighed on her shoulders. The only consolation Alice had was that Delilah was seemingly safe inside that room. It was more than could be said for Alice. Even though she was left alone and scared, blinded by the hood that covered her head, at least Delilah wasn't forced to entertain their monster.

Not like Alice.

Clearing her throat of the emotion welling inside her, she added, "Besides, you're wrong. I'm not a fighter."

The chopping stopped, his right arm moving to place the knife on the counter to his side. His palms pressed against the black granite, but he didn't turn to look at her. "Am I?"

A long pause occurred between them, only broken when Max spoke again. "There are nightmares in your eyes, Alice, a bleak darkness that is obvious to any person who has experienced it firsthand."

After placing the vegetables in a pot to steam and arranging the steaks on the grill top of the stove, he turned to study her. The sound of sizzling meat filled the space between them, the smell causing Alice's traitorous stomach to churn with rancid hunger.

She wasn't sure when she'd eaten last.

Watching Alice's every expression, mentally tracking each movement and behavior, Max stood silent, his large body propped against the counter at his back.

"I knew a person like you once. He had the same mannerisms, the same characteristics that marked him as something *other*."

Her attention drawn to his mouth, she studied the way his lips moved when he spoke, the way he kept his head slightly bowed so that he was watching her from beneath thick, inky lashes. His hair was so dark, it manipulated the shadows around him, blending him seamlessly into his environment.

Silence allowed his words to sink into her thoughts, to collide against the nagging whispers that she should be doing something besides listening to his cryptic statements. But just as the first sparks of rage ignited inside her, she forced her eyes from his face, diverting her gaze to the television screen.

"Other? Are you trying to claim we're not human?" It would explain how any man could so easily torture another human being. He had to view that person as an object or an animal.

His eyes followed hers to the television screen, an expression of pity softening his features. She thought he would speak again, but instead he turned to flip the steaks. Black smoke rose up in a thick cloud to mingle with the steam that had accumulated above the boiling pot.

"There is no *we*, Alice. There is only you."

Her eyes locked to his as he slowly spun back to face her. His head angled in the direction of the screen. "She is not other. Only you."

Confusion saddled her. She'd grown tired of the meaningless statements and words. His explanations revealed nothing. "What do you mean by other?"

"You've seen darkness, experienced Hell...you've battled nightmares all your life. It's shaped you, molded you and set you apart from the majority. You are human, obviously, but your mind is not the same as the worthless sheep who fill our society. You don't care about the inane, you don't waste idle time discussing bullshit. You, of all people, understand what it is to be haunted by evil."

Her brows furrowed, her eyes narrowing on him in disbelief. "There's no way you can know that about me. I've told you nothing."

He grinned. "You didn't need to tell me. I already knew."

Dismissing her as she sat in shocked silence, he returned his attention to the food, pulling the meat from the grill to place it on a plate on the counter. Alice watched the meat bleed onto the plate, crimson red dripping down into rivulets that ran the white porcelain.

"We should eat," he said, busying himself with the steamed vegetables.

"I'm not hungry."

"You will be," he responded. Casting her a taunting glance, he nodded towards a doorway behind her. "The dining room is through there. I expect to find you seated at the table. I'll unlock your cuffs if you promise to behave."

She didn't move. It wasn't in her to obey, to easily submit to a man she didn't know. "And if I don't?"

Without speaking he turned to look at her, a single amused brow lifted in question. After they held each other's stare for several seconds, his gaze slowly traveled to the television screen.

It was all the answer Alice needed.

FIFTEEN

12:30 p.m.

Gray walls.

Black table.

Plastic, fake red roses.

Everything in place.

"Alice? ... Ms. Beaumont? ... Alice Beaumont..."

"Yes, Doctor."

Five steps across the room, three steps over the soft, patterned carpet. Four cushions. A white throw draped loosely over the armrest.

Alice lowered herself to sit on the couch, clutched a pillow to her chest, and raised her eyes to look at the doctor.

He stared at her, his posture rigid on the chair, his notepad left sitting on the table to his side.

"How are you today?"

She didn't like that he hadn't assumed his typical, relaxed position. Where was his pen? Why did the environment feel different?

"Better?" she guessed, uncomfortable in the doctor's presence. "I think."

Had she given him the answer he sought?

Her pulse ticked in time with the clock, her eyes scanning the room in search for anything that would explain the doctor's strange demeanor.

Nothing was out of place, even the dripping faucet still beat down upon the sink with the same rhythm as usual. But beyond those hallmarks of passing time, the silence between them was deafening.

"How has your daily life been, Alice? Have you been active in any hobbies recently? Have you been exercising or reading, by chance?"

She blinked. It was the only outward symptom of the surprise she felt at his questions. "No. At least, I don't think I have. Why?"

His unwavering attention made her nervous. More seconds ticked by, more rapid heartbeats pounding beneath her ribs. Having come to some unspoken conclusion, the doctor nodded once before sitting back in his chair to grab his notepad and pull it into his lap.

She released the breath from her lungs. The tension dissipated.

"You appear stronger today. I thought, perhaps, you'd become involved in a therapeutic activity. I assume from your answer that I was wrong to think that."

The room righted itself, the atmosphere returned to normal. She focused on his statement, his claim that, at least on the surface, she appeared stronger.

"You seemed different to me for a minute there. Rigid and -" Her voice trailed off, barely a whisper when she added, "I don't know. Just different."

He studied her; the way his eyes locked to every movement of her lips, to her posture and the small tics of her muscles unnerving her more than most days.

"Perhaps you're becoming more aware of yourself. Of your surroundings. At every session we've had, you've been closed in and cut off. A world exists around you, Alice, yet it seems you've locked yourself inside a small, sheltered box."

She hadn't locked herself anywhere. It had been life that shoved her inside herself and threw away the key.

Wanting to return to the only thing that was important, Alice ignored his statement. "He called me a fighter." It wasn't until she'd spoken the words that she understood how they were in complete opposition to what the doctor believed her to be. One man believed her a scared mouse, while the other called her a lion.

"Maybe that's what you want to be," the doctor suggested. "Maybe Max isn't someone separate, but rather, a part of yourself."

No, she thought, Max was definitely something apart from her.

Refusing to respond to the ridiculous statement, she shrunk into herself, her body physically curling as her mind pulled away. Hidden behind a wall that, while not physical, could still be felt, she retreated to a place where the doctor's veiled insinuations couldn't touch her.

He only pretended to believe her, while suggesting every time they talked that she was crazy. "He called me other," she said, her voice forceful because she knew she wasn't crazy.

The leather of the executive chair creaked as the doctor relaxed back against it. "And what do you think that means?"

The words were on the tip of her tongue, but she couldn't speak them. Thick and sticky, they clung there refusing to brush over her lips on even the barest of whispers.

Shaking her head, she tightened her body into a ball. Her head rested on her knees and her arms quaked with how tightly they held her bent legs to her chest. Blonde hair slipped from the ponytail that trailed down her back and she hid behind that small bit as if it would conceal her.

"I can't tell you," she admitted, her words broken by the emotion that continued assaulting her from the inside out. "But I can show you. The dreams, Doc. All the answers you need are in the dreams."

Regretfully, he answered, "I don't think they are, Alice."

His pen tapped.

With a concerned furrow to his brow, he spoke softly. "But if that's all you have to give to me now, then tell me more about the dreams."

SIXTEEN

"You haven't touched your food."

The tines of Max' fork scraped across his ceramic plate. It wasn't the best China. He'd told her that when they first sat down. He'd chosen a cheaper set, instead, because he was sure she'd fight him and break it. In time, when Alice accepted her place, he'd feed her on the best he had.

Despite his apologies for the table setting, the ceramic plates were still better than Alice had ever seen. They were a simple pattern, light blue against pristine white. The delicate swirls of color around the perimeter reminded her of a set her grandmother owned, understated, yet elegant, speaking to a generation of people that was long lost to time. Modern society had moved on from the beauty of the past, however everything about Max - his mannerisms, his clothes, his home and the dishes that sat on the table in front of Alice - reminded her of a time long ago.

But the elegance was lost on her. The fine food and wine, the delicate table cloth and napkins to match. The food smelled delectable, but the atmosphere tarnished it all.

She was a trapped woman, held victim to a man that had somehow taken her captive, and who held her there with the threat of hurting someone she loved in her place. Whenever Max spoke of her, it was only *when* she'd acquiesce and submit, never *if*. Alice knew that Max had the biggest bargaining chip of all, the collar that held her in place. And based on his certainty that she would eventually accept the life he was creating for her, he knew it too.

"I'm not hungry," she admitted, her voice so soft it was barely audible to her own ears.

Max' fork fell to his plate. The small sound was jarring in the quiet room, Alice's eyes drawn up to see the silent anger in the gaze of her captor.

"You'll eat when I tell you to."

The light blonde of her eyelashes fluttered over her vision. "But if I'm not -"

She couldn't finish the thought, not with the way his hand clenched over her face, her cheeks painful against her teeth, her eyes as wide as the beautiful saucers that sat on the table.

She'd wondered why he'd chosen to sit on the chair next to her rather than at the head of the table. She didn't have to wonder any longer. He remained in reach of her in case the opportunity arose where he would have to correct her behavior.

Leaning in, his expression - the flared nostrils and sharp cut of his cheekbones - was a barely controlled threat of rage. However, his eyes remained lazy, the light blue color hazed over as he studied the terror that ran in small quakes across her body. She'd never understood that emotion could be a physical thing, but her silence didn't disguise her fear, not with the prickles that ran across her skin or the blood that rushed to her cheeks as tears wept from her unblinking eyes.

"When I tell you to eat, you eat. You won't be allowed to wither away in this house. You won't destroy the body that now belongs to me. I won't let you."

If he'd screamed the words, they would have been less menacing than the cold way in which he'd spoken them in that moment. Like the blade of a sharply honed knife, they sliced across her senses, opening her up in places she'd rather remain hidden from the world.

She knew then that this is what the monsters could do when they got you alone. They tore you to pieces slowly, methodically, because they had all the time in the world.

If only her father had been able to tell her what to do when you woke up in the monster's arms. She'd never had the chance to run or refuse. She'd been taken without knowing the threat was there. And now she was stripped from the world. Alone. Terrified. At the mercy of a man that had captured her when she hadn't been aware.

With one hand, he held her, his fingers clamped down on her cheeks until her lips were pressed open from the strength of his grip. Picking a piece of steak from her plate, he slipped it between her lips, the spices he'd used to cook it a burst of flavor inside her mouth. Releasing his grip on her face, he sat back, studying her as the small bit of meat sat lingering against her tongue.

"Chew, Alice."

Hating herself for fighting against that small spark of rebellion within her, she did as she was told. Swallowing down the bite took effort, and when it finally slid past the knot in her throat, it fell like a boulder into her stomach, writhing in the churning acid of her fear.

When she didn't move to take another bite, her fork lying useless against the delicate pattern of the ceramic plate, he lifted a questioning brow. "Should I continue to feed you myself? Or do you think you can manage without being forced?"

A veiled threat, a tender question. The dichotomy of one against the other was staggering. She didn't want to eat, didn't think it was possible to force another crumb past the throat that restrained her silent scream. But what choice did she have?

Only the one he gave her.

Fifteen minutes passed, Max' eyes set and focused on the small woman as she picked at the dinner on her plate. He studied every movement she made, the food she selected, the manner in which she chewed slowly and thoroughly to ensure she didn't choke on the nutrients he'd prepared for her body.

Had it been up to her, she would have starved that body until there was nothing left but skin and bone. It didn't belong to her anymore, so why would she care for it? If she was truly his possession now, she wanted nothing to do with it.

"Thank you," he whispered, his hand coming across the plate to rest on her own. The fork dropped from her fingers, her head bowed so that only the scraps of food left on the plate were visible to her tear filled eyes.

Pulling his hand from hers, he plucked the napkin from his lap, placing it on the table without releasing her from his cold and calculated stare. "We should clear the table, Alice. I can't function unless everything is clean and in its place."

She hated everything about the man who refused to release her from his tethered hold.

The formality of him, the manners, the routine he attempted to force between them. Families ate dinner together. Families cleared the table and washed the dishes. But not like *this*. Not with *him*.

Daring to question him, she swallowed her fear, her hand reaching up to brush the burning moisture from her eyes. "Why are you doing this to me? Why are you torturing me with all of this bullshit?" Her hand flew across the table, the dishes that had been set so beautifully were scattered until they crashed against the wall and floor.

She expected to be restrained for her behavior, slapped or kicked, raped or beaten, but none of those things would occur.

Without commenting, Max watched the dishes fly across the room, the delicate patterns shattering into the same tiny pieces as Alice's heart and mind. Only when the last shard had settled its frenetic clamoring against the floor did he resettle his gaze back on her.

A shy smile tugged at his lips, unspoken thoughts obvious behind the brilliance of his blue eyes.

"You prove me right in everything you do."

He allowed that comment to hang between them, allowed her anger to ratchet higher until it was a blanket covering her fear. With a voice that betrayed nothing of the emotions he was feeling, he said, "You're so easy, Alice. So predictable. I keep waiting for you to do something to surprise me."

"Fuck you." Her words came out on a shaky breath, rage settling over her vocal chords as her mouth curled into a sneer.

Finally having forced him to his breaking point with two simple words, she learned about the violence in the man who'd stolen her.

He struck out before she could react to his movement, his strong fingers gripping her fine blonde hair, twisting the length of her tresses until they wrapped his hand and forearm. Alice screamed in shocked response at first, but soon that sound was a manifestation of the burning pain that spread like fire across her scalp.

Pulling her close so that her body lifted from her chair and hung over his lap, he ignored her anguished pleas. He dropped his lips against her ear.

"I warned you. Do not try my patience, Alice. I'm trying not to harm you."

Despite his words, despite the controlled manner of his voice, the beast inside him rose to the surface, his eyes shadowed with rage and righteous anger as he forced her to the floor. Standing up from his seat, he took deliberate steps around the table, still clenching Alice's hair in his hand. She had no choice but to crawl at his feet, a woman made into a pathetic dog by the man who'd claimed her fate.

Crossing the room, he finally released her at the wall where the dishes had shattered, her body falling helplessly to the floor as broken as the shards she'd been dropped down upon.

"Clean it the fuck up."

Her body trembled at Max' feet, one hand cut and bloody where it had been torn apart by the shards, the other reaching up to her head, to learn if he'd ripped the hair from her scalp. Sobs disabled her, and pain kept her from finding the strength to do as he'd instructed.

Kneeling down, Max stared at Alice, his palm touching her back as if his contact could comfort her. "I try to be civilized, Alice, I do. But there are rules, basic fucking rules that you need to learn and follow."

His palm stroked over her back, eventually smoothing down the mess he'd made of her long, blonde hair. "You make me do these things. You make things worse for yourself when you don't behave. I can control it, if you can."

"Let me go and I'll control myself just fine, you sick bastard!" Daring to look up at him, she glared into his eyes. "How about that? You sick fuck! Have I surprised you now?"

His hand left her back and she shrunk over herself waiting for him to strike. If she could push him to a point where he lost himself entirely, perhaps he would end this all - right here and right now. Hurt her so badly that she'd escape into the ether and away from the torment and crippling pain.

But Max didn't lift his hand against her a third time, didn't dare release his bottled rage against her. He wouldn't give her the thing she wanted most: escape from the nightmare he'd created for her.

Instead, he stood above her, pausing for a few tense seconds before slowly walking away. Alice forced herself up, following the path he made with her eyes swollen and tired from the salty, hot tears she'd cried.

"Where are you going?" she screamed.

Max stopped before walking through a doorway, his face staring down at his shoes, refusal to react to anything she'd said apparent in the set of his broad shoulders. Without answering her, he pulled a phone from his pocket, his thumb running across the screen she couldn't see just before a small beep sounded in the distance. Metal slid against metal, a lock releasing in a room adjoining the one where Alice lay crumpled like an abandoned doll.

He sighed, his shoulders rolling back as his head pulled up to cast his eyes on the ceiling.

139

With a voice as soft as satin, he answered, "Watch for yourself. I warned you, Alice. You only have yourself to blame."

It was all the response he'd given her before his large body disappeared into another room, the weight of his words left hovering behind him to strike panic into the woman he'd left crumpled on the floor.

Clarity suddenly thundering through her rampant mind, Alice knew who would suffer now that she'd dared to misbehave.

"No," she shook her head, understanding lighting a fire inside her that had her scrambling to her feet.

"NO!" she screamed, tearing across the room to follow him, to stop him from what she knew he would do.

SEVENTEEN

12:30

Gray walls.

Black table.

"Alice? ... Ms. Beaumont? ... Alice Beaumont ...."

"Yes, Doctor."

Five steps across the room.

...*drip*...

Still the same, but nothing was safe.

Not anymore.

Taking her usual seat on the sofa, Alice didn't bother with pleasantries before curling her lean body into a ball.

Something had happened that frightened her so thoroughly that she couldn't gain control of her pounding heart, couldn't control the way air froze in her lungs with every unsteady breath. Her limbs trembled in response to any noise she heard, her muscles cramped from the constant fear that held them tight across her aching bones. However, when she tried to pinpoint the cause, her thoughts scattered across a violent wind that continued to knock her back.

"Alice? Is everything okay? You haven't looked at me once since you've been here."

She shook her head, as if the small movement would answer every question he could possible ask her. Beneath her arms, her stomach churned, the bitter taste of her terror bubbling up into her throat until she could barely keep from retching.

Concerned, the doctor leaned forward, his hand extending the space between them until his fingertips touched softly upon her shoulder. "Alice?"

"He hurt her."

She didn't know from what part of her the words came. All she knew is that they hurt so badly she had to say them out loud simply to find a release from their agony. As if sharing the words would take away at least a small part of the pain they caused.

The doctor didn't immediately answer her. His hand maintained the contact between them, his body remained perfectly still so as not to startle the woman crumbling in front of him. Only when Alice let out a hard sigh did he finally speak again.

"I didn't let you finish that part, Alice. I don't know that you're ready for it. Not yet."

A bark of laughter rattled her chest. "I dreamed it. It's not like I don't know what he did to her."

"Yes, but is it real to you when you haven't told anyone about it? I didn't notice until our last session..." He paused, a sigh blowing over his lips before admitting, "I had to restrain you, Alice."

Her eyes opened at his words, the sudden rush of soft light surprising her because she hadn't realized they'd been clenched shut before.

"Restrain me?" Her arms shook, panic coursing through her veins with such violence she feared her skin would rupture from the onslaught. "How did you restrain me?"

His voice was whisper soft. "It doesn't matter, and it wasn't for long." Another pause, his words measured to ensure they didn't frighten her more. "But that's not the point, Alice. The point is these dreams are destroying you."

She was already destroyed. The dreams couldn't possibly tear her apart any more. But she chose not to say that to the doctor. She didn't want him to know how truly far she'd fallen.

"I'm going to increase the dosage of your medications -"

"Don't," she answered abruptly, all but cutting off the words he'd intended to say.

"Alice -"

"I said don't!" Anger forced her body to straighten out, for her to snap her shoulder away from the small contact she had with Dr. Chance. Her head wrenched at a painful angle, she glared at him, fighting to control the volume of her voice.

Acting crazy wouldn't help her. It would only prove the doctor right.

"I don't want to forget the dreams and that's all you're trying to do with the meds you're giving me. I want to know them. I *have* to know them. I don't take the pills, Doc. I won't take them."

His eyes flew open in surprise, but his voice didn't match his expression. Calm, cool, moderated in a way that could only be perfected by a trained professional, his voice disguised whatever truth existed to his personal feelings. "Can you state that for a fact, Alice? That you don't take the medication?"

Staring at him with eyes that were tired and hazy, she nodded her head at the question. "Yes," she answered feebly before the confusion found its way back to mingle with whatever lucid thoughts she'd clung to. "No. I don't know."

Clarity had been a fleeting thing, breaking apart the fog to allow one shining beam of light to invade what was always a cryptic, impossible puzzle. Her body relaxed against the cushions of the soft couch, her finger playing idly with a frayed string of her oversized green sweater.

Green. It was the first time she noticed anything about herself in how long?

"Why," she asked over words that were crushed glass inside her blistered throat, "why did you have to restrain me?"

A pen tapped over the doctor's notepad, once, twice, before the tip was scrawled across the page. His strong handwriting was a wash of blue over white, creating words that carried little meaning to Alice if they couldn't take the pieces of her fractured life and put them back together.

"I thought, for a moment, you remembered something outside this office."

There was a particular position she normally took when surrounded by the serenity of the doctor's office. Her legs pulled up to cross into a tangled position that reminded her of a bow and her days spent in Kindergarten. She had thin arms that had lost so much muscle mass the skin was sagging and waving just below her shoulders. Like two, raw chicken cutlets, the skin flapped as she moved her arms to curl around her frame, caging her in a false sense of protection.

Once she'd assumed the posture that shielded her from the world outside herself, she cast a soft glance at the man who had always been so patient.

"I remember the dreams," she insisted, ripping the conversation away from the present and slamming it right back down beneath the chains of the nightmares she'd endured for too long.

She was drawing a line between them, a long straight mark between two points, unlike the one that had been drawn for her when her body was sleeping. That line had been a different beast, an infinite mess because it had a clear beginning, but no definable end.

The doctor crossed the line she drew, a far braver act than anything she could hope to accomplish.

"I want to talk about *before*, Alice. To the memories you have that occurred before your life was bisected."

When she didn't openly complain, he specified, "I want to talk about your father."

Her eyes clenched shut again. "My father was a drunk. When he was sober, he cared for his family, and when he wasn't, he wished us all dead. He scared me all the time talking about the monsters in our world. Meanwhile, he was one of them. There's not much more I can say about him."

"But there is more, isn't there?" Leaning forward to close the distance Alice wished would remain between them, his face was a mask of sympathy beneath the soft light, his hair a tawny brown that framed his angled face and soft lips.

It was the first time she'd paid attention to his features in a light that allowed her to see them. She was struck by the way his brows knitted over his eyes, the way his glasses clung to the tip of his nose because another inch forward and they'd tumble away. "You seem so familiar."

His voice wouldn't give away his private thoughts, but the expression on his face certainly did. Confusion becomes obvious when painted across questioning eyes and a mouth that pulls into a taut and narrow line. "We've been meeting for a while now, Alice. I hope I seem familiar."

"The dreams, Doc. Let me finish the dreams and I'll tell you everything else you want to know."

Resigned, he relaxed back against his chair. "At our next session, you'll tell me? You'll talk to me about *before*?"

She nodded her head in silent agreement. She'd agree to anything if it meant she could save Delilah.

"Fine, but start with what happened after Max came back from the basement. I don't want you so upset that we can't finish this session."

"He raped her, Doc."

"Alice -"

Her frantic eyes locked to his. "He raped her right there on camera for me to see. She...she..."

Her body trembled as the images flew past, snapshots detailing the way her sister's skirt had been lifted, the way her covered face had been shoved against the mattress so that she couldn't scream or breathe. When he'd finished, red fingerprints had dotted the white skin of her legs from the force he'd used to hold them apart.

"I don't need the details of the assault, Alice. Please, start with what happened after."

EIGHTEEN

The corner of the room where she lay crumpled and broken was the only crutch she could find to keep her from shattering apart completely. Before her stood a steel door painted to look like simple wood, its hard, cold surface disguised to resemble warmth.

A pneumatic hiss followed the electric beep, a small red light flashing to green before the door was pulled open into a shadowed interior. A monster filled the doorway with broad shoulders, a trim waist and thighs so thick with muscle, they challenged the seams of the linen pants he wore to cover them.

His heavy, booted footsteps were the first warning he gave as he entered the room, stopping just shy of where her feet stuck out on legs that were useless to hold her.

Tilting his head in the way that mocked her with familiarity, he pursed his lips, a silent observer to her suffering.

"Did you finish cleaning up?"

The words were staggering in their normalcy, a question asked a million times by a million different mouths and voices. Mothers to their children, husbands to their wives, teachers to the students that filled their classrooms day after day until lazy summer weeks switched from something promised into something actually lived.

Alice wondered if ever in those million times had the question been asked in a situation as bleak and hopeless as the one in which she found herself trapped.

"No," she confessed, wanting to throw the question right back at him as heavy and solid as the way he'd tossed it to her. *Did you clean up, you petty bastard, after hurting a woman that did nothing to you?*

His hand outstretched, he wiggled his fingers inviting her to grab hold so he could lift her from her crumpled seat. And knowing what her rebellion would bring if she dared refuse him, she reached up to give him all he expected, despite the way her skin crawled at the moist heat of his palm.

Lifting her was effortless, a quick flex of a bicep that was three times the size of her arm. Unsteady in her heart and body, she tumbled forward until she was pressed against him, his arms wrapping around her as his chin came down to rest at the top of her head. "One of these days, we'll get you on task, Alice. You'll be able to remember things without me having to remind you."

Desperate to pull away, she collapsed against him because she knew she had to accept the unwanted embrace.

A clock sounded in the distance, the eight o'clock hour announced by the bells tolling the Westminster chime, a morbid crawl of melody that forced her emotions to manifest into hot and sticky tears.

Only when that clock had pounded down the eight lonely gongs, did her captor speak again.

"Come with me, Alice. We need to clean up the mess you've made."

The mess you've made, she thought, her mouth clenched tight so she wouldn't accidentally speak the words that scratched at the surface. An assault inside her, she wanted to dig them out and shove the words into the space that hung between them.

I wouldn't have been here to make that mess if you weren't such a depraved and cruel prick.

However, silence lingered heavily as her feet half stepped, half dragged herself into the dining room where the plates lay broken and still, the delicate pattern that had once been so beautiful cut through with the evidence of her violence.

Dropping her to her knees, Max stood above her, watching as she brushed together the fragmented pieces. Each piece could have been a part of herself, her heart and soul split down the middle, her freedom and dignity crushed beneath the baked red potatoes that had been flavored with salt and rosemary.

Forming a pile of the larger bits of food and ceramic, she left behind the dust that lay scattered too small for her to manage with shaking hands.

"I need a dustpan," she admitted, flinching to finally hear the way her voice was gritty with emotion.

He eyed her from the height he stood above her, his angry mask dissolving into pity and sympathy. As if each jagged, sharp angle of his face was peeled away to reveal another person behind it, someone who could feel the same pain he inflicted.

"There's a dustpan and broom in the pantry closet. While you manage that, I'll clear what's left of the table. When you're finished, I'll be in the kitchen washing dishes. You should meet me there so you can help."

She nodded her head, unable to speak around the lump of hatred that festered at the base of her throat.

His heavy steps ticked off the growing distance he placed between them, unhurried and sure, they spoke volumes about the control he knew he'd gained over her so easily. After his taunting steps had faded completely, she picked herself up off the floor and found the closet with the broom and dustpan waiting.

Perhaps it was her bitter tears that made her move slowly to clean up the mess, or a subconscious effort to delay the time she'd have to pretend that washing dishes with a madman wasn't a pitiful thing. But like any chore, she came to the end of it, dumping what was left of her rebellion in a plastic trashcan lined with a white, plastic bag.

Max stood facing the sink, his shoulders moving beneath the black fabric of his shirt, his shoulder length hair a tangled mess where it hung in wild waves. Alice stood and stared at him for several minutes wondering if he knew she loitered behind him watching the way his arms worked back and forth polishing away the remnants of the dinner he'd cooked for their first night together.

Her eyes traced the lines of his shoulders and back, the muscles that lay corded and partially hidden beneath the folds of his once finely pressed shirt. Wrinkled now, the dark fabric was stretched taut over his shoulder blades before falling into a disheveled mess where it followed the tight dip towards his hips. Had they not come together in such a horrible way, she would have found herself attracted to the man that silently washed dishes, would have been impressed with the physique that spoke to everything masculine and strong about him.

A kitchen island stood between them with white cabinets and black granite counters. It was a touch of modern against the vintage features of the Queen Anne style house. She wondered when he'd remodeled the place, but knew from the stainless steel appliances that it couldn't have been that long since he had the expensive appliances installed. Her eyes looked at the litany of gadgets that littered the front of the large refrigerator and wondered why any person would need a coffee maker in the freezer door. Fools and their money were so easily parted.

Stepping closer, she continued keeping Max in her peripheral vision as she glanced here and there about the room, her eyes tracking a random path until landing on the bright steel of the cleaver that lay inanimate on the counter behind Max. Temptation flashing beneath the lights of the room, her fingers curled into her palm, her fingernails carving half moon circles into her skin as she pondered what could be done with a weapon as sturdy as the one laying within her reach.

Taking a tentative step forward, she crept as silently as a mouse, and moved closer with her muscles clenched tightly over her body, waiting for him to notice. He neither turned, moved, nor said a word as she approached the fierce object that could lead her to salvation.

Reaching out with a shaking hand, she brushed her fingertips over the smooth surface of the handle, pulling back at the last minute for fear that he somehow knew what she was doing. But Max didn't react, instead taking one dish from the soapy water to scrub it with the brush he held and rinse it beneath the steady stream of the faucet.

Inching her arm back towards the cleaver, she imagined imbedding the sharply honed blade into the back of his skull. Wrapping her thin fingers around the handle, she cringed to hear its weight slide across the counter as she found the strength to pick it up.

"Do you know how much force it would take to do whatever it is you're planning on doing?"

The instant his voice broke the silence, her fingers released the handle, the heavy blade falling to clamor over the dark stone tile that sat pristine beneath her feet. She flinched at the sound of metal and wood against the floor and glanced down to see the stone hadn't been broken.

Max glanced at her from over his shoulder, one dark, questioning brow perfectly arched over an intelligent set of sparkling blue eyes. "Do you know the strength it would take to actually kill me with that cleaver? I'm not sure you have it in you, Alice." His chin nodded in the direction of the weapon that now lay useless on the floor. "Pick that up, would you? It needs to be washed, as well."

She hated him for everything he'd already done to Delilah and her, but hated him more for the casual tone in which he spoke. As if he hadn't just dragged her across the floor by her hair, or worse, the despicable violence he'd committed against a person she loved simply because she'd dared challenge him. A shiver ran up her spine and she imagined the same bruises that dotted her sister's skin running a constellation of pain up her own until she was just as beaten and marked, marred by the large, strong hands of a man that had no concern for the devastation that remained in his wake.

When he glanced at her again, a smirk pulling at the corner of his sculpted lips, she bent over to retrieve the cleaver and walked it around the island to stand next to him at the sink. He plucked the weapon from her fingers and sunk it down into the soapy water before handing her a dishtowel to dry the unbroken plate he handed her next.

When they'd settled into a routine of washing, rinsing and drying the dishes and cookware, Alice thought she would scream if for nothing else but to break up the cruel silence that wrapped them both like a suffocating shroud.

"A lot of people think it's easy to stab someone either in the chest or back, possibly the face or neck, and cause them to die from bleeding out."

He spoke like he was discussing something as mundane as the weather, or a movie he'd seen on a lazy Friday night. He didn't bother looking at her, his gaze held steady on the task at hand, the dishes that needed to be cleaned and polished to a shine so that they appeased his need for a clean and tidy house. Glancing at the plate in her hand, Alice hated the reflection that stared back at her, the lifeless eyes of a woman who had so easily submitted while barely putting up a fight.

"But it's not easy. It takes knowledge on where to stab if you hope to disable your opponent. And it takes strength to sink the blade deep enough so that it punctures a vital organ or damages a muscle in such a way that renders the limb useless. Even then, if your opponent is strong enough, or has a high pain tolerance, the single stab will only serve to piss him off, so you have to keeping stabbing, over and over again, until you're covered in his blood, a spray of thick, hot liquid against your skin that's enough to make any decent person vomit from having committed the act."

He turned to her at that moment, his body dangerously close to hers, his hair brushing over his shoulder as he angled his head in question while mocking her with lazy and admiring eyes. Scanning her body, his liquid gaze started at her hips, settling on her breasts as they worked their way up until coming to lock with the terror behind her eyes. "Do you think you could do that, Alice? To me or anybody else that pisses you off?"

As if daring her to commit the act, he pulled the cleaver from the soapy water, washed it slowly until all traces of the meat he'd used it to cut were absent from the blade and handed it to her to rinse and dry to a perfect polish. The blade was heavy in her hand as she worked the towel over the surface, fear reflected back at her behind the darker blue color of her gaze rimmed red by tears that hadn't stopped falling.

She shrugged before swallowing down the venomous knot of seething, jagged hatred that clogged her throat and cut off the air she needed to breathe into her lungs. "You said I was a fighter. What makes you think I couldn't?"

"I never said you couldn't," he finally answered, his hand working slowly over a platter that he'd used to carry the food to the table. "I said you don't have it in you, not unless you were pushed that far. However, in this house and in this particular situation, you're powerless to do anything with that cleaver because you'd only end up killing yourself in the process."

A shiver crawled along her spine nestling at the base of her neck, the hair standing on end where it settled. "You'd use the cleaver on me?" It was a hope she couldn't allow herself to digest fully because too many other factors came into play. Namely, that if she died, what would happen to her sister?

"I'd never use it on you." Spoken with a matter of fact tone that covered the darkness in his voice, he washed another plate before talking to her again. "But this house is impossible to escape unless you know the codes, and dying from starvation or thirst can't be the most pleasant way to go. Killing me would only trap you in a cage, Alice, a cage you have no hope to escape in time."

Her mind spun down a dizzying spiral, the truth of his words smacking against her every so often as they spun along right beside her. Thoughts brought back to her mind's eye all the metallic panels and flashing lights that proved turning a simple key or deadbolt lock wouldn't deliver her to freedom. She'd hated technology as she'd watch it manifest in the modern world while she grew, and she hated it now more than ever. Modern devices had served to put people all over the world in contact with each other at the touch of a button, while removing them from participating in their every day lives with the people who were sitting right next to them. Now, as the situation in her case had turned out, it also prevented her escape from a man she wished existed on some other part of the planet far away from where she or her sister had once lived their ordinary, non-tragic lives.

After finishing the last dish, he watched her as she polished off the beads of hot water and placed it in a rack.

"We've both had a difficult day. I think it's time for us to see if we can get some sleep."

A few seconds before and she would have sworn the situation couldn't get worse, but he'd proven her wrong with two sentences.

Her legs became jelly beneath her, sticky sweat reaching out to grasp onto the fabric of her dress and hug it tightly against her skin. "Bed? Am I...are we..."

He studied her with amusement, the height he had over her making her feel like a small child. With a calculated gaze that was as mysterious and beautiful as an iceberg turned so that its belly breached the surface, his eyes were as cold and unforgiving as the ocean that harbored those deadly islands of ice that had sunk so many ships.

"Take the stairs up to the bedroom. Sit down on the edge of the bed. I'll be up in a moment to give you your night clothes."

Panic set in, her body trembling as she put distance between them, happy to walk away but not happy about where she was going.

She could refuse, could attempt to find a place to hide in the large three story house, but with the cameras and monitors she knew he had tucked away and hidden, she would only be risking another terrifying show like the one he'd played out for her earlier.

Mounting the stairs with a hesitant foot, she climbed them one by one, each step reminding her of what she'd seen on the television screen that stood proudly in the sitting room off the study. Max hadn't wasted any time teaching her the valuable lesson of what would become of the woman he kept caged in a room that belittled a happy, functional childhood; a place where the pinks ran with blood and the bed sheets were stained by the evidence of his violence and lust.

Reaching the top floor, she shook her head of the images that were seared on her psyche, of the muffled screams and pleading words that she only understood because she would have been crying the same desperate pleas had a man bent her over to flip her skirt to her back and force himself inside.

Her hand grasped the doorway of the bedroom where she'd earlier gotten dressed, the chains above the bed still foreboding where they swung from a ceiling that arched up beautifully with thick wood beams that followed the curve of the domed roof that was so typical of a house as beautiful as this.

Forcing herself inside, she sat on the edge of the bed, her legs heavy where they were pressed together, her mind a wash of pain because, rather than breaking a window and screaming for help, she was planted right where he'd told her to go.

Her entire life she'd considered herself stronger than the woman she now discovered herself to be: a victim, a weakling, a liar.

She'd lied to herself on the day she promised she'd choose death over torture, on the day she swore she'd never allow a person to torment her as much as the nightmares that plagued her every night.

Yet, there she was waiting and anxious to see what *bedtime* in this man's house would bring.

NINETEEN

12:31 p.m.

Gray walls.

Black table.

"Alice? ... Ms. Beaumont? ... Alice Beaumont ..."

"Yes, Doctor."

Five steps across the room.

Still the same.

"It's a pleasure to see you again, Alice. Our last session was less eventful than the one prior. Do you feel better today?"

The doctor sat hopeful in his chair, leg crossed at the knee, his trusty pen held ready over paper. He stared at her with an anxious set to his brow.

His question flew aimlessly about the room, a balloon released and forgotten by a spoiled child. Softly, it hovered there, caught in the draft of the air conditioner, until settling its ribbon string on Alice's shoulder and bursting with a loud *pop* that jogged her attention.

"I'm fine. Frustrated, I guess, but fine."

Her head ticked to the side, her eyes hooded with exhaustion. How many times had she sat on this couch without finding the answers she needed to decipher her sordid puzzle?

How many more sessions would she have to endure until she learned whether her life would be normal again? Well, as *normal* as it could be for her.

"Your body is curled over itself, your affect is rigid and you haven't looked at me once. I wouldn't call that fine."

Who was he to tell her how she felt? He hadn't lost a family member, hadn't been forced through the wringer by his own perverted imagination since the day he could remember dreaming. He probably slept well at night, didn't wake up in strange places, was able to move upon waking because his body wasn't paralyzed by excruciating fear.

Fine wasn't exactly how she felt, but what other word was there to describe the crushing weight that sat on her shoulders, the whispered voices that reminded her how she failed at happiness, at family, at life?

Apathy maybe, but it would require she didn't care. Confused, morose, defeated.

Yes, that was it. That last one. Alice felt defeated.

"Your leg is crossed. You're wearing dark navy slacks with a white button up shirt, the cuffs buttoned by gold links, and your notebook sits in your lap with a blue ball point pen at the ready."

She glanced up at his attentive face. "I looked at you, Doc."

With an expression heartfelt in its sympathy, he nodded. "But this is the first time you've looked at my face."

Her shoulder shrugged away his statement and his attempt to win against her in this stupid game he liked to play. "I've seen it before."

A soft breath blew over his lips, audible only because it was deathly quiet in the room. "You promised me we'd talk about *before* in this session. I've made notes about what I'd like to discuss..."

"I'll give you half, Doc," she interrupted. "But only half. The other half is left for me, to discuss what I'd like to talk about."

She peeked at him from beneath heavy lashes, expecting and waiting for his angry reply. All he did was tap that blasted pen he used to turn her pain into science.

Laughing at that thought, she straightened her legs, her hands smoothing down a wrinkle in her jeans.

There was no science to be found in a study of emotion, not unless you could crack that skull right open and look inside to see what chemicals flooded the soft gray tissue that made up a person's brain. Beyond that, it was all smoke and mirrors, a simple discussion that allowed the patient to feel better and to peel the inky black mess of emotion from their fragile psyche.

Like lifting the weight of pain and suffering to set it beside you and attach to your leg, the old ball and chain that followed you no matter how many times you voiced it.

"Half, then. That should be plenty of time."

A snarl curled her lips, but she waited politely for whatever questions plagued his mind.

"I'd like to discuss your father."

Wrenching her head to stare him down, she flung the limp strands of white blonde hair from her shoulder. "Why would you want to talk about him?"

His pen scribbled over the surface of the paper that sat like a silent witness in his lap. How many times had he committed his judgment to those pages that were building and expanding the story of a woman he had no hope of helping?

"Because he came before. And I'm interested in several claims you've made about him."

"Such as?"

"Such as his drinking," he answered firmly, giving her no room to wiggle away or bargain in his tone.

...drip...

Her attention was drawn to the leaky faucet. She had to wonder: What kind of dime store doctor was she meeting with if he couldn't even afford to fix a broken sink?

"I'm taking you back to before, Alice, because I'm trying to talk about you. These sessions, everything we're doing here, it's all intended to help you." He emphasized the last word, pronouncing it clearer than the others and drawing Alice's thoughts to the selfishness of the entire thing.

She wasn't interested in helping herself. The dreams wouldn't kill her...not like they would her sister. But to help Delilah, she had to understand the dreams. And to understand the dreams, she had to appease the man lobbing questions at her like pesky tennis balls. The man who stared at her with heavy anticipation behind his eyes about what she'd have to say. Like an internet stalker, or a suburban gossip queen, he'd latched onto the chaos and drama in her life and waited in rapt attention to learn the excruciating details.

The only things he was missing were popcorn, a soda and some 3D glasses.

"My father had a drinking problem. And a gambling problem." She answered, her unsteady voice suddenly resigned. A whispered confession and an afterthought, she added, "And a problem holding onto jobs."

Dr. Chance listened attentively as she spoke, his blue ink pen coming to life with everything she had to tell him.

Careful. Controlled. A deep voice that urged a person on without startling them into silence. "Did he love you?"

The pendulum swung, rendering power back to the doctor – or, at least, it should have with that one weighted question.

"I think he did. He just wasn't able to take care of us. I paid my way through college and racked up a healthy pile of student loans in the process." She laughed, an honest laugh that she hadn't heard in God knew how long. "I bet those have all gone to hell because I can't remember ever paying them."

"Your father, Alice," the doctor redirected her back to the topic at hand. "Your father and you."

Her head hurt with the truth that threatened to tear from her scalp just so it could look her in the eyes and dare her to acknowledge it. "I hate my father," she admitted. "As soon as I was legal age, I got out of the house and I never looked back. He was an arrogant man, a strict authoritarian, abusive both physically and mentally, and I couldn't stand a person treating me that way or telling me what to do when he couldn't even take care of himself."

The cap of the doctor's pen tapped twice, the tip turning to press against paper, two bold lines drawn to underscore words Alice couldn't read from her position.

Pulling the pen up to his mouth he pressed the cap against his lips, his dark eyes appraising her shrewdly. "Do you think it's possible, Alice, that these dreams you're having aren't about your sister at all, but about yourself?"

Her eyes flared open, rage coursing through her at the audacity of his suggestion. "What is that supposed to mean?"

Remaining firm, the doctor didn't immediately recant or flinch away, he just stared at her like she was a lab rat fresh on the first dose of some new experimental medication. "Hear me out before you get angry."

"I already am angry, Doc! I'm here for my sister, not to discuss some ridiculous theory you have about my non-existent daddy issues."

"When did the sleep disorders start, Alice? What is the first memory you have of them?" Effectively cutting off her tirade, he leaned forward in his chair, the leather groaning at his movement. He stared at her like she'd disappear if he released her locked gaze. "When, Alice?"

Frustration a driving force inside her, she leaned forward to meet his unspoken challenge. "When I was eight. Okay? Does that answer your question?"

"And when did your issues with your father begin?"

Alice visibly flinched, his words a verbal slap that rattled something loose in her thoughts. The truth had always been there, lingering and festering beneath the surface, the connection never made until it had been forced.

"When I was eight," she answered softly. Her body relaxed back against the couch slowly, until she'd pulled her legs up and curled into her protective ball. Not so much talking to him, but to herself, she sat in stunned shock and said, "The nightmares and the problems with my father both started when I was eight."

The brush of pen against paper, the knowing nod of a head, the doctor appeared pleased to have made his point clearly. After scribbling down whatever thoughts were so important they couldn't become lost, his eyes flicked between Alice and the clock ticking down the seconds on the wall.

"I'm a man of my word, Alice, and we're halfway through our session, do you still want to discuss the next dream?"

Although her voice was lost to a void the realization had opened for her, she nodded her head *yes* to his question.

"Very well, then, tell me the next dream."

TWENTY

His steps were a warning in themselves. This was a fact Alice had quickly learned, each heavy, booted *thud* a reminder that she was not alone. That he was coming for her.

He'd taken eighteen of those warning steps as he climbed the stairs towards her.

Eighteen beats that counted down her future.

Eighteen beats that cried out in their slow, foreboding tone, *beware the monsters*.

Her hair hung down at the sides of her face where she sat waiting on the soft luxury of his bed, a bed so large it took up nearly half of the room. From behind that curtain of tangled, limp blonde silk, Alice peered at the man standing in the doorway, his shoulders as wide as the frame, his eyes as cold and deep as an arctic lake.

For a while he stood watching her, his gaze shrewd in its cruelty, his body tight beneath a wrinkled shirt and linen pants, and mannerisms that were more fitting for an affluent man that had stepped out of the past into the modern world. She could imagine a man like him with a coat that had tails hanging down over the firm round mass of his behind, a fitted vest several shades lighter than his coat, worn over a crisp white shirt with jeweled cuff links glittering at his wrist. She had no problem believing he would wear a pocket watch, the gold chain dangling at his hip, reminding each person around him that he was intelligent, powerful...wealthy. He had the swagger that came with the silver spoon life, the hawk-like gaze of a man that could rule any room he happened to deign to enter.

Unsure why he reminded her of a time long gone, she trembled where she sat, attempting in vain to ignore the frantic beat of her heart, the pulsing need for escape that echoed across her bones with every solitary second he stood deathly still and studied her.

The steps began again, each one closing the distance between Alice and her nightmare. Her muscles tightened with every beat, the shaking of her body becoming more violent with every foot of space between them that was lost. But when he'd come within arm's reach of her - when he paused as if this single moment would be the one that tore her to shreds over a bed of elegant silk - he paused long enough to make her mouth go dry, to add fuel to the already blazing fire of panic that burned across her chaotic mind.

However, he didn't touch her. He simply walked away.

Replacing the distance between them, Max blended into the shadowed interior of a large closet, lost to Alice's sight as quickly as he'd appeared.

Alice released a shaky breath, her trembling hands wringing in her lap, her heart rate dropping back to a steady rhythm that could sustain a fleeting life.

His absence wasn't long. Within a minute, possibly two, he returned from the black shadow of the closet, a flowing garment of pristine white held tightly in his hands.

And like every time he approached, Alice's heart sped back to a dizzying, frantic rhythm, her breath caught in her lungs and burned for release. A caged animal now, cornered and abandoned by the entire world, Alice watched his boots move across the floor, finally arching her neck to gaze up at the beautiful face of a man who was as silent as he was menacing, who wore forbidden lust as a second skin, who gazed back down at her with discontent behind his sharp, chilling eyes.

"Get dressed," he instructed, the nightgown falling from his hands to puddle at her feet, the command leaving no room for her to argue.

"Right here?" She swallowed down her panic, forcing her fear-swollen heart from her throat back to that empty place in her chest.

He inclined his head, taking two measured steps back to allow her room to stand.

Barely able to force her muscles to move, she picked up the nightgown from the floor and pushed herself to her feet. The soft fabric bunched tightly around her delicate hand, a rope binding her until the skin around that fabric became white from lack of blood.

Max didn't move, his body so still she would have sworn it was made of steel or stone, hard, impenetrable plaster like that of the statues she'd admired in a museum so many years ago. Not a twitch of his muscles. Not a tic of his jaw. The only part of him that screamed there was life inside his body were the ever-watching, haunting eyes that spoke of dirty secrets, sordid trysts, and dark, depraved desires.

Unable to pull her gaze away from the silent witness in the room, she loosened her grip on the nightgown to place in on the mattress. There was no point delaying the inevitable. He would see what he wanted to see, regardless of whether she welcomed the intrusion or not. She knew that now, knew the lengths he was willing to go in order to take what he considered his.

Her eyes flicked up to the television screen mounted in the top corner of the room, a momentary distraction from the living, breathing threat that stood only a few feet away.

Her sister sat on the bed, her body dressed in a white nightgown much like the one Max had given Alice to wear. But her head was still covered by the rough, brown hood that, as far as Alice knew, hadn't been removed since she'd been forced to her knees in front of her, put on display as the whipping girl who would pay for the misdeeds of her sister.

A shiver ran down Alice's spine, but she returned her attention to Max, allowed her eyes to settle on his eyes before chasing the mottled lines of the scar that ran across his left cheek. Rather than making him more frightening, that scar somehow made him more human.

What caused it? She wondered. *What nightmare did he suffer that undoubtedly created the man he was now?*

The taste of sympathy was acrid across her tongue, she'd rather hate the beast than feel sorry for him. But the emotion was there anyway, because she knew what it was to be mistreated and hurt.

Letting out a resigned sigh, she squared her shoulders and told herself that she wasn't doing this in submission to the man that believed he owned her, she was doing this to save the woman on the screen because, in many ways, Alice was stronger.

She'd endure.

She'd play the part.

She'd walk the line he was drawing so clearly in front of her.

And she'd survive whatever torment he gave.

Lifting up the loose skirt of the yellow dress that was far too cheerful for a place such as this, she hooked her thumbs into the elastic waistband of the nylons. Ignoring where they had clung too tight and left a red, angry mark across the flesh of her hips, she slipped them down, the fabric releasing its tight hold as it bunched over her thighs, her knees, and eventually settled loosely at her ankles. Stepping out of them, she kicked her feet free of the material that still carried the warmth of her body.

Max' eyes followed every movement she made, his liquid gaze tracing hot tracks along the length of her legs, silently watching as the stockings went from taut across her skin, to loose and folded at her ankles.

His expression was a blank mask, but the heat behind his stare was sweltering, the small breeze kicked up by the air conditioning system no match against the assault of his illicit inferno. Alice didn't need to ask him what he was thinking, she knew, and the knowledge was a weighted blade against her senses, a razor sharp realization that shredded everything brave within her to tattered, forgotten rags.

Although his eyes were still the color of dangerous arctic ice, his stare had become anything but cold.

When Alice hesitated, her dignity and modesty preventing her from unbuttoning the dress to pull it from her body, a questioning arch to Max' dark brow broke through the impenetrable mask he'd worn.

Their eyes locked, the intensity of the give and take between them so lurid that Alice felt tingles across her skin, goosebumps of fear erupting over the surface of her entire body. She knew he'd rip the clothes away, or not bother with them at all. From what she'd already seen, he hadn't needed to strip her sister down in order to take everything she had to give.

With nimble fingers, she unfastened the buttons down the back collar of her dress, the position pushing out her chest, her breasts tight across the cloth that was the only thing keeping her body from his view. Once the buttons were unclasped, she dropped her arms to her sides, matching his stare with a question that broke through the surface of her terror.

"What happens if I don't get undressed?"

He angled his head in that way that was all his own, his lips betraying his thoughts when they curled at the corners. *You already know the answer*, he was saying, *you already understand the pain I can inflict for any small spark of rebellion.*

Daring to give him a smile, she said, "You're not much of a talker, are you?" It was stupid to say, but she needed some relief from the suffocating silence, from the blanket of hatred and rage that sat heavy across her shoulders.

He didn't react.

She hadn't expected him to.

Another breath to steady herself, and she slipped the dress from her shoulders, allowing it to slide along her body until it puddled around her feet on the floor. He hadn't provided her a bra when he'd given her the clothes to wear earlier that day, and despite the lacy underwear that held tight around her hips, she felt completely exposed to his roaming eyes, to the blatant lust that radiated from him at the sight of her breasts now bared to him.

She wasn't sure if it was her fear or the chill in the air that caused her nipples to form tight, painful peaks.

A shudder ran over Max' body. Slight, but still noticeable, it was the first outward sign beyond his mysterious gaze that gave away anything of what he was feeling.

Forcing her arms to her sides, she felt hot, salty tears burning at the rim of her eyes, her nakedness another facet of her submission because she hadn't attempted to fight. What happened now was completely in his power. She wasn't allowed to say no, wasn't allowed to refuse this stranger whatever he decided to take from her.

Give and take.

Take and give.

It wasn't a mutual agreement. And it wasn't a reciprocal exchange.

She gave.

He took.

There was no other arrangement to be made.

Her body turned to pluck the nightgown from the bed, and with her eyes averted, she felt the heat of his body wash against her back before a large hand fell on her shoulder. No sooner had she gripped her hand over the soft, white cloth than it was ripped from her grasp, tossed to the ground to lie in a puddle on the floor.

The tears that burned her eyes finally slipped down her cheeks and she craned her neck to look up at him, her soul seared and tattooed with dread by the intensity of his stare.

A slight shake of his head was all he gave her before her body was shoved down against the mattress, her weight sinking down heavily into the soft luxury of the blankets, while Max stood at the foot of the bed.

This was it, then. The moment she knew would come. The moment he'd prove his supreme dominance over the woman he'd taken as his.

"Until death, Alice."

Three words spoken on a gritty, deep voice. Three words that she understood their meaning, but was confused as to why they were said.

We're married, you and I. You are now my wife...

He'd told her that in the beginning, but the words hadn't registered until just then. What type of insanity ran through this man's mind that he believed he could claim such a commitment without bothering to ask for her acceptance in return?

Until death...

She didn't know whether he was promising her that release, or whether he was promising her he'd never let her go. And as her body trembled with bitter cold against the seething, burning hatred she felt, she stared at him, her heart empty, her soul betrayed.

Seconds ticked past, tension building between them until Alice wanted to scream, *Just do it, you bastard!*

But Max wouldn't be hurried, wouldn't be denied and wouldn't be forced. He would take his time. Take his fill. Take whatever he deemed worth taking.

His eyes were locked to her body, his stare a palpable burn against her skin. Out of instinct and dignity, she pulled her arms around herself to hide her nudity, but a simple and subtle shake of Max' head stopped her before she could cover herself completely. He didn't need to speak to lay down the laws that governed her. The set of his eyes, a small movement of his head, the rigid posture of his shoulders and strong arms: those were the clues that told her to behave.

The strong and silent type had never been so demeaning.

She was as easy for him to control as any person would be, the fight she'd always trusted inside her destroyed by one constant threat that hovered above them all: hurting those she loved as punishment for her wrongdoing.

The English monarchs had it right, it seemed, because it was the only threat that cowed her so thoroughly.

She wouldn't break beneath him, wouldn't allow her mind to shatter as easily as her heart. She wouldn't give him her soul as easily as she was giving him her body.

With slow, controlled movements, Max unbuttoned his shirt until it hung open to reveal the strong physique hinted to by the taut pull of the material across his shoulders and chest. Shadows highlighted every curve of his pecs and abs, the V that ran down from his waist to bury itself beneath the waistline of his pants. Before this day, she would have been powerless to refuse the advances of a man as beautiful as Max Frost, and even now with the darkness so obvious within him – the cruelty of his touch, the crimes he'd committed against her – she was still powerless to resist his seductive charm.

However, fear was still her constant companion. Fear and anger for everything he'd taken and she'd lost.

The buckle of his belt clanged like a soft whisper across the room. His pants pulled open, but not pulled away. He stalked towards her with smooth, unhurried movements, allowing the pressure to build with each solitary step he made.

His wasn't a violent rape, but it was rape just the same. He left her no options for refusal, no room with which she could retreat. His was the most insidious type of violence, violating her body while at the same time violating her mind.

You're allowing him to do this…

You haven't told him no…

The tears fell faster as those words assaulted her thoughts, the reality that she had given up and given in to his dark and sinister desires.

When he was finished taking her, she wouldn't have him to blame alone. She didn't fight like her instincts screamed for her to do.

She didn't have to be forced by crushing blows or the threat of death.

No. She simply lay down and let him win.

The bed sunk beneath his weight. A prowling tiger whose shoulders moved with a feline grace, he crawled up to hover above her. His heat was a blanket that covered her, his blue eyes the cool, icy threat that sent chills across her sweat dampened skin. Caged against the mattress by strong arms that were as thick as they were rigid, Alice forced herself to close her eyes. But he wouldn't give her that escape.

"Look at me when I fuck you."

There was no anger to his tone, however every cold syllable dripped with the threat of sensual violence.

She opened her eyes, her breath catching in her throat as Max' head dipped down so that his tongue could taste the tears that were still relentlessly falling.

Her head fell back against the bed, his hand brushing over her hair where it fanned out across the mattress. With one swift flick of his wrist, he tangled the hair around his fist, pulling her head back further until her neck arched painfully, his teeth sinking down against the skin hard enough to draw blood.

Crying out, her body bucked beneath his weight, and she stared at him with frightened eyes to see the blatant desire written across every inch of his dangerous expression.

His lips glistened with the remnants of her tears. Locking his gaze to hers, a gaze that was every bit as cold as it was staggering, he said, "You wanted to know your monster, Alice. This is what he is."

There wouldn't be any more lies between them, not until he'd taken all she had to give.

His lips brushed across her neck, trailing down until they ran the length of her shoulder. A chill rushed over her body, her head turning slightly as her eyes locked to the television screen that had become her never ending horror.

Beaten, abused, alone – the woman whose face was never seen, whose body had been broken beneath the weight of futility.

For her, Alice thought. *I'll live through this only for her. I'm the strong one. I'm the survivor. I'm the one who can endure his violence and his rage.*

His greedy hands explored her body, the rough pads of his fingers sliding along her rib cage, feather soft in their pressure, and aggravating in how they claimed her regardless of her acceptance of him. Teeth grazed her neck, a sharp row of enameled bone that warned her with a harsh bite every time she squirmed or tried to move away from the places he touched.

Unable to resist the way he caressed her, Alice grit her own teeth, the muscles of her jaw locking down until pain shot across her cheek. She refused to look at him like he'd demanded, refused to look away from the woman for whom she was tolerating this slow and seductive abuse.

But despite the nagging whispers in her head that she should fight or scream or claw at him with her nails until he had no choice but to pull away, her body responded to the strength of his hands, the blistering warmth of his skin that covered her own, the masculine notes of his scent that melted her to that bed, wanton and desirous for him to fill up the spaces that had long remained vacant, unused and empty.

"Look at me, Alice." The command was a subtle threat, a hissed reminder that she couldn't escape in her head, that every sense she had would submit to the man that worked her into a panicked frenzy.

Her rebellion still an electric spark inside her, she couldn't turn her head, couldn't ignore the tears that were cold and wet against her cheek, couldn't force herself to face her monster.

His fist, still clenching her tangled mess of hair, tugged sharply, pain like spider webs crawling across her scalp, a spreading fire that would never be contained. She cried out when his other hand gripped her chin, forcing her face to turn to him, her wide eyes locked to the icy wrath of deep artic blue, pale and insidious.

"You'll look at the man who owns you, Alice."

Her lip trembled, his hawk-like gaze locking on that one small movement, his mouth opening slightly as he brought his head down to take her lip between his teeth, to bite down and laugh softly when she cried out again.

Pulling up, his eyes admired the swelling where his teeth had just been.

"Such a dirty little mouth you have. I can't wait to enjoy all of its talents."

Her teeth ground against each other and he released her chin to brush his finger along the muscle of her jaw. A whisper soft voice that was so deep it vibrated in places inside her where it didn't belong, "So angry. And so beautiful because of it."

Alice couldn't submit any longer, couldn't suffer the violence of his physical assault while he mocked her with a soft, seductive voice. Her hands flew up to claw at his sides, but Max was stronger...faster. He released her hair to grip her wrists, his strong fingers like steel so tight they threatened to snap the bones.

With minimal effort he locked her arms above her head, his body weight falling down on her until she was pinned between him and the soft mattress. She moved her feet in an effort to find any way to fight against him, but he dug his knees between her thighs, preventing her movement entirely.

"Please," she begged, "please don't do this."

His head angled on a question, the thick inky black of his wavy hair brushing across his shoulder from the movement. "You let me do this. I know you, Alice. You'll beg for it again before long."

Seconds passed, the fight leaching out of her slowly until she was a quivering mess of pain and suffering beneath him.

His mouth brushed the rim of her ear, his warm breath an unwanted caress against her skin. "I'll make it all better, Alice, I promise."

Her arms still trapped above her, Alice closed her eyes when he slipped his pants down from his hips, when the hard, thick reminder of his twisted lust pressed down onto the skin of her stomach. Her tears had turned him on, but it was the small fight she'd attempted that had pushed him into a mindless, toxic fervor.

She didn't dare look away from him again, her eyes narrowed on the shadows that darkened the artic blue, on the blaze of heat that turned the pale color into jewels that sparkled with wicked, malicious delight.

He broke their locked stare to seek out her breast with his mouth, his teeth snapping down on the sensitive tight peak, a cutting pain that forced a moan from Alice's throat as he licked the sting away. He enjoyed the taste of her torment, enjoyed the taste of terror that burst across her skin in sticky beads of sweat.

"So sweet," he breathed out, his voice as breathless and devoted as a prayer.

One hand squeezed her wrists harder, while the other trailed a whisper soft path down the length of her body. A quick swirl of his fingertip around her navel caused her abdominal muscles to clench at her sides. He smiled to see the reaction. And what a beautiful smile it was. It wasn't fair that evil could come wrapped in such a pretty package.

Dimples indented his cheeks, two points that caged a mouth that was full and soft. She hadn't noticed them before because Max had never shown her a side of him that was happy.

Not until the moment he had her in his bed.

Dipping down, his finger found the scalloped lace edge of her panties and slipped between the thin silk and her skin.

He looked up at her from beneath a fan of thick black lashes, conquest written in his eyes. "I remember that you're sweet here, too."

Remember?

How could he remember when this was the first time he'd assaulted her - in this way, at least - but then she remembered too. She'd been drugged, so hazy and lethargic that she'd vomited on herself and couldn't piece together the moments between retching and waking to find herself naked and displayed.

"You begged..."

Did he smile when he took her then as well, and was the smile just as beautiful?

She didn't have time to scour her memory for more details of that tryst because his rough finger slid down the line of wet and sensitive flesh, finding and circling a tight hole that hadn't been touched for so long.

Pleasure, like a mushroom cloud burst from her core, the smoke pushing up into her veins as a poison that dulled her senses and forced her eyes to roll back.

Shockwaves erupted across her skin, through her abdomen and along her limbs, small tremors a sharp vibrato within her when he explored that far too sensitive place. He hadn't pushed inside her, but already her body was a traitor that whispered, *you want this, just let him...how long has it been?*

Her eyes flew open in panic and refusal, but a small spark of desire burst into flame when she saw the way his broad shoulders moved above her, the line of his muscles undulating beneath tan skin that spoke of everything masculine and feral.

The thickness of his long black hair brushed across her hip, tickling the skin just before his eyes reached up to meet hers. Her breath hitched at the pale color of those glistening orbs that watched her with arrogant satisfaction, caging her in his lethal, sultry stare, as the one finger finally pushed inside.

Her head fell back against the mattress, and Alice was lost to the liquid desire that flowed through her body and between her legs. A blush the color of sunset pink raced across her body.

Moaning, she squirmed when he curled that finger to touch her in places she wasn't sure had been found before, because right now, in this moment, all she could focus on was him.

"So easy," he whispered, his amused voice mocking her as much as the finger he used to thrust down deeper. And despite the anger that was born to mingle with the rush of unwelcome need, Alice had lost all the fight she had in her.

She hated herself as much as him, but spread her legs anyway begging for him to push deeper still. His breath fanned across her slick skin and she bucked at the burst of heat.

"*Please...*" It was one whispered plea that crawled out from somewhere deep down inside, a frightening reminder that she'd been so easily seduced. One touch - one pleasureful touch - and she was a slave to the sensation he gave her.

His shoulders shook with silent laughter, his finger picking up its tortuous rhythm until he was driving it so deep within her, she was begging for more so she wouldn't scream.

She groaned in complaint when he pulled his hand away, and he shushed her and cooed, "Just a little bit longer."

His body moved to kick his pants down farther and the weight of him inched up over her until his body heat was a comfort across her skin, a lie that promised safety and love. And when he finally pushed into her as thick and hard as she knew he would be, the sudden fullness from that one violent stroke inside forced the breath she'd been holding from her lungs.

Max wasn't the sweet type in bed, the kind of man who told you how beautiful you were beneath him and made promises of how he'd love you forever. No. Not with the darkness that lurked inside him, the clawing need for pain that forces a woman to whimper. He drove into her so hard, she thought she'd split open, his hand wrapping over her throat to hold her in place and steal away control of the air that flooded her lungs.

Unable to draw in a breath, Alice swam in euphoria, the feeling of floating beneath him while he took what he wanted. She was coming apart at the seams, trapped in a nightmare that split her between the side that begged and the side that whispered to her that she was finally the victim she always promised herself she'd never be.

His strong hand released her neck and she gulped in the hot air between them, her mind still lost when he pulled out to flip her body over.

Memories rushed back, the woman with the mask, with her face crushed to the mattress as he drove in from behind, and now Alice was that woman, her body on its knees as Max rode her with one hand on the back of her head and the other clutching the thick flesh of her hip, driving and forcing himself so deep it was all she could feel.

A flutter in her belly grew into a wave of ecstasy and rebellion, an orgasm churning until it exploded within. She opened her mouth to scream into the mattress, her voice breathless and torn, her submission finally and thoroughly complete.

Max used her body to chase his own release, catching it on a deeper stroke before he dropped his weight down, crushing her beneath his body and the bed, his hand releasing her head to allow her to breathe.

Having come down from the orgasm that relieved the torment, Alice lay beneath the cage of his body, a single tear slipping from the corner of her eye, one liquid, hot drop that was all she had left of the woman who'd existed before she'd been stolen away.

TWENTY-ONE

12:32 p.m.

Gray walls.

"Alice? ... Ms. Beaumont? ... Alice Beaumont?"

She couldn't bring herself to announce her presence. Defeat sat heavy on her shoulders as she walked into the interior of the doctor's office, her feet dragging beneath her as she forced her eyes to seek out the usual landmarks that told her she was somewhere protected and safe.

White door.

Dark wood desk.

White and beige striped couch.

The doctor sat back in his leather chair, his slacks wrinkled at the knees and his notebook on his lap. He studied her for several minutes without saying a word, forgoing the usual questions he'd ask when he said, "Something's changed."

Nodding her head in response, Alice pulled a pillow into her lap as if that small square of fluffed fabric would protect her from the truth she didn't want to admit to herself or to him. "How far did I get in our last session, Doc?"

Speaking softly, the doctor's voice was cautious, as if Alice were thin ice that would become cracked and broken beneath the weight of his words. "You described a sexual assault."

She shivered at the familiar words, at a nagging memory she hadn't yet fully retrieved. But even more than that was what came *after* in that particular dream. For the fact that he hadn't mentioned it, she knew she hadn't been brave enough to speak it out loud. Now was as good a time as any, because what she had to say was the worst confession of all.

"I fell in love with Max in that dream."

The quiet shuffle of his pant leg when he moved was the only sound in the room beyond the ticking clock and the sink that still hadn't met a plumber. Relaxing back against his chair, he dropped the pen on the surface of his notepad to bring his steepled fingers to his lips and appraise the woman balled up and fragile on the couch in front of him.

"Because he raped you?" he finally asked, his words as vulnerable as Alice.

Her eyes were hot from the tears that rimmed them and threatened to drip down cheeks that were already swollen from crying. Shaking her head, she clenched her eyes shut, expelling the tears so their heat would trail down in small rivulets of shimmering pain.

"No," she croaked, her voice weak and gritty. "It was because he chased away the nightmares."

Silence was a heavy ticking elegy that beat with the rhythm of the wall clock and drowned out the sound of a sink dripping endlessly.

Studying her, the doctor remained silent as if he was waiting for more from her. Alice stared back at him, also waiting. They'd reached some kind of stonewall where both people had more to say, but neither was willing to say it.

Whereas Alice's thoughts were a jumble, nothing truly concrete or static, the doctor had reached an obvious decision and proceeded forward in an attempt to lead his patient to the proper understanding of the emotions she was feeling.

"Are you sure that's the only reason you fell in love with him? Was the lack of the disorders the *only* reason?" He paused, his focus unrelenting when he quietly asked, "Is there more to the love you're feeling, Alice? People don't normally experience love after being violated in the most personal of ways. Can you think of something else that might have happened to make you feel that way?"

Slapping at the tears that slid down her jawline and clung to her chin in fear they'd fall away and be forgotten, Alice pulled her bent legs to her chest and rested her forehead against the warm, hard planes of her knees. She didn't understand what the doctor was asking of her, but something pulled at her thoughts, a gentle tug that was as annoying as it was frightening.

"I didn't tell you the last part, apparently. If I had, you would understand completely."

The soft sigh that blew over the doctor's lips did nothing to calm Alice. Silently, he considered her words while the beat of his pen against paper counted down the full minute it took him to make his decision.

"I wanted to discuss more about your father in this session, more about your life before the loss of Delilah and the dreams." He paused, waiting for her to look at him.

Alice pulled her head from her lap at the absence of sound, her eyes meeting his before he continued.

"But, I think the disclosure you just made trumps everything I wanted to go over. Tell me what happened, Alice. I want every possible detail."

TWENTY-TWO

After Max removed his weight from Alice and rolled over on the bed, a blessed rush of cool air washed across her skin, the parts of her that were wet and swollen growing cold when the air found them.

"We should clean up," Max finally said, his voice gritty and raw.

Alice struggled to pull her face from the comfort of the mattress, as if staying there long enough would suffocate her slowly and grant her the escape that Max refused to give.

Crushed and broken from the way he'd played her body like he knew every touch, every kiss, every painful place that turned her on, she dared voice a question that was as ordinary as it was strange. "What is with you and cleaning?"

The soft chuckle that whispered over his lips was unsettling. "I like a clean house," he explained. "Everything has its place. Everything is spotless and new. Everything is controlled and regulated, with no surprises or mistakes." He paused, his eyes raking a tender trail down her body, a slow caress of ghost fingers left in its wake.

Almost resigned, his voice was a feather soft confession when he admitted, "There are scars we can't wash away that mark us for life, Alice. There's no need for our outward environment to be as marred and ugly as us."

The mattress jumped after he stood to leave the room and disappear into the adjacent bathroom. Rolling to her back, Alice enjoyed the wash of cool air over her breasts, her ears picking up the sound of rushing water from behind the closed door.

Assuming Max was in the shower, she stared up at the chains that hung above her and wondered about their purpose. Perhaps if she hadn't so easily been seduced, he would have bound her in those shackles. A shiver coursed through her at the thought, and her eyes followed the hypnotic swing of the chains and the glint of light against the metal cuffs that dangled just above her.

The shower turned off after a few minutes, a cloud of swirling steam billowing out when the door was pulled open. Max stepped through with a white towel wrapped loosely around his narrow hips.

"It's your turn," he stated calmly, his eyes having returned to the ice cold temperature that felt like frozen fingers against her skin each time he stared her down.

Not wanting to move, Alice dragged the blanket on the bed over to cover herself, her head resting back against the mattress when she asked, "Why?" A slight shrug of her shoulder and she mused aloud, "Maybe if I stay dirty you won't want to rape me again."

It was the wrong thing to say, but the words had already been released like small squawking birds that wouldn't be silenced.

Max didn't so much as blink in immediate response to her words, but after a minute he turned and retreated back into the bathroom. The shower turned on again, great rolling clouds of steam dancing out the door, spinning and churning against the cold air of the bedroom.

Alice closed her eyes, exhaustion settling over her and lulling her into a false sense of comfort, but it wouldn't be for long. The shower turned off and heavy steps announced Max' return, his naked form a silhouette in the doorway with the towel he'd previously used to cover his hips now hanging steaming and soaked in his hand.

He stepped into the light of the bedroom, his malicious gaze locked on Alice, so scathing that she sat up from the bed and inched her way to the side. By the time her feet hit the floor, he'd started across the room, closing what little distance there was. "Then I'll wash you my goddamned self."

He lunged forward to grab her, barely missing her arm before she fell back. Her bottom struck the ground so hard the impact ricocheted up through her bones and into her teeth. Ignoring the jolt of pain, she spun over to land on her hands and knees, crawling as fast as her limbs could carry her, but not fast enough.

She heard the wet towel snap in his hand, and expected the sting of the end against her body, but it never came. Daring to glance back, her eyes opened wide as the towel was held open in his hands, the soaked fabric brought down until it wrapped across her face. He wrenched it tight by twisting the ends at the back of her head, and she lost her balance, her naked body falling until splayed over the ground.

"Get up," he warned, the dark notes of his voice not a loud, striking thing, but something colder and ominous.

A quick tug of his arm had her neck arching back, her hands clawing at the towel because she couldn't breathe through the hot, soaked material. She wanted to scream, to beg him to stop, but drawing in air through the wet fabric was nearly impossible. Panic rose in her, a wild animal caged, her head shaking back and forth in an attempt to find freedom.

Dragging her by the towel wrapped around her head, his footsteps were thunder against her senses, a steady warning beat that said death was soon approaching.

Her fingers were useless against the cloth, the hot water that soaked it burning her skin where it touched. Her body was dragged over the threshold between the carpet of the bedroom and the tile of the bathroom. Max forced her up onto her knees.

"You can breathe, Alice. Stop fighting me and breathe!"

His arm wrapped around her abdomen and she was lifted in the air, the towel still secured where it suffocated her. Her body dropped down onto slippery wet tiles, the shower turned on above her head. More water poured onto the towel to flow down her body, the scalding heat an inferno against her skin.

She bucked and twisted, her mouth open and desperate for air, her mind scrambled by the fear that she'd finally pushed him far enough.

"Are you ready to take a shower now?"

Nodding her head fervently, she started to cry, her lungs burning in her chest from a lack of air.

Relief was given when he removed the wet shroud, a burst of dancing steam dragged into her lungs as she gasped and choked on the freedom he'd returned to her.

A bar of soap was tossed at the floor by her knees, a washcloth slapped down unceremoniously beside it. "Meet me back in the bedroom when you're done."

His steps faded off as he retreated from the room, but stopped short, his deep, cutting voice filling the empty space his lack of steps had left behind. "And be sure to get those places I dirtied up real well, just in case I want to *rape* you later."

He practically spit the word rape from his mouth, a look of revulsion tightening his features. She wanted to laugh because, despite his disgust with the word, what else could you call it?

The door slammed shut, vibrating the walls, and she was left trembling beneath a spray of water far too hot for her skin. Her fingers slid up the slick tile and found the nozzle. Turning it to the right, she cooled the temperature of the spray, but it didn't help calm her after everything that happened.

Taking the soap in her hands, she sobbed as she rubbed it over the washcloth to spread the suds over her body and clean the *places he'd dirtied*.

After finishing, she climbed out and squeezed the water from her long hair before tossing the tangled heap to fall down her back and stepping softly into the darkened bedroom.

The sheets that were previously covering the bed were a wrinkled pile on the floor, replaced by a clean, pressed set that was the color of a summer sky.

It was then that she realized Max hadn't lied about his need for everything to be neat and tidy, clean and sterile, controlled and unmarked by the scars and dirt that life left behind.

"Get in bed. I have something I need to do and then I'll join you."

The voice came out of nowhere, causing Alice to flinch at the sudden, unexpected intrusion. Obediently, she climbed onto the massive bed and watched Max leave the room. He didn't appear again until her eyes met the television screen that still glowed a faint light in the room, his large body approaching the woman whose face was still covered.

"No," Alice whispered, her voice hitched in her throat. "Please, no."

Her eyes were trapped to the screen, her attention stuck on a scene she knew would cause her to rage silently, to fill up with an angry, toxic poison that she wouldn't be allowed to release.

Max approached the woman slowly, her head moving up despite the hood that concealed her face. Reaching out with a tender hand, Max caressed the woman's cheek before dropping to his knees in front of her. His shoulders shook like he was crying, but Alice thought it had to be a trick of her eyes. Angling his head down, he pressed his forehead to her lap, a man begging forgiveness.

Sitting up, Alice watched with rapt attention, her lips parting in shocked silence when the woman's hands moved to run her fingers through his hair. It was an act of forgiveness, a solemn moment...another piece of a puzzle that had no known solution.

Max and the woman stayed in the position for several minutes before Max rose to leave, and when the screen returned to a picture of a lonely woman trapped and broken, Alice breathed out a shaky sigh. Confusion saddled her as a chill slithered up her spine.

What had just happened?

In time, Max returned and didn't speak a word of what he'd done as he climbed into bed beside her. Wrapping his arms around her body, he pulled her back against his chest, a soft sound of contentment brushing across his lips.

Alice lay awake, her eyes still glued to the screen, a thousand questions running through her head until they exhausted her completely and delivered her to sleep.

* * *

The next morning came as ordinary as any morning. Except it wasn't ordinary for one stark reason that Alice didn't understand until she opened her eyes to find the first rays of morning sunlight trickling past the curtains of a large picture window in the room.

Dust motes glimmered where they hung suspended in a cascade of shimmering beauty, tiny fairies of light that had paused to worship the warmth that was returning to the world after hours of the cold moonlit night. Her eyes followed those small points of reflected light where they danced and swirled within the gentle air current that worked a path through the room.

She was aware of her surroundings, but not yet awake enough to feel panic over it. More importantly, she wasn't pinned to the bed by some unseen specter. She was able to wiggle her fingers and toes, and she didn't open her eyes onto the scene of nightmare that had followed her from sleep into her waking life.

The sleep paralysis she'd suffered so often that it had become a part of herself was absent. There was no ringing in her ears so loud she feared she'd never hear anything beautiful again. There was no weight on her chest that threatened to crush her. Her body was solid and not floating above itself looking down to where she lay comfortably in the arms of a man.

The confusion that came with the absence of a demon that had plagued her for as far back as she could remember was staggering. So much so, in fact, that she forgot to feel the panic of the reality to which she'd woken. The monster to whom she'd woken.

Max' arms were a warm weight across her body that prevented her from sitting up, but from what she could see, the pillows she laid her tired head upon the night before were still in place. The sheets were as neat over her body as they had been when she tucked herself in. There were no obvious points of pain on her arms or legs from where she'd hurt herself fighting some unseen force through the night. She was still in place and hadn't woken to find herself standing in the threshold of a doorway, or lying down in another room.

She'd slept through the night without fighting. Without dreaming. Without panic or fear. And she woke peacefully to find the glimmering rays of quiet, morning light.

TWENTY-THREE

12:33 p.m.

Gray walls.

Black table.

Plastic, fake red roses.

"Alice?   ...   Ms.   Beaumont?   ...   Alice
Beaumont?"

"Yes, doctor."

Alice's feet shuffled beneath her as she
dragged herself in to take her usual place on the
couch to be examined. But unlike other days
where she'd sunk into the cushions, weighted
down by the grim reality that they would never
understand or cure the nightmares that haunted
her, Alice felt lighter, more awake, more in touch
with the world around her.

She still didn't remember what she did from
hour to hour. She couldn't stitch together time
until it became a clear picture of what her life
was like. However, for once, and for those few
moments she knew would be fleeting at best, she

felt like she'd triumphed in the face of an ever-present threat.

"You look good today, Alice. Rested."

The doctor's observations weren't entirely accurate. She wasn't *good* or *rested* in the traditional sense of the words. She was better than most days, but still didn't feel like a normal person would.

She didn't comment on what the doctor said, couldn't find the proper words or phrase to explain the way her fears still existed beneath the surface of her skin. Guilt rode her for finding the smallest amount of joy in the relief she felt that her fears weren't the first thing on her mind, or a crushing weight pinning her in one harrowing place.

The doctor arched a brow in question at her silence, but he didn't prattle on to make her discuss the change as she'd thought he would.

His throat cleared, a sharp bark of a sound before the gentle lilt of his voice filled the silence between them. "Before we talk about any more of the dreams, I think it's important that we go over a few points I've determined are necessary topics."

Idle fingers toying with the ends of her long hair, she glanced at him to let him know she was listening.

"You admitted in our last session that you'd fallen in love with Max. That after the abduction, the violence and the abuse..." His voice became softer, more hesitant and careful. "...that after the rape, you loved him."

A quick nod of her head, a throat working over the remnants of a previous confession that were uncomfortably lodged in place.

"That's worrisome, Alice. And it speaks to several conditions that give me significant pause."

Some awkward emotion pulled at the corners of her chapped lips, some disturbing thing that caused her to want to laugh off his words as an obvious statement. "That I could love a man like him?"

Turning her head slightly to give the doctor a brief look at her soft eyes, she noticed the rigid set of his shoulders, the seriousness of his attentive posture. He was on edge and she'd been the one to make him that way.

A new guilt rode her, and one she hoped could be lessened with a simple acknowledgement of his concern. "I didn't love him for the abuse, Doc. That's not something that makes you love a person, is it?"

Rather than responding, the doctor sat motionless in his seat, patient and waiting for whatever explanation she would give.

Returning her attention to the hair she continued toying over her fingers, she said, "I didn't love him for that. I loved him because he was dangerous enough to chase away the nightmares." As an afterthought, she added, "He was dark enough that he overshadowed my light, and the nightmares couldn't find their way."

The tip of his pen scribbled over his notepad, the pages rustling as he turned them to continue jotting down thoughts. "He is a nightmare, Alice. The relief you're describing was nothing more than one element of a dream."

"But it's a small bit of peace I never had before. A dream within a nightmare, I guess. Unless you lived a life like mine, you can't understand how special, how rare, that small ray of light was for me."

In his typical fashion, he didn't immediately respond, allowing her words time to fully form so that every hidden nuance of meaning could be seen.

However, the quiet moment couldn't last.

"Have you considered my theory at all, Alice? That these dreams aren't a tie to your missing sister, but instead, are about you? About something inside yourself that is so terrible, you can't face it except through dreams?"

Delilah. She hadn't once thought of her since stepping foot inside the doctor's office. But the spoken reminder was enough to set her back on that edge of panic and guilt, the very real understanding that her sister was the one in danger...the one who would pay for Alice's crimes.

"I don't think you're correct in that, Doc. I still think the dreams are a link to her, a clue into her disappearance. I feel ashamed for finding even a small amount of peace while her nightmare continues."

With more censure in his tone than she'd ever heard from the man, he argued, "You felt love for a man who a stole you, Alice. For a man who hurt you, who raped you. Do you understand what that could be? There are conditions -"

"What? Like Stockholm Syndrome?" She laughed. "Isn't that what every dark story is about these days?"

"Not every story," he answered, his words solemn and dripping with sorrow.

The clock ticked.

The faucet dripped.

The doctor tossed out a reminder that shot terror through her veins.

"You're running out of time, Alice."

Breath shaking over her lips, she said, "I know."

Blood rushed through her head, the quiet rolling thunder that followed a flash of blinding fear. "We need to save her, Doc. We need to find Delilah."

His pen tapped, an annoying tick that was a key to the mystery of his personal thoughts and feelings. Ever the professional, Alice knew he would follow his training and push those feelings aside to redirect his patient to where he needed her to be. And having gone to school for a similar field of study, Alice could respect him for his persistence.

"We need to save you," he reminded her.

Another tap of his pen and Alice smiled at the sound of it wondering if he knew it was an outward symptom of his own frustration.

"Am I really that difficult, Doc?"

A twitch of his lip betrayed his amusement. "So, you're saying that you didn't fall in love with this man because of the abuse, but rather, because he was somehow able to quiet the sleeping disorders that you suffer?"

Damn, he was good. She grinned to realize that he wouldn't be so easily distracted from his path.

"It's never happened before," she admitted. "And I don't care if it was just a dream. That was the first time I woke up not drenched in sweat. The first time that my teeth and jaw didn't hurt from grinding. That I was able to move without fighting to regain the use of my arms and legs. I don't think anybody can truly appreciate how terrifying it is to wake up in places you don't remember falling asleep. To feel like you're tied to a bed, or that some unseen force is holding you in place.

It's like you see in horror movies, except it's not a ghost and I'm not possessed. But I wake up sometimes to look down on myself sleeping. To see demons hovering nearby with sharp teeth and eyes that glow or are completely black. It's like being a prisoner within your own body. And I'm always tired, Doc. I'm constantly tired because I never actually sleep."

"They're hallucinations, Alice. You know that. You've suffered them long enough to know that sleep paralysis is just a dysfunction in your sleep cycle. You wake up physically, but your mind is still dreaming."

A chortle escaped her throat. "Yeah, I'll try telling myself that next time I'm unable to move while some wicked thing peers down at me with evil in its eyes. I'm sure it will make me feel so much better."

Another slash of the tip of his pen across paper, blue ink swirling into patterns of words she couldn't read and wasn't sure she wanted to know.

"Let me ask you something."

215

Alice glanced up, her mood light despite the nagging feeling that he would say something to bring her down again.

"When you left home to go to school, did you ever return to live there again? When you had problems in your career, was returning home an option?"

Confusion furrowed her brows. "Why does that matter?"

"Because it paints a clearer picture of your life before all of this, for me and for you. Maybe if we can understand where you were mentally and emotionally at the time Delilah disappeared, we can better understand why these dreams are the ones that particular event conjured."

Her eyes rolled, but she played along. She could give him that in repayment of every frustration she was sure she'd caused in his life. "I think you're barking up the wrong tree, Doc, but I'll go along with it, if it makes you feel better about things."

His lips pulled into a grin.

"But after that, I think it's best we return to the dreams. It's like you said, I'm running out of time. This session will be over soon."

"That's not what I meant, Alice."

"I know," she admitted. "Delilah is running out of time. And if I hurry, I might discover how to find her, how to save her before that time runs out and it's too late."

Staring at her with an expression that made it clear he was losing just a bit of the patience he'd always had, the doctor said nothing. He didn't need to. The look behind his eyes and the manner in which his shoulders rolled back and his body refused to relax against his chair was as direct a response as anything he could have said.

"Fine," she breathed out. "In answer to your question, no, I didn't return home. Even when I was living off bullshit money after quitting my job at the hospital, even when I was bouncing between other jobs, I never went back there. It's like I told you, my dad could barely take care of himself, and when I left he still had my mother and brother to manage. I wasn't going to add to that."

"Is that the only reason?"

"No," she confessed, the dark cloud of panic finally settling over her shoulders now that the doctor had brought the memories of her early life back to the surface of her thoughts. "My father was an abusive ass. Both mentally and physically when he was drinking. And he was always drinking. Why do you even care about any of this? It has nothing to do with the dreams."

"I care because I find it interesting."

"Why?"

With his mouth pulled into a stern line, he settled back against his chair now that he had her running down the path he'd designed for her, his little mouse running a scientist's maze.

"Because you started having nightmares based on one abusive relationship, and it took another to chase them away. Don't you find that relevant? Impossible, even?"

Not having given much thought to the reasons behind her nightmares, she hadn't made a connection between their cause and Max' ability to silence them. It didn't matter to her. All that mattered was that she'd had one peaceful night, one peaceful morning, a chance to wake up and smile rather than fight against some unseen force that existed completely in her mind. Shaking her head, she attempted to ignore the fact that the moment had been another manifestation in her head. But thinking about it now, she wanted to cry.

Perhaps that one solitary glimpse of being normal, of being able to find peace in sleep, had been nothing more than a cruel bit of torment... because it was something she'd never find in her waking life.

She couldn't admit it to herself, and she certainly wouldn't admit it to him.

"Maybe one monster is just scarier than the other," she mused aloud.

"Or maybe," the doctor countered, "that fact is more significant than you realize."

The rim of his glasses flashed beneath the soft light when he sat forward to lock her eyes with his. "Maybe, it's the key to understanding what these dreams are about. Tell me something, and be honest in your answer. Who did your father abuse when he'd been drinking? Was it the entire family? Your mother? Your sister? Your brother?"

Alice's heart clenched in her chest, the truth trickling over her like acid now that he was releasing it from where it had been trapped in her mind. Her skin melted beneath the flow of toxic filth, falling away to reveal all the pain that had been hidden inside.

"Who, Alice?"

"Me," she snapped, her teeth gnashing together from the bitter taste it left in her mouth. "Just me."

"Why?"

"Because I was the freak!" she shrieked, her hands clenching into fists in her lap, her jaw working over itself as she craned her head to look as far away from the doctor as she could. On a sob, she released the truth that clawed at her with the talons of a man who'd destroyed her long before Max entered her life.

"Because I was the one who kept him awake at night, who wouldn't let him get to work on time because he was so tired. Because I was the one screaming so loud the neighbors called the cops. And because I was the girl who didn't fit the picture of a perfect family that he'd created in order to hide the problems that were all his own. So he drank. And when he did, it was me who was locked away in a small closet at bedtime. It was my body that took the pounding blows when my mother was too tired to wake up and deal with me in the middle of the night. Everybody else was perfect. They knew to stay quiet and they knew to stay out of his way. But not me. I was too loud. I was too strong. I was the one who always drew attention to herself."

Her breathing was erratic. Her pulse racing as the truth poured out in a viscous liquid that amplified the pain of memories in her heart.

"I was the one who became his target because, instead of getting better, I got worse. The more he hurt me, the worse I became. The worse the nightmares became. The worse my entire life became."

The doctor didn't react openly, but she saw a glimmer of anger behind his eye. Somehow managing to keep his voice steady, he asked, "And if you hadn't been your father's target, would your other family members have been safe?"

"No," she breathed out, the confession a sharp razor that dragged across her tongue.

He sat back in his chair, his eyes flicking back and forth between her and the tip of the ballpoint pen that flew across his notepad. Giving her time to settle down, he jotted down his thoughts, his face twisted into an expression of grim concentration.

When her sobs had quieted down and when the tears had slowed to a trickling rhythm, he ripped a tissue from the box beside him, leaning forward again to hand it to her. Alice took it, but didn't thank him for the small courtesy.

"One more question and then we'll move on to the next dream."

Through hot, swollen eyes, she glared at him.

"Is it possible that these dreams are nothing more than a metaphor, Alice? A memory seeping out from whatever secret place you'd kept it hidden?"

"No," she shook her head and sniffled. "That's not possible."

"How do you know?"

She clenched her eyes shut to expel that last of the stinging tears, opening them again to look him dead in the eyes.

"Because of what happened next. Let me finish, Doc. Stop playing around with crap that has nothing to do with this and let me finish."

He nodded. "Fine. But whatever you say needs to convince me that it's not connected to your past. Otherwise, we'll be having this conversation again."

TWENTY-FOUR

"Get dressed."

Two clipped words spoken, one white dress tossed at her feet.

Sitting on the edge of the bed, Alice had waited patiently for Max to get showered and dressed after he finally woke up. She'd locked eyes with him as soon as his eyelids fluttered open, her heart still swelling with the small happiness of having escaped the disorders that usually plagued her nights.

Not knowing what to expect when he opened his eyes to the early morning, the last thing she'd thought he'd do was grumble at the sight of her, thrash his way out from under the blankets they shared and march into the bathroom with heavy-footed steps.

He was angry, and she didn't know why.

The small bit of pleasure she'd felt from waking up rested was lost as soon as the bathroom door slammed shut and a spray of water could be heard whispering from behind that wooden barrier.

Shivering at the memory of the events of the previous night, Alice had crept out from beneath blankets that were far too warm against the heat of anger that ran across her skin, and she'd shimmied her body down to the foot of the bed to wait.

Max emerged from the steamy bathroom with a white towel wrapped around his hips. She wondered for a brief moment if it was the same towel that he'd used to wrap her head when he'd dragged her into the shower. Remembering his need for clean and new, she brushed that thought aside as absurd.

Dropping the towel from around his hips, Max tossed it into a wicker hamper, the firm cheeks of his ass staring back at her from beneath broad shoulders, a strong back, and the indented line that ran along the length of his spine. Smooth skin barely contained the steel musculature of his body, and Alice became lost to the way his biceps flexed when he pulled clothes from his bureau.

Dark blue jeans and a simple white t-shirt. It seemed too casual for a man as complicated as him.

After getting dressed, Max disappeared into his closet, reappearing with the outfit he'd selected for her to wear.

He left the room after making his demand, his voice trailing over his shoulder with the instruction for her to meet him in the kitchen when she was finished.

"Well, good morning to you, too," she whispered, unsure why she felt rejected by his irritable and arrogant mood.

Snatching the dress from the floor, she stood up on achy legs to stand before the full-length mirror. No underwear, no bra, just a shell of a dress with buttons up the front, a blue sash as a belt to cinch it at her waist.

Pulling the cloth over her shoulders, she fastened the buttons one by one before tying the sash and looking at her reflection in the mirror. The dress was quite beautiful, despite its simplicity, but her hair was a frightful mess of blonde limp tendrils. Reaching up, she braided the mess back to give it the illusion of being styled before huffing out a breath and making her way out of the room and down three flights of stairs.

From the kitchen came loud clanging sounds, pots and pans being pulled from cabinets, the sizzle of bacon heard seconds before the smell hit her nose like an avalanche of temptation. Her stomach rumbled as she stepped barefoot from the wood floors of the entry hall onto the cool stone tile.

"I'm here," she stated softly, her eyes flicking between Max and the television screen positioned at the top left corner of the room. The woman, still hooded, sat still on the edge of the bed, her body covered in the same dress that Alice now wore.

Her brows furrowing with confusion, she wondered why the woman on screen was always dressed identical. Her mouth opened to ask the question, but she shook her head deciding against the risk of angering a man who was already agitated.

"Take a seat at the center island, Alice. Breakfast will be ready in a minute."

An obedient lamb sitting down to the slaughter, not a word from her mouth in protest of the butcher. That's how she felt every time she acquiesced to his demands, each moment she submitted to him without argument or complaint.

Plates were set down on the table before her, a different design than the ones she'd shattered the night before. Eggs and bacon, toast and juice, an ordinary meal despite the circumstances that were far too dismal to be normal.

"Eat."

Every command he barked was as curt and emotionless as the one before it.

Picking up her fork, she ignored the whispers inside her head, the nagging reminders that she was giving in too easily. She was stronger than this, a fighter, a woman who'd endured her entire life despite the crushing blows and painful torment that had accompanied her from sleep into reality.

However, her body knew what to do despite her mind's inability to conform. Her body was hungry. Her body was needy. Her body made her a slave to the demands of the man who now stood above her watching.

Slipping the tines of the fork into the scrambled eggs, she fed herself slowly, chewing thoughtfully on the food that would sustain her. Instead of the aversion she felt the previous night, she enjoyed the salty slide across her tongue, the warmth that traveled down her throat to land on an empty belly. Relief was found in the comfort of the nourishment he'd provided her.

"I have a surprise for you today. Something I know you'll appreciate. It comes with a price, just like anything in life, but one that's not too steep."

Glancing up at him from beneath the thickness of her light colored lashes, she attempted a polite smile that was more strained than pleasant. "Will it hurt me? The surprise or the price?"

Unamused by the tone of her question, Max leaned back against the kitchen counter, a steaming cup of coffee held in his hands, his lips pursed to blow over the surface of the liquid. His face was clean shaven, the dust of shadow gone following the shower he'd taken that morning.

Alice watched him when he wasn't looking, her eyes playing over the sharp lines of his cheekbones and the strong, square jaw that gave him a rugged, but cultured appearance. Despite the scar that marred the left side of his face, he was elegant in his features. With a straight nose that ran above full and sculpted lips, he had eyes that were pale and cold, a sparkling blue that were in stark contrast to obsidian hair and tan skin. An enigma wrapped in beauty, he was as alluring as he was fierce.

A question toyed over her thoughts. Afraid to ask, she worried her bottom lip between her teeth, her curiosity too much for her to keep her silence.

"What happened to you, Max?"

His eyes pinned her in their callous stare, studying her over the rim of the cup from which he sipped. His throat worked to swallow down the steaming liquid before he pulled the cup away to place it on the counter. "What do you mean?"

Clearing her throat of the fear she felt for bringing the subject up, she summoned everything brave within her to continue forward in the conversation she'd been dumb enough to start. "Your scars? How did you get them?"

His glacial stare was a wash of cold anger across her body, a shiver running down her spine to know she'd stepped in places not traveled by any person who valued their life. But wasn't she already in danger just for being in the house with him? Hadn't he already threatened everything she loved and admired for no other reason than because he could? What was one more thing that would draw his ire?

He wouldn't kill her. That much she thought she knew. There was no reason to stifle the question that had traipsed quietly through her mind from the minute she'd met him.

Silently considering her question, his jaw ticked a slow beat. She wasn't sure whether he'd answer her, and the tension that mounted her shoulders forced the fork from her hands, her pulse an annoying drumbeat that fluttered over the soft point of her neck.

Black lashes framed his hollow eyes, shadows creeping and swirling beneath the blue that didn't give her any clue to the thoughts assaulting him inside.

"My father," he finally said, his voice morose and vacant, "was an exceptionally driven man. I was an only child, his only offspring that survived the journey from my mother's womb to the bedroom where she'd given birth to me. I was the seventh in a line of eight, and the only one who'd taken a breath once the umbilical cord was cut."

Pushing up from the counter upon which he'd previously leaned, he took three steps to stand by the island where Alice sat listening. A sheet of paper sat to his side, a stack of mail neatly organized beside it. Slipping the top sheet from the stack, he slid it to lay between them, his hands working methodically over the blank surface, making folds with sharp creases, before opening it again. Spellbound by the precise motion of his fingers, Alice jumped when he spoke.

"So, because I was the only child they managed to successfully bring into this world, I carried the full weight of the family's legacy on my shoulders."

His eyes flicked up to catch hers, the fleeting contact sending a chill along Alice's skin. Returning his attention to the sheet of paper he continued to fold and unfold for no obvious reason, he continued.

"Seven graves sat on the property where we lived. Six older than me, and one younger. I hadn't been there for any of the burials because I was barely a year old when my sister, Greta, was stillborn. But every day, from the time I could walk and understand what was being shown to me, my father led me outside to look down at the markers that held the names of the seven children who'd failed him."

A memory brushed across her mind, a nagging sense of something familiar and ominous skirting the edges to leave tattered ribbons of understanding blowing softly in an unwelcome wind. Like rain, the drops of memory fell over her shoulders, cold against her skin. Unsure about whether she wanted to hear the rest of his story, she drew her arms around herself, hating the shared emotions the dire tone of his story conjured within her battered heart.

"You see, my father didn't accept failure. He'd never failed, and as far as he was concerned, those that had were better left behind and forgotten. If it hadn't been for me, those children would have never had a parent visiting their lonely graves. However, because of me, they enjoyed a daily visit so that my father could show me what failure looked like, so that he could show me how little a person was worth when they didn't live up to his expectations."

His lips curled on a sad grin. "Until I was seven years old, I assumed my father had killed each and every one of them. But my mother explained to me the circumstances of their births when I'd become so scared of going out there that I cried each time my father called for me."

Sympathy, a baleful echo inside her, Alice regretted the question she asked him. She wanted to hate this man for everything he'd done to her, for everything he'd done to her sister. However, his story rang a bell in her heart. It was a link between their pasts that she wished didn't exist, a familiar story about the empty place left by an uncaring parent in a child. Without responding to his words, she stared at him with heartache blooming in her chest, with a pesky belief that she could guess how his story would end. Her story hadn't started out as strange and hopeless as his appeared to be, but she knew the outcome because she'd lived it.

With hands still working over the paper he toyed with as easily as he toyed with the two women he kept trapped, he refused to look at her as he gave her a window through which she could view the life he'd known before.

"I became everything my father wanted me to be. But, not at first. Not until he showed me what happened when I dared disappoint him."

His eyes met hers for a brief second, the same pain she carried inside herself reflected back at her as if she were looking into a mirror. Dragging his gaze away, he explained, "When I was ten or eleven, I'm not sure of the exact age, my nanny gave me a birthday present. I cherished that present because it was something secret between the two of us, a bit of whimsy in a life where childhood fantasies and interests were not allowed to exist. My nanny felt sorry for me, I assume. She was a silent witness to the hours of rigorous study I had to complete. From the minute I was conceived, I was shouldered with the responsibility of carrying on my father's legacy in business, and there was no room for idle time. Math, literature, foreign language, economics and the like: those were the toys I was allowed to play with."

He sighed, and Alice didn't fail to notice the small hint of vulnerability she wouldn't have thought possible in him.

"The present was a set of books. Something fun for me to play with when my father wasn't lording over me ensuring that I was becoming a model image of the man he'd grown to become. Late at night, after he'd gone to bed, or whatever it was he did in the late evening hours, I would crawl out from beneath my covers and pull those books out from below a loose board in the floor. Hidden underneath that board were all the treasures I held secret, like a small part of me that had to remain hidden for fear it would reveal the truth that I wasn't as interested in success as he had been. The first book was on magic. Parlor tricks, really, basic stuff that required a sleight of hand. They were tricks that were simple enough for a child to master if enough practice was given to the task. After learning those, I moved on to the second book. A book on the art of paper folding. Origami. Something that filled the time I had to myself."

Dragging her eyes down to the paper he was working into a familiar form, she suddenly understood what he'd been doing all along. Whatever he was creating still hadn't taken full shape. Her attention was drawn between the face of the man whispering his confession and the form that confession was taking on the paper he crafted into a beautiful thing.

"It was by accident that he discovered the talents I'd learned from those books. We were in the kitchen. My mother was preparing dinner on a gas burning stove and I sat at the small table where I tended to find myself when not at the formal dining table. I forget what subject I was studying at the time, but I'd grown bored of whatever nonsense I was reading and, without thinking, I started making folds in a piece of paper. Eventually those folds became something specific, and at the same time that piece of paper transformed into the image of something other than itself, my father walked into the room."

Lifting his hand, he placed a paper crane on the table in front of her. Its beak pointed at where she sat, its wings perfectly formed at its sides. Small and plain white, with no ornamentation to speak of, the creation was beautiful for its simplicity alone. Reaching out to touch it, she'd almost put a finger against its surface, but pulled back at the last second. There was something sacred about the paper crane, something solemn that kept her from corrupting it with any part of herself.

Her gaze fixed to the inanimate bird, she didn't look up when he spoke again.

"My father was livid when he saw the crane. To him, it was a betrayal of sorts. A fanciful interest that wouldn't prepare me for the path he'd expected me to follow. It was a distraction and a curse, a symptom of a childhood he'd never allowed me to live."

Alice closed her eyes when Max' voice dropped to a dreadful whisper. She knew the ending before he spoke it, but didn't stop him from telling the tale.

"In his anger, my father picked up a cast iron skillet my mother had been using to prepare the family meal. He normally hit me with objects, never with his hand because that was too personal – even that small amount of contact. The skillet was still steaming from where it had been sitting on the stovetop."

She opened her eyes, slowly lifting her head to look up at the face of a man in pain.

"Needless to say, when the back of the skillet hit my cheek, it took off some of my skin with it. The smell..." He paused, his face wrinkling in disgust at the phantom of a memory.

"The smell was horrendous and my mother screamed when she looked at her perfect son to see what had become of me. It took days for my father to realize what he'd done. Days to realize that he'd permanently scarred the son upon whom he'd placed the entire future of his company. How could a man run a business when nobody wants to look at him when he speaks? How can a man be the mirror image of his father when half of his face was scarred?"

The thin line of his mouth curved at the corners on a thought, the hint of a dimple indenting his cheek giving her a flash of the boyish charm hidden behind the blank mask he normally wore.

"In retrospect, this scar may have been my only salvation. As soon as he realized the damage he'd done, he no longer expected me to take over the family business. In his eyes, I was as useless as the children buried in the garden on his property, as easily forgotten as those who'd been long dead."

Their eyes locked and Alice shed a tear for the man who stood so open and vulnerable before her. She didn't know how long this moment would last, but it was a piece of humanity inside a man she would have never guessed could be human. She wanted to reach out to that part of him. Nurture it in case it would somehow help her escape the torment he'd caused.

"My father was a cruel bastard as well," she offered, "except I wasn't fortunate enough to escape his notice. He tried locking me away in places I couldn't escape from, tried muffling my screams in hopes he could sleep through the night without being jostled awake by his freak of a daughter. But no matter what he did, I was always right there in his sight. Always the dumb child who didn't know how to behave or stay quiet. It wasn't my fault. I was sleeping most of the time. But that didn't matter to him." Her voice trailed off, her mind locked into a memory that she'd prefer to forget.

Max didn't openly react to her statement. His head angled to the side, his hair brushing against his shoulder when his lips pulled up into a playful grin.

"I already know that about you, Alice. It's what draws me to you. We're alike, you and I. Two very different backgrounds, but a shared trait that pulls us together."

It was the first time he'd told her he knew all there was to know about her. While he stood in front of her as a mysterious puzzle that had no known solution, she felt naked to his eyes…naked and vulnerable to the knowledge he had of her, gained by means she wasn't sure she wanted to know. Perhaps he was lying each time he told her he knew more about her than she knew of herself. Another aspect of the game he was playing against her, his knowledge of her – or at least the threat of it – was just another method through which he could control her.

How can a person hide their weaknesses against another person who knew all their insecurities and secrets?

If it was even possible for him to know as much about her as he claimed to know, how had he gained that information?

She'd never been a social butterfly in any sense of the world. More reclusive than anything else, she'd kept to herself since the moment she left home to attend school. Expending as little energy as she could manage with the other students and teachers that surrounded her in the years until she'd graduated, she always painted a prettier picture of the life she'd led. Nobody, except for the members of her immediate family, knew of the secrets she carried.

Her heart broke at that thought, an answer rearing its ugly head to stare her in the face and show her just how foolish she'd been to feel even an ounce of remorse for the monster in front of her.

"She told you, didn't she?"

His brow arched on a question. "Who?"

Turning her face in the direction of the screen that still had a picture of a hooded woman sitting alone on a small bed, Alice caught Max in her peripheral vision, waiting until he removed his gaze from her and fixed his attention on the television screen.

"Did you force the answers from her? Torture her so she'd tell you all about her freak of a sister? Is that how you found me, you son of a bitch?"

Fingernails pressed half moon circles into the palms of her hands, her entire body shaking with anger and newfound rage. "Tell me!"

Here again, Alice expected violence to rise back to the surface, a cold, simmering evil that lay dormant inside him until she did or said something to bring it back to life. But instead of returning to her the scorching flame of revulsion and anger that had sparked to life inside her, he turned his head slowly in her direction to match her fire with his ice.

A secretive grin tilted his lips when he answered, "You told me, Alice. You told me everything there was to know about all of the little secrets you hide."

"Liar." She spat the word at him, her teeth clenched together from the rage that was bubbling up inside her.

He didn't react, at least not on the surface. Instead, he simply sighed. "You can be as angry as you want about the fact that I know you so well, but, in the end, does it even really matter? Stop playing around with facts that have no significance. All you'll achieve is to spin yourself around in circles with no true benefit. Stop wasting your energy on petty things. You've already lost this game, my love. You lost long before you ever started playing."

Pulling her eyes away from the cold steel of his gaze, she stifled the tears that threatened her eyes. Anger raced across her nerves, her hands clenching tighter in her lap to realize that he wasn't wrong in what he'd said. The game they played was never one she'd ever had a chance at winning.

The instinct of self-preservation set aside, she opened her mouth to speak the thoughts that battered at her weary skull. "I thought that, maybe, you were softening up. That, perhaps, you could see my sister and me as something more human. Abusive men raised us both. Our lives were both intended as a trophy for the parents that raised us, rather than about anything that would make us happy and whole."

Chancing a sidelong glance, she peeked over at Max. His expression was a mask of pity, his head shaking so slowly in disbelief that she wasn't sure she was seeing it at all.

With a slap of his open hand against the counter, the sound so sudden and loud that it caused her to jump, he quashed any hope she had that he would make this life easier on her than the past twenty-four hours.

Her eyes darted from his face down to where his palm had landed, and from beneath his fingers she could see the crane crushed and broken, something fragile and beautiful rendered to be nothing more than a piece of forgotten trash. Never before had she felt such a tie to an inanimate object. The crane could just have easily been her or the woman he held prisoner in the basement.

"Do not mistake what I told you as a vulnerability inside me, Alice."

Her eyes dragged up his arm, over his broad shoulder and along the cords of his neck to lock on to a set of eyes that cut as deep as the sharpest razor. Anger was obvious in the set of his jaw, a cold slice of steel that you didn't know had maimed you until the blood seeped out, fast and hot.

"My father shaped me regardless of whether I walked the path he'd drawn for me. And he paid for those mistakes as a result. I don't exist in this world for anyone but myself. And any vulnerability I had in life vanished when I left childhood behind. Don't waste your time looking for weakness. You'll walk away empty and a little more crushed and broken for the effort."

Her throat worked over the thick fear that swelled up from her rapidly beating heart, her skin prickling in response to a chill that had nothing to do with the temperature.

Forcing herself to speak, she worked quickly to repair whatever damage she'd caused by her assumptions. "I'm sorry. I didn't mean anything by what I said."

Inclining his head slowly, he studied her for several moments. His appraisal complete, he said, "I want to show you the surprise I have for you. I think you'll appreciate the small bit of freedom that comes with it." He paused for a moment, his head turning to look at the television screen – at the image of the solitary hooded woman – and back to Alice. "But you'd be smart to never allow yourself to forget the price."

Her eyes closed, the burning tears slipping down along her cheek to trace the line of her jaw. Futility was the cloak she now wore, the painful, twisting knowledge that there wasn't a shred of decency or humanity in the man that now ruled her life.

With measured steps, he rounded the kitchen island to offer his hand to her. "Come with me, Alice. You'll like what I have to show you."

A snake that would bite her, his hand hung between them for several seconds, the fingers coiled to strike as soon as she reached out to accept it. But with little choice, she reached for the predator in her midst. A warmth that wasn't welcome against her skin, it hurt her in so many ways that she felt paralyzed by the contrast of emotion flooding her.

Comfort because he'd chased away her nightmares.

Hatred because he'd threatened the one person she loved most.

Bitter resentment because he'd made her body respond to him in ways that no other man had succeeded in doing.

There wasn't one single emotion she could grasp onto when he was touching her, not one single thought that didn't become a jagged edge that ripped at her heart and mind.

Trailing him at a leisurely pace, she kept her eyes trained to the ground, her attention not drawn up again until she heard the familiar sound of a code being tapped into a panel by an outside door. Her brows knit together in confusion.

"You're taking me outside?"

The question slipped before she could contain it, and she hoped that he wouldn't become more angered by the fact that she questioned anything he did.

Without answering her, he led her through the door into the warmth of the humid breeze of the morning air.

Stunned by her surroundings, Alice forgot the harrowing circumstances of her life. Her eyes opened wide to view a garden so beautiful, nothing she'd seen before could compare to the small piece of paradise hidden beneath the shade of giant live oaks, their moss hanging from solid branches and swaying in the same warm wind that brushed across her face.

"What is this place?" she asked, her voice reverent and breathless.

"Your garden," he answered, his eyes catching her from the side, his fingers squeezing her hand tighter before a sharp tug pulled her forward, deeper into the labyrinth of flowers, shrubs and ornamental grasses.

Fingers trailing across the feather soft white tuft that rose above the thin spindles of tall grass, she caught herself smiling. Happiness didn't belong in this place and not beside this man. But when the wash of color swallowed her, when the melody of birdsong drifted softly past her ears, she was lost to the serenity of the environment. The sun against her skin warmed her. The smell of roses and gardenias lulled her into a false sense of harmony and promise that life here wouldn't be completely bad.

"Mine?" she finally asked, the word nonsensical when given birth through sound.

Max inclined his head, releasing her hand to spin and face her, to watch her eyes track across the collection of plants and trees that had learned to exist together. Some tropical and others only tolerant of a colder environment, she wondered what masterful gardener had managed to cultivate the impossible.

"This is your place, Alice. A refuge you can come to when I'm away. It's yours to manage and care for, yours to nurture and support."

The generosity of his offer was a development that confused her. Scared her, really, because she didn't understand how someone so cruel could give her something so valuable.

Gardening had always been a haven for Alice, a place she could escape to in the hours that her father was home. Originally planted by her mother, a large garden existed outside their modest home, and on the days that her father's rage reared its head, her mother would lead her outside and away from the terrible words and the physical blows that would soon follow.

At first, and because she'd been so young, she wasn't interested in the knowledge or skill that came with tending to the lives of useless plants. They smelled nice, yes, and in the spring they were beautiful, but they couldn't play with her, couldn't talk to her when she needed just one person to listen.

And just like her father, those plants had thorns, sharp points that would prick at her skin, mocking her with their beauty.

However, as the months passed and as the plants she'd grown from seeds began to emerge and bloom, Alice fell in love with the belief that she was a part of the world where she'd long believed she didn't belong. Her few years had been filled with the label of *freak*, her father often calling her a pest that would have been better left unborn.

As soon as she learned to love the feel of her hands dug deep into the cool wet soil, she'd spent most of her time there through each season, through the bite of cold in winter and the blistering heat of the long summer days.

There was always something to escape to in the garden of her youth, and in this new life, Max had returned to her the one place that had been her only true friend.

"Thank you," she breathed out, her mind so lost in the wonder of the garden, she'd forgotten the price that still hung over her head.

Weary eyes became brighter as they followed the stone and pebble paths that wove like streams over the entire space, her feet pulling her deeper into a maze of colors and greenery. The breeze carried with it the smell of jasmine in bloom, and Alice glanced over to see the vine that covered a black, wrought iron gate.

Stopping in her tracks, she marveled at the gate, at the bit of gothic mystery that was hidden behind the thick vines. Almost covered completely, the thin, sharp spires still rose above the tangle of flowers.

She took a step towards it, her curiosity too powerful to contain. However, her forward path was stopped by a strong hand that landed on her shoulder, by the press of fingers into the soft spot above her collarbone that shot pain along her arm.

"You can never go beyond that gate, Alice. The garden is enclosed and there is no escape. Never think that anything beyond that border is the key to your freedom from this place."

His words were spoken softly, a warning hidden beneath the velvet softness of his voice.

"What's behind the gate?" She turned to look at him. "If you don't mind my asking."

The icy chill of his gaze drifted past her shoulder, locking onto that lonely gate that stood lost and abandoned beneath the shade of trees. He was so quiet she thought he'd never answer, but then his throat moved and his lips parted, the truth revealed on the whisper of his sorrowful voice.

"Seven children. A mother. A father. *And one other*. That's what lies beyond that gate, and if you ever decide to break the rules that I have set for you, you'll remain behind that gate, as well."

TWENTY-FIVE

12:34 p.m.

White door.
Dark wood desk.
White and beige striped couch.

He hadn't called to her like he normally did from the threshold of his office door. Simply sliding open the dark partition, the doctor had stared at her, concern ruffling the skin of his forehead, his expressive lips pulled down into a thin, stern line.

She walked her path across the carpet and sank down against the couch cushions.

...drip...

The silence between them was thick. His leather chair groaned when he took a seat. The clock ticked its measured beat. And the sink dripped endlessly, the sound so grating against her senses, she swore she would tear it from the wall.

"Why haven't you spoken?" she asked, shame preventing her from looking towards the face of the one person who could judge her for the insanity that lay dormant inside her mind.

"I was waiting to see what you would say."

"Why?"

He sighed, a rush of breath that betrayed the aggravation seated inside him. "Are you ready to look at these dreams for what they are, Alice? You've already told me everything I need to know."

Limp strands of blonde hair hung down to shield her head. She hid behind it, desperate for something more solid, more full, where she could crouch down and cower, where she didn't have to learn the truth these sessions were forcing her to face.

"It's time, Alice. For you and for your sister."

At the mention of Delilah, Alice's eyes crept out from behind the curtain of her hair, her head spinning slowly over her shoulders and neck to lock eyes with the man that was guiding her forward. "You finally believe me?"

Her body trembled beneath the weight of a question she asked despite her fear that the answer would be his typical response.

"I'm not saying that," he breathed out, his aggravation transitioning into a pitiful cadence to his words. "Would you like me to talk? To bring up the symptoms and facts about your dreams that you have yet to acknowledge?"

A single nod of her head was all she could give him, the movement sharp and spastic.

Leaning back in his chair he tapped his pen to a beat of three before scribbling out some note. Like a surgeon's scalpel, that pen sliced her open, dissected her so that the doctor could look down inside to see all her ugly and weak parts.

"Fine. You're out of sorts today, so I'll play along."

Flipping through the pages, he ran his finger along some line of thought that was a wash of blue against white paper. "Several times now, you've mentioned to me that Max seems to know a lot about you. Why do you think that is?"

She shrugged, the movement so subtle and weak, she wasn't sure she'd actually done it. Bringing her hands into her lap, she stared down on the tendons that pushed up beneath the skin, at the calluses that marred the tips of her fingers, dirt a brown line beneath her fingernails. When had her hands become so ugly, so aged? And would the stains that had come from someplace unknown ever be washed away completely?

"After our session, I had another dream –"

"I'm not interested in the next dream, Alice." He paused, regaining control of a voice that had become far too impatient. "At this point, all I'm interested in is the answer to the question I just asked you."

Barely able to swallow past the thickness of her throat, she closed her eyes and let go of every bit of air trapped in her lungs. Another breath brought her more into focus, the filth washed out of her as she exhaled to be replaced by the clean air of the doctor's office.

"I don't know. The only reason I can imagine is that Max isn't real. He's a part of myself, perhaps."

"That's bullshit and you know it."

Her eyes shot open at the harsh words, the muscles in her neck wrenched by the effort it took to face him fully. "How would you know? They're dreams, Doc. Dreams! Images and actions that take place entirely inside my head. Every person, every face, every word and every horrible thing is made up by my mind, my recollection, and my brain's fucked up inability to record memories the way it's meant to. Of course he knows everything about me because he *is* me. He's the vision of somebody in my head so he has access to every memory I hold. That's the only explanation that makes sense –"

"Or..." he interrupted, his voice booming through the room loud enough to drown out every tick of the clock and every drip from the sink that was slowly driving Alice mad. "...it's the only explanation you'll accept as making sense because you are too far gone to acknowledge what it could actually mean. You're a scared little girl, Alice. One who has sunk so far into herself that you refuse to look closely at the images these *dreams* are showing you."

Her jaw fell open in shock, her eyes searching his face with disbelief that the normally patient and kind doctor she'd known was yelling and treating her like an errant child.

His body leaning forward in his chair, the notepad dangled from his lap from the speed with which he'd moved to close the distance between them. He glared at her, every ounce of frustration inside him a red mask over his skin. With his pen gripped in the fist of his hand, he shook his head when she said nothing, when she failed to respond to the angry and volatile words of a person she believed had no clue as to the thoughts and emotions crippling every part of her body.

"You are running out of time. With every second that ticks forward you are losing ground. And those seconds are ticking, Alice. They're adding up, moving forward and leading you somewhere I'm not sure you want to be. I'm done playing around with you. Either open your eyes or let it go entirely."

Tears streamed over her cheeks, her lips trembling where those tears slid along the crease to drip over her chin and down her neck. Fierce sobs shook every part of her and she couldn't gain control of the fear that blossomed out from deep within her.

Before settling back against his chair, he reached for a tissue to hand to her. Alice didn't accept it, so he tossed it to land on her lap. Retaking his normal position, he drummed a furious beat with the pen against paper, one final tap louder than the others before he said, "You're missing every important aspect of these *dreams* and focusing only on the things that don't scare you."

Shock tore across her skin. "How can you even say that? Everything I've told you has been frightening. He raped my sister, he forced me to have sex with him, he hurt me and hit me, and threatened to end my life if –"

"You said you loved him already, Alice. Don't continue lying to me, and more importantly, yourself, about how you really feel about him. He *rescued* you from your nightmares. He gave you a pretty garden to play in while he was away. If you're going to rely on dreams to tell you what really happened to your sister, than look at the parts you're too scared to see. The parts that are, actually, frightening. The parts you have buried deep down inside because you don't want to admit you were part of them. Those are the dreams I want to know. Those are the dreams you need to discuss. Not the ones that paint a dismal picture of a man who did everything to harm you while also committing abuse against some faceless woman on a television screen."

Pulling the glasses from his face, he placed them on the table beside him and reached to rub at the bridge of his nose. His eyes were clenched shut, his foot tapping a frantic rhythm where it was crossed at his knee. Finally opening his eyes, he wrote a few more lines in his notepad before retrieving his glasses and resettling them over his eyes.

A breath of frustration rolled across his lips, his voice dropping back to the soothing tone he'd always used until this session.

"I've known you for a long time, Alice. I've been treating you since you were a small girl and I can't sit idly by and allow you to continue lying to yourself. We're running out of time. If you're going to continue with the dreams, then fine. But tell me the ones that frighten you the most, and for the sake of yourself and the sake of your sister, look at them for what they really are. Look at who Max really is, and look at the truth for what it is. Who is Max, Alice? And how is he connected to you?"

A shaky breath rattled over her lips, her hand reaching up to knock the tears from her skin. "Fine, Doc. I'll play your game. But don't blame me when you discover that you're wrong. These are just dreams. Dreams that have nothing to do with me, and everything to do with my sister."

He shook his head, a subtle motion that Alice had barely seen.

"Start with the price, Alice. The price for the garden. Perhaps it's the key to helping you remember."

TWENTY-SIX

"I'm leaving the house for a few hours. You're allowed outside in the garden during that time. Everything else will remained locked."

Alice sat in the parlor room staring up at a man that was dressed in a gray suit, white shirt and a crimson tie. Everything about him spoke of money and elegance, refinement that she hadn't known in her younger life. She was as attracted to him as she was scared of him, her hands trembling in her lap, but she couldn't understand why.

"Don't dawdle outside for too long, Alice. You need to remember the price, the tasks I've given you to complete. Don't fuck them up and don't forget them. You won't like the result."

With that, he stepped out of the room, the heels of his dress shoes a rhythmic clap against hard wood until the sound disappeared entirely. A door opened and closed in the distance, and for the first time since she'd been brought to live in the large house that had been Max' childhood home, Alice breathed out a sigh of relief.

The price.

She wasn't quite sure what all it entailed, but she hadn't thought it so terrible when he first explained what she'd been brought here to do.

Be his wife.

Love him.

Care for him.

Ignore the demons that lurk inside him and cater to his need for a real family.

She glanced up at the screen to see the woman still sitting there quietly. Never moving. Never attempting to rip off the hood that covered her face. Just sitting. Shaking her head in disbelief, Alice spent an hour at least just watching the image, waiting to see any small mistake that could reveal the image as something other than what she assumed it to be. The screen never flickered, never jumped and never wavered. It wasn't a loop, and it wasn't an image on pause. But something wasn't right about what she was seeing.

Standing up, she made her way into the kitchen to find a list written in neat script on the counter, the image of a small, perched crow, an emblem that sat at the top of the stationary. Laughter bubbled over her lips, the words so depressing and normal that they didn't belong in this fantasy house, didn't belong in the nightmare of this particular reality.

Clean the floors…

Wash the sheets…

Prepare dinner by six p.m. sharp…

All basic. All bullshit. A list that jogged something inside of her that was lifting hidden truth to the surface.

Placing the note down on the counter, she spun on her heel to look over the house. Familiarity was a nagging whisper in her head, secrets better left hidden if she wished to retain her sanity. But those whispers were endless, relentless. There was more beneath the surface of a beautiful home that trapped the nightmares behind mechanically locked doors and television screens that screamed for her to see the truth.

Unable to focus on any one thing, her eyes clenched shut and she reached down to smooth her palms over a light blue skirt she didn't remember having put on. The dress had been yellow. The dress had been white. At what point had the color changed?

Her head wrenched to the side, the muscles in her neck locking in sharp pain. The woman on the screen sat motionless, her dress a light blue frock with a white lace collar, exactly as Alice was dressed now.

Unable to understand, or perhaps not wanting to, she ripped her eyes from the screen and walked the lonely steps from the kitchen out into a haven that had been created for her – by her.

A train of thought slammed into her, out of control and with a punch that knocked the breath from her lungs.

By her.

The garden had been created by *her* loving hands.

Tentatively, she stepped out, images filling her head of warm, sunlit days beneath the canopy of the stately oaks, their moss swinging in a subtle breeze, becoming shadows that played over her skin. There was nothing she didn't recognize in that place. Not the roses that were planted in an array of colors: red, white, yellow and purple; they were the most difficult to cultivate, their beauty masking the pain of their thorns.

A drop of blood over her finger. A set of lips that suckled softly to clean it away. The scratch of a man's stubble against her palm as she laughed and told him he was disgusting for having tasted her in such a private and personal way.

You're a part of me now, he'd whispered, *always and forever...*

Until death.

Until death.

Until death.

She fell to her knees with the words repeating like a funeral dirge in her thoughts.

Realization a sinister villain that flashed harder and faster, so bright and brilliant that her body fell forward against her bent legs, her hands clenching her head at the sides as if covering her ears could stop the words from booming inside her skull.

Until death, Alice. Until then, you are mine.

Her head shook, her pain leaking from the lids clenched tight over her unseeing eyes.

Just a dream. It had to be, this couldn't be anything more.

She hadn't understood until this moment. Not until the birds sang their melody above her head, until the breeze brushed past and carried the notes of all the flowers that had been chosen and planted by a woman who needed the safety of her haven.

Her body shook on tumultuous sobs, her muscles pulled taut over bones that were tired and weary. She recognized this place, this garden of good and evil, and that recognition was the small broken fissure that fractured wider, that allowed the light to brighten the shadows of her mind.

This can't be…

I didn't do this…

But she had.

She pushed her body back up to her feet, and she walked the grounds that were so familiar she knew every nook and cranny, every carefully hidden corner that contained the secrets even she couldn't face.

They were buried beneath these flowers. Every single memory and secret frozen in time, their shadow swinging above her in hypnotic patterns, their beauty preserved until it was time: Time for them to feed the flowers. Time for them to give the beauty they once had to something far more beautiful than they could ever be.

Her haven.

Her safe place.

Her home amongst the trees and nature.

The place where she could escape the screams.

The wind picked up as she surveyed her surroundings, the scent of jasmine and gardenia a subtle note within the fresh clean smell of moss and soil, among the sweet, lulling fragrance of heirloom roses in full bloom.

Creeping further beneath the canopy of branches, she blinked at the streams of light that broke through the leaves. Glancing up, she couldn't smile at the sight of white and purple orchids that clung to the bark, couldn't take pleasure in the fragile beauty of the refuge that had been designed by her hands.

Alice didn't have a particular path in mind, yet her feet kept moving her forward. Beyond the trees were large swatches of bougainvillea, the sweep of the flowers concealing the thorns that had torn at her skin so often.

Yet, despite the bite of the beauty of nature, she never blamed the plants she'd tended, never regretted her own drops of blood that fed the soil at her feet. She deserved the bites, she deserved the scratches, she deserved the pain that came with the secrets that lay buried beneath her feet.

Before she noticed where she was going, her mind so lost in thought she hadn't paid attention to her path, she came upon a wall of jasmine, the vines so thick and tangled, she wouldn't have seen the fence that lay beneath them unless she'd already known it was there.

Reaching out, she ran a finger along the spires, her feet still moving her closer to the place she'd been warned about so many times before.

The unending whispers cautioned her to turn back, to run from this place that would be her destruction, but her curiosity won out.

She needed to remember this place.

To remember the secrets that had long been silenced.

Her hand found the small gate that was practically locked tight by the vines that grew over it. Ripping at them, Alice ignored the sap that bled from the plants, white and sticky against her skin. The dark green leaves and white flowers littered the ground at her feet, her body struggling to uncover the gate and the truth.

What lay beyond would be what destroyed her because the gate wasn't only designed to keep a person out, it was designed to hold the phantoms in.

The hinges groaned loudly, a high pitch screech that echoed across the expanse and carried in the wind a warning cry that begged for her to step back into the dreams that she'd created for herself.

A shudder traced along her spine until it blossomed out over her chest, shoulders and arms. Despite the weakness in her legs, she took a hesitant step forward to observe the secrets that had been waiting for her behind the veil of beauty she'd planted as a disguise.

Seven smalls headstones lay crumbling and forgotten, each one bearing the name of a child that had never had the chance to breathe life into their lungs.

Seven names.

Seven dates.

Seven heartbeats that had never been.

Unmarked space followed those headstones, large enough for the plots of two adults, of two people that weren't loved enough for their final resting places to be marked. Low lying plants now covered those lonely spots, weeds with yellow and white flowers. It was obvious that no person had cared for them in a long time, and Alice felt a pang of anger and also regret for the bones that lay beneath. She didn't need to guess who was buried there, the whispers told her as memory flooded back, as her body shook and trembled on the knowledge of everything she'd become.

Stepping further, she froze in place, the land open and begging, a shallow grave not yet covered or filled. It was the final piece of the insidious puzzle, the reminder that blew apart the veil so thoroughly that she could look inside and see the truth.

Bending down to run her hand over the freshly turned soil, she felt a tear slip down her cheek, and she jumped in response to the cruel hand that landed on her shoulder.

"I told you not to come here, Alice. I warned you." His voice was soft, regretful, a warning in the way his tone crept along her skin as the heat of his palm seeped into her cold shoulder. "Why? Why did you have to break this one rule?"

Her heart ached at the soft agony in his fractured voice. Closing her eyes, she clenched her fist over the damp earth that lay in clumps at the edges of the open grave. Memories like spider webs across her thoughts, the pain and torment becoming more pronounced with each one that made itself known.

"The garden," she whispered, her voice not sturdy enough to be anything else. "I remembered the garden, about what is buried there beneath the ground."

As a hush fell between them, and as the wind sang its haunting song, Alice understood the price of what had been hidden here in this place for so long.

The price wasn't to love the man that stood above her.

It wasn't to pretend to be the family he'd never had.

The price was to bear witness to the monster that was concealed within him, to remain silent while loving him, to endure the carnage and remain strong.

TWENTY-SEVEN

12:35 p.m.

Gray walls.

Black table.

Plastic, fake red roses.

Everything in place, the dust on the tables untouched by human fingers.

...drip...

"Alice? ... Ms. Beaumont? ... Alice Beaumont ..."

"Is it my time, doctor?"

He nodded.

White door.

Dark wood desk.

White and beige striped couch.

Still the same.

...drip...

She couldn't lift her eyes to look at the doctor, couldn't bear to see the disappointment and disgust that was surely written across his face.

Distracting herself from the tension building between them, her fingers pulled at the fabric of her shirt, knotting the cloth over her hand until the blood had been squeezed out from beneath the skin. Over and over she wrapped and unwrapped the fabric around her palm, pulling it tighter each time until it shot pinpricks of pain along her fingers.

"You're remembering, aren't you?"

Still refusing to look at him despite the question he'd posed, she nodded her head slowly, tears threatening her eyes. How could she still be crying when it felt like there was no emotion left inside her? The numb feeling had replaced the torment. The apathy and shame had stripped away the terror to replace it with the harrowing truth of her crimes.

"They aren't just dreams. Are they, Doc?"

Silence beat between them, the seconds counted down by the ticking clock.

"I'm sorry, Alice. I wish I could tell you they were."

She wanted to be angry with him for playing along the entire time, for not holding her in place and screaming the truth at her until she remembered.

"Why didn't you tell me before? Have you known this entire time?" Her voice shook on the question, her mind racing with the prayer that he wouldn't give her an answer that made him more enemy than friend.

The familiar sound of his leather chair creaking filled the room. Alice knew he was settling back, his eyes studying her in the dimly lit interior of his office.

His voice was regretful when he explained the reasoning behind his betrayal.

"You know better than most people that the mind is a fragile thing. And whereas in your field of study, you were more interested in the physical properties, the flesh, the nerves, the synapses and veins, my field is more focused on the function of those parts on a more *subjective* level."

She smiled. At least the bastard finally admitted it.

"In both of our fields, we agree on one theory. Dreams are the mind's way of transferring short term memories to the long term. Where we differ in our fields is interpreting what happens when a broken mind is processing that information. Neurologists are more concerned about why the mind dreams, whereas psychologists are more concerned with what the dreams can mean."

He gave her a pointed look, a slight smile tugging at the corners of his lips. When she didn't respond, he continued, "Dream interpretation is a guessing game. So, yes, these dreams are more than just dreams, but rather than something predicting a future event, as you've believed them to be, perhaps the explanation all along has been that these dreams are memories of a past event, but the information isn't completely accurate due to the emotional health of the dreamer – you."

Alice sniffled, but nodded her head in agreement with his theory.

"Your mind is torn apart, Alice, barely held together while you come to terms with the truth of what happened to your life. You came to me to help you remember and put the pieces back together, to repair something that I'm not sure can ever be *truly* repaired. I don't think you could have done it on your own, not without losing every part of you that was important and pure. Why else would you seek out a doctor who you haven't seen since you were a child?"

The explanation made sense, and now that she finally understood the dreams were memories coming to the surface, a dam broke in her mind, the images and events she'd fought so hard not to see finally coming into focus with a vengeance that shredded her from the inside out. Daring to glance up at the doctor's face,

Alice saw patience instead of judgment, concern instead of disgust.

"I should hate myself for everything. For being so stupid and so weak."

He tapped his pen against his notebook, the sound soothing because she remembered it from when she'd been young.

Without commenting on the self-hatred she'd just exposed, the doctor moved the notebook in his lap to set it on the table beside him. He adjusted the frames of his glasses over his nose and sighed heavily, the whisper of sound across his lips an avalanche of disappointment and pity.

"Let's start with the easy memories, Alice. It's as I've said already, time is running out, but if it helps you face the truth of the memories that plague you, let's start in a place that's safe. A place that feels like home."

Her lips rolled over each other, the chapped skin sticky as she opened her mouth to answer him aloud. "This was the only safe place I remember from my childhood. It's probably the reason I sought you out. Although, for the life of me, I can't remember the first time I came here. Not since I was young. Not after..."

Her voice trailed off, her eyes clenching shut now that she understood what she'd done.

Forcing herself to keep talking, she drew in a steadying breath and opened her eyes. "My mother brought me to you because of the sleep disorders, didn't she?"

His voice patient and astute, he answered, "That was the reason she gave me on the day you first stepped foot inside this office. But after meeting with you several times, I knew there was more to your problems than either you or your mother would let on. You were a smart girl, Alice. Impressive, really, and I had to fight to keep you talking most of the time. You were protecting someone. I assume now that person was your father."

Her head nodded in agreement with his assumption. "If I'd told you or any person about the abuse, it would have destroyed my family." She laughed, a choked sound of hatred and regret. "Not that there was much to destroy as he grew worse over the years, but at least they were safe. I was the only target he seemed to care about."

"You loved your family."

Not a question, but a statement, and Alice wasn't sure how to respond. When she didn't answer, he filled the silence for her.

"But there was more to how you felt about them, wasn't there? Something secret that made you feel ashamed? Frightened?"

With trembling hands, she pushed her hair away from her face, and then wrapped her arms around her body as if that would somehow protect her from the ugly truth of her life.

"I was jealous of my brother and sister. My sister, mostly. They were never forced to sleep in small closets, and he never seemed angry when they were in the room. It was only me that he hated. Only me that he wished had never been born."

Giving her words a few minutes of consideration, the doctor spoke slowly when he replied, "It wasn't your fault. You know that, right? The disorders, what your father did to you, or the jealousy you felt for your siblings as a result."

Her fingers dug into her sides, her arms wrapped so tight around her abdomen that she could feel the pulse of blood beneath the skin. "I know that now, especially after everything I learned in college about the disorders. But that didn't help me when I was a child. I had no way of knowing..."

"I tried to tell you in your sessions."

"Yeah," she argued, "but I thought it was just a bunch of lies."

The air left her lungs on a rattle, her body buckling in the seat as she curled into a tight, protective ball.

"I think I'm ready, Doc. I think I'm finally ready to face everything."

"Are you sure?"

Nodding her head so hard the hair bounced at the sides of her face, she bit her bottom lip and closed her eyes. Pulling herself out of the cocoon of her body she'd constructed to keep herself safe, she opened her eyes again and said, "All the pieces were there the entire time. All the memories. I'd just turned them into something else entirely because I couldn't face what had become of me, what he had done to me so easily."

Turning to face Dr. Chance, Alice pulled her arms from around herself and knotted her fingers together over her lap. "If dreams are just the mind's way of processing memories, then why do they have to be so abstract?"

The leather chair groaned when he leaned forward, his own hands wrapped together where they settled atop his knees. "Perhaps you needed the abstraction so you wouldn't break apart entirely. But the pieces were all there. I saw them. I have them written down. It's time for you to take them and put them into some order so that you can put the entire picture back together. It's time for the story to make sense."

A shiver ran across her.

"I'm a bad person, Doc." The confession stung as it crawled up from her throat to brush across her lips.

"You're not a bad person, Alice. You wouldn't be here if you were. People can do bad things and still be considered good."

Annoyed by tears that wouldn't stop falling, her lip trembled as her vision blurred. "Where do I start, Doc?" Her voice squeaked as she spoke, fear a creeping entity that threatened to pull her farther into its grasp. "Where can you start on a story such as this?"

He looked at her with shrewd appraisal behind his eyes, the time ticking between them so slowly until he finally opened his mouth and said, "Start from the only place that makes sense, Alice. From the beginning...and from the moment you first met Maximilian Frost."

TWENTY-EIGHT

"As you can see, it's nothing more than a dirty, forgotten closet." The sound of velvet laughter filled the room behind where Alice was crouched to look down into the shadows of a dusty crawlspace. Old paint containers lined a part of one wall with a ragged tarp barely covering the rusty cans. A few hangers swung lazily from a metal rod that ran the length of the back. The ceiling arched down with the shape of the roof above their heads making the right corner of the closet useless for storage.

Crawling backwards, she brushed her skirt to remove the dust that had settled over the navy blue fabric. She stood upright and turned to the man who was as unsettling as he was appealing. They stared at each other for several tense moments before she finally broke down and smiled.

"I have to be honest with you, Mr. Frost..."

"Max," he corrected her. "Please."

Swallowing down the odd sense of attraction she had for the mysterious stranger, she chuckled softly when she confessed, "Max. I have to be honest with you."

His eyebrow arched in question, a smirk peeking out at the corner of his sculpted lips that drew her attention to how soft and supple his mouth appeared. She wondered what those lips would feel like against her body, about the contrast of their heat against the sensitive places of her skin.

Shaking her head of the unwanted thoughts, she admitted, "There's no way in hell I'll be able to sell this place."

He laughed a booming sound that filled every nook and cranny of the decrepit house that was as startling as it was divine. It was the sound of a man at ease, of a man who had no worries in the world. She liked that sound, and found herself stepping closer to its source if for nothing else but to feel the vibrations of true mirth roll across her skin.

She'd probably lose her job the next day when Sarah found out what she'd said to the owner, but Alice couldn't lie. The house should have been marked for salvage and tear down, not dressed in a pretty red bow and put up for sale.

His laughter faded and his blue eyes trapped hers in a gaze that was crinkled at the corners, hypnotic and sparkling with humor.

She smiled at him, not the shy, professional smile she normally gave strangers, business associates and friends, but a bright smile, the kind that pulled her lips until they ached at the corners, the kind that revealed her straight, white teeth.

When had she last smiled at a person that way? And then she remembered: never.

Her heart skipped in its rhythm behind her ribs, and she found herself stepping even closer, her lungs dragging in air so she could smell the subtle and exotic notes of his cologne.

Stumbling over what to say next, she spit out an apology, even if she didn't mean a word of it.

"I'm sorry, Max, but I don't see how I can sell this property to a buyer for more than what the land is worth. And even then, I have to take into account the cost of tearing down the house and grading the land so that another house can be built."

She sighed and glanced around at a room that at one time had been magnificent. With true regret in her voice, she added, "I really wish someone had taken better care of the place."

Max stepped forward to continue closing the small amount of distance that remained between them. "Well, I'm happy that you're being honest with me, and please don't think that I'm offended by what you've said. I know this place is a dump..." He paused, his eyes tracking the room around them. Under his breath, he continued, "Actually, I'd consider it more a worthless piece of shit, if you don't mind my being frank."

Laughter bubbled out of Alice's throat and she snorted at the absolute truth of his statement.

"I really am sorry…"

"Don't be. It was an investment property of my family's, and is of little value to me." He grinned at her, causing her stomach to flip flop in her abdomen, for her heart to beat so hard she could count the heavy pulse in her throat. "Have dinner with me, Ms. Beaumont."

Halfway between a request and a demand, he locked his eyes to hers as he made the offer.

Light lashes fluttered over her eyes, her mind startled by the offer that hadn't been expected. Unsure how to respond, she considered whether dinner with a client for non-professional reasons was even allowed.

Giving it some thought, and while keeping her eyes locked to those of the man she was becoming more attracted to with every passing second, she realized that this job was just another in a string of crappy ventures that never went any further than a few weeks at most.

Alice wasn't one to date. In fact, she'd only had one real boyfriend in her life, and that had been in high school. Given her sleep disorders, and the embarrassment she felt because of them, she could never allow a man to sleep beside her for fear he'd run screaming as soon as he saw the truth of her problems.

But dinner would be okay, wouldn't it?

Just dinner.

"Okay," she answered, her lips pulling into a broad smile that stung at the corners of her mouth. "I'd like that very much."

He grinned, the expression extraordinary and charming.

Offering his arm for her to wrap hers beneath, he pulled her close to his side when she accepted and said, "Allow me to escort you out of this shithole so we can go someplace more suitable for someone of your beauty."

The burst of laughter that boomed from her lungs shocked her. The true depth of happiness that she could feel with the practical stranger a shock to her cynical and closed up nature.

How he'd affected her so easily, she wasn't sure. But she was willing to spend more time with him to see if there wasn't more than a budding attraction to the mystery of his expression and the wickedness of his sensual smile.

By the time they walked through the front door of the house and down the crumbling steps that damn near swallowed them whole, Alice couldn't stop grinning at the feel of him by her side.

* * *

As it turned out, dinner lasted much longer than the hour she'd assumed it would. Max was fascinating to her, a man of obvious wealth and class, but one who didn't allow the affluence he held in life to go to his head.

They talked about everything that night, at least that's how it seemed, and Alice often found herself prattling on about the details of her life she normally kept hidden. She was careful not to discuss the elements of her childhood that were better left unsaid, but she caught herself going on and on about her time in college and the hospital, her decision to leave neurology and the string of worthless jobs that followed in its wake.

Never once did Max seem bored with what she had to say. He laughed at all the appropriate points of her story, and he appeared thoughtful during the parts that were hard for her to admit: namely, the fact that she was very much alone in the world, with very little money and no true hope of a bright and promising future.

Her cheeks flamed red when she realized what she'd admitted to a practical stranger, but he never judged her for her poor choices or the sad fact that she had nobody she could name as a friend.

Not much of a talker himself, Max would offer small bits of information about his life back to her, quick glimpses into the life of a man who was as reclusive as her. It surprised her to discover that he wasn't one to socialize very often and that, in fact, he almost didn't ask her to dinner for fear she'd turn him down.

Magnets drawn to each other, Alice and Max' date grew into another date and another. Weeks had passed and Alice finally felt comfortable enough with their burgeoning relationship that she allowed him to pick her up from the small apartment where she lived. Prior to that, she'd always met him at the restaurant where they'd often dined, each time with Max voicing his dislike of not being able to pick her up himself and take her on a *proper* date.

When he pulled up in front of her apartment building, Alice watched from the window and noticed the scowl that marred his lips when he saw the exterior of the building. When she'd moved there, she knew the neighborhood wasn't the best, but the rent was something she could afford while still between jobs.

After eyeing the paint that peeled away from the stucco walls, and the grass out front that was more brown than it was green, Max stepped over some trash that littered the parking lot to ascend the stairs to the second floor. Alice tracked his path as far as her eyes could follow him, but when he turned the corner of the stairs to take the hall that led to her door, he was out of her view for several minutes longer than she'd expected.

Finally, a knock sounded at the door. She opened it to discover that his eyes were hidden behind shadow, his lips pulled into a thin line of disapproval.

"This is where you live? In this...*hovel*?" He spat out the word as if it burned his tongue to hold it inside.

Startled by the disapproval that flowed around him like a sickening aura, she gripped her fingers tighter around the doorknob and quickly rethought the decision she'd made to allow him to pick her up.

Her voice quiet and ashamed, she couldn't meet his eyes when she admitted, "I'm sorry, but I can't afford anything else."

Reaching out for her, he slipped his finger beneath her chin to lift her face. She opened her eyes to see that his expression had fallen, the anger that had been there just seconds before replaced with something else. Unsure whether it was pity for the state of her life, or regret for having so glaringly pointed it out, his expression was a mystery to her in that moment.

"I won't allow you to continue living this way. I can't, Alice. I *feel* too much for you to accept you being in this place."

The revelation had been staggering, knocking Alice off balance so much that she neglected to step back to allow him into the apartment. "You feel for me? What does that even mean?"

The thick dark lashes of his eyes blinked over the brilliant blue, his face twisted into a painful expression. She hadn't known him long enough to understand that Max wasn't the type of person to feel anything.

Struggling with how to express what he wanted to say, his eyes darkened even more than they already were. "May I come inside so we can discuss this? I'm not sure the hallway is the right place, and besides that..." he paused, his nose wrinkling in disgust, "...it smells like vomit and piss out here."

Alice paled at the reminder that she'd not invited him in. Stepping back, she motioned for him to walk inside. Flustered by her own rude behavior, she shut the door behind him and stepped softly as she followed him into the small space of her living room.

Max' eyes scanned the space without any obvious emotion playing across his features, but she could tell by the rigid set of his shoulders and the way his hands clenched into fists that he wasn't pleased with what little she'd done with the place.

Because the apartment never felt like her true home, she hadn't taken the time to decorate or do anything that would dress it up. Instead, all that existed was a threadbare couch in an awful, faded pattern, a faux leather chair that didn't match, and a small potted plant that she'd neglected to water, its leaves hanging wilted at the sides of the pot. It was the only part of the place that she regretted. She loved plants, and in her own depression, she'd forgotten to nurture the poor thing until it got to a point where she'd never be able to bring it back.

"This is –"

"Pathetic," she finished for him. "I know."

Making his way into the bedroom that was only big enough for a queen sized bed and a small chest of drawers, Max studied the small room for several minutes before turning to her.

The chill in his stare confused her because, until that moment, all she'd ever seen in him was warmth.

"I *care* about you, Alice. Deeply. And I won't be able to sleep at night knowing you live in a place as *dangerous* as this."

Stepping closer, he took her hands in his and brought her knuckles to his lips. After placing a chaste kiss on them, he pulled them away to say,

"There are monsters that exist in our world and I'd hate for you to live in a place that makes you such easy prey."

There was nothing Alice could say to alleviate his concern. She'd failed to sell the Victorian home after explaining to Sarah that even the owner considered it a dump. As a result, she was let go from yet another job. With little left in savings, moving was out of the question.

"There's nowhere else for me to go." Anger washed over her, anger and shame for not being able to match him in wealth or esteem. "Listen, it was a bad idea for me to invite you here. Maybe it's best that you go."

Stepping closer to her, his massive form overshadowed her completely. She felt so small compared to him, so feeble. Unable to handle the way he dominated the air around her, Alice attempted to step away, but his fingers gripped her arm and pulled her closer.

"I'd like to take you somewhere."

Shaking her head in refusal, she tried to pull her arm away, but his grip was too strong. Warning shot along her thoughts, the sense that there was far more to this man than the genial nature he'd shown.

"You're scaring me. Please let me go."

His fingers loosened and she jerked her arm away before placing distance between them. Glancing up to see the disapproval behind his eyes, she felt her skin blush over her cheeks, her arms wrapping around her abdomen as if that would protect her from whatever side of him this was.

Pleading with her, Max angled his head to the side, his thick hair brushing his shoulder as he studied the expression on her face. "I didn't intend to scare you. I only meant to..." His words trailed off, frustration obvious in the sharp edge to his words.

"I'd like to take you to my house, Alice. To show you where I live. I thought we'd reached a point where our lives can come together."

Her eyes widened at what he'd said, fear and distrust still a nagging whisper in her head, but her heart beat faster at the thought that he saw her as something more than a woman with whom he'd gone on a few dates.

"What are you trying to say, Max? Just spit it out. I don't appreciate people who beat around the bush with me. I don't have time for it."

Straightening his posture, he rolled his broad shoulders back and moved closer to her, his hands reaching out to take hers, hovering there until she reached out to accept the contact.

"I'd like for you to live with me. Nothing would make me happier than to have you someplace where I know you're safe. Where I can take care of you and give you the life you deserve."

Logically, she knew what he was asking of her was foolish. They'd only known each other for a few weeks, and very few relationships that moved as quickly as he was suggesting lasted long. However, what she felt for him couldn't be denied and, on her own, she wasn't in the best position to decline any assistance he could offer.

She'd already screwed up so much of her life by remaining distant and reclusive from the world. Perhaps if she broke free of the shell she'd created for herself after leaving her childhood home, she could finally find a small part of the happiness she sought.

Decision made, her lips pulled up into a shy smile. "I can't make any promises, Max. But I'll go with you to take a look. Anything has to be better than this place, right?"

He grinned. "I'm not just offering you a new home, Alice. I'm offering you the entire package. A new life. A new love. A new family. Keep that in mind tonight. Nothing would make me more proud than to call you my wife."

Gripping her chin gently between his thumb and finger, he lifted her face to his.

"Are you ready?" He asked, his eyes alight with some emotion Alice couldn't name.

Shaking her head of the emotions that were a wave of confusion crashing inside her, she asked, "For what?"

"Your new life. The life you've dreamed of having."

TWENTY-NINE

12:36 p.m.

Gray walls.
Black table.
Plastic, fake red roses.

"Alice? ... Ms. Beaumont? ... Alice
Beaumont?"
"Yes, doctor."

Taking her usual place on the couch, Alice
didn't feel the need to curl over herself for
protection. The nightmares and confusion were
slowly fading, the truth of the life she'd lived
coming back in haunting pieces that slowly
stitched themselves together to form the full
picture she wished could be different than it
was.

Guilt rode her shoulders with a weight that
couldn't be ignored or forgotten, her heart
breaking with every new shadowed secret her
mind brought into full light.

"Shall we simply jump into this, Alice? I think the formalities and pleasantries are long past us at this point."

Nodding her head, she drew in a steadying breath, her eyes unable to meet the doctor's stare because her shame was far too much for her to face.

"It's all starting to come together for me, Doc, and I'm terrified to go further. I don't understand the reasons why I didn't remember any of this until now, why my mind seemed to wrap it all into another reality."

His pen scribbled quietly over his notebook, his focus more on his written thoughts than on her. "The mind is an interesting place, Alice. You know that as well as me. When something tragic happens that we're not ready to face or deal with, the mind has the unique ability to transform it into something else. For some, their personality fractures and, in their head, they're two different people entirely. For others, they sink into themselves so deep that they become a shell of what they were before that tragedy struck. It appears that in your case, your mind conjured a storyline that contained elements of the truth, but disguised it in a way that you could accept. At least until you were ready to face what really happened."

Wringing her hands over themselves in her lap, she stared at a ring on her finger that she'd neglected to notice until her memory had pieced itself back into place. Until that moment in the garden when reality had slammed against her like a runaway train.

"He never abducted me, did he? I wasn't a prisoner to Max. I was his wife."

Her eyes stung from the tears that seemed like they would never stop falling. She was so sick of crying, but it was the only way the wave of emotions inside her could find their release.

"He told me, Doc. Over and over again in the dreams, and I didn't listen."

...drip...

With a voice as quiet as it was solemn, Dr. Chance tapped his pen against the notebook once before letting out a gentle sigh and saying, "Perhaps it was easier for you to believe that you were forced to live that life instead of having chosen to stay there. Or, perhaps these dreams are a jumble of all the memories coming together, but not in the proper circumstance or order. Whatever the reason may be, the story doesn't end there, Alice. And you can't move past what happened until you face the entire truth."

The ticking clock beat down the seconds of silence that fell between them, Alice huffing out a shaky breath because she knew the doctor was hurrying her forward.

Time was of the essence, it seemed, but she didn't know what would occur when it finally ran out.

"Keep going, Alice. Walk me though the entirety of your life with him so that I can help you find all the pieces you need in order to put the broken parts back together."

THIRTY

When Max had first brought Alice to his home, her response to the lovely Queen Anne where he lived had been full of wonderment and promise. The house sat on a large lot surrounded by woods, a secluded piece of the world where a person could hide away from society.

Her eyes had rounded to see the property, her lips parting on a soft sigh at the possibility of living in such beauty with a man who could see to her every desire and need.

Like a love struck teen, her heart had beat a soft patter beneath her ribs as he'd guided her up the front walkway and into the home.

And just like the outside of the house, the inside was elegant and painstakingly cared for. Clean and immaculate, the interior reminded her of something you'd see in a magazine, of a home that any normal person would love to own, but could never hope to afford.

Giving her a tour, Max had warned her that the basement had not been restored or remodeled like the other rooms, and as such, was dangerous due to aging wooden stairs and crumbling bits of foundation that were a hazard to anyone who attempted passing through in the dim light that was down there. He warned to her to stay out of the basement for her own safety, but assured her that the rest of the home was hers to travel as she pleased.

Alice hadn't been surprised by his description of the basement. Older homes often required a lot of money and care to bring them back to the state they'd been when first built, so she'd ignored the warning and didn't wonder if there was something down there Max didn't want her to see.

Perhaps it had been the house itself that washed away every bit of logic and instinct that Alice had left in her, because almost as soon as they crossed the threshold, she found herself saying 'yes' to anything and everything Max would offer her.

Theirs was a whirlwind romance that was the stuff of dirty novels and sickly sweet movies. Almost as soon as Alice agreed to marriage, Max set to work to plan every detail of the ceremony.

But even before they could be joined as husband and wife, Max insisted Alice leave the apartment where she'd lived, leaving everything behind except for her clothes and the possessions that were precious.

Her first night living in the house with Max felt like the first night in her life when she'd been able to take a full breath. Gone were the days of a family that didn't want her. Gone were the sleepless nights where she worried how she'd be able to afford her rent.

Money was no longer her concern.

She was wanted and cherished.

But there were still secrets inside her she needed to express, secrets that needed to be shared before the first night they spent in the same bed together.

"I'm going to cook dinner for us tonight. It's been a long day for you with the move and it's the least I can do to help you get settled."

Max smiled down at her as he led her into the large kitchen and assisted her into a chair at the kitchen island that broke up the interior space.

Rounding the island, he pulled open the fridge and selected several vegetables and a large slab of meat to place on the counter. A knife set sat on the island nearer to Alice, and after placing the meat on a cutting board near the sink where he stood, Max turned around.

Nodding his chin towards the island, he had an easy grin on his lips when he asked, "Would you mind handing that to me?"

His sparkling blue eyes locked to hers, an arrogant tilt to his full lips that made her shift nervously in her seat. He was beautiful in any situation, but in his home, in the place where he felt most comfortable, he was absolutely divine. Wavy hair, black as a raven's shimmering feather, hung loosely over one side of his face and concealed his scar. Alice swallowed down a knot in her throat. She was nervous around him suddenly, nervous about what the night might bring. Lost in thought, and mesmerized by the man that stood before her, she blushed when she realized he was waiting for something from her.

"I'm sorry, what?"

He laughed, the sound charming and full of humor. "The cleaver," he explained. "Would you hand it to me, please?"

"Oh!" Lips rounding on the word, she felt her cheeks heat up even more, her arm moving quickly to pick up the heavy utensil and reach over the island to place it in his palm.

Settling back down into her seat she realized there was something about this man that flustered her completely. How she'd be able to keep her senses around him, she wasn't sure.

It was an entirely new situation for Alice, one where she wasn't judged or criticized. But there were still things in her life he didn't know or understand. Her stomach churned with anxiety because she had no choice anymore but to tell him.

Before she could conjure enough bravery to mention the subject, Max glanced at her from over his shoulder. "I hope you like your steak rare. Personally, I prefer when the meat is warm, but tender, easy to slice and chew, the blood running hot and thick against the tongue."

Her smile wavered, dark thoughts a shadow over the enjoyment she should have felt about the evening. "Rare is fine. Just as long as it's warm and not mooing at me from the table."

Winking his eye in response to her answer, he turned his back on her again to chop the slab of meat into individual steaks.

"Hey, Max?"

The motion of his hand didn't stop when she spoke, the rhythmic chopping never paused or faltered when he answered, "Hey, Alice."

Swallowing down her pride, she squeezed her hands into fists on her lap, her nails cutting ridges into the skin of her palm.

"I need to tell you something."

The chopping stopped, his head spinning just enough where he could cast a cursory glance at her from over his shoulder. "Cold feet already?"

Soft laughter bubbled up from her lungs. "No, nothing like that. Although," her voice lowered to a practical whisper, "You might have cold feet after what I have to say to you."

The cleaver fell heavily on the counter to his side, his entire body turning now so he could give her his full attention.

"I doubt there is anything you can tell me that would cause that to happen. We all have secrets, Alice. Some of us far darker than others."

Shifting restlessly in her seat, Alice failed to notice the shadows behind his eyes as she clenched and released her hands in her lap, pins and needles shooting along her arms with how hard she curled her fingers.

So focused on her own insecurities, she missed the dark secrets behind his words that should have been the first sign there was more to Max than she knew.

"I assume, and I may be wrong, but I assume you want me to sleep in your bed tonight."

His eyes were wary, his full lips pulling into a thin line. She wasn't sure what thoughts were running through his head, or if she'd just invited herself to a place where he hadn't yet intended for her to go. However, it was a subject that needed attention, regardless. Max had every right to know.

Forcing herself to speak clearly, she finally blurted out, "I have certain issues that I've had since I was a young child. Issues that, for the most part, are the reason I don't speak to my family much anymore."

Stepping forward, he rested his forearms on the kitchen island, his eyes level with hers when he said, "You have my undivided attention."

Her eyes closed and she breathed in a steadying breath to ready herself for a conversation that revealed something about herself that only her family, and a psychologist who treated her as a child, had known.

"I don't sleep like normal people," she admitted. "From what I know, it wasn't always that way, but at some point when I was younger the problems started."

Silence fell between them, her entire body trembling from the fear that he'd reject her as soon as he knew.

"And those issues are?"

His voice was so soft, so hesitant, that she wasn't sure if he hadn't already been chased away by her confession.

"I have sleep disorders. Strange ones, and they happen every night no matter what I do. It's the reason I've never really dated, and the reason I've always lived alone."

Max didn't comment further, just sat patiently with rapt attention on her.

"Have you ever heard of parasomnias? There are multiple types and I, unfortunately, suffer from several of them."

Beyond nodding his head, he didn't move otherwise. "Like sleep walking? Stuff like that?"

She swallowed down the churning of her stomach, the acid that had forced its way up her throat. "That's one of them, yes."

Where she'd expected concern behind his ice blue eyes, there was interest instead.

"I've heard of conditions such as those, but never seen it myself. Why do you feel the need to tell me this?"

Her hands continued wringing nervously in her lap. "Because of the severity. It's caused *problems* for me in the past and I wanted to warn you because I didn't want it to be a surprise if you witness it. I don't remember most of it because I'm asleep when it occurs, but from what I've been told, it can be somewhat bothersome...or scary."

Pushing up from where he'd leaned over the island, he rounded the side to stand next to her. His hands grabbed the armrests of the chair and swiveled it so that her knees rested between his partially spread legs. They were as close to each other as they could comfortably get with her sitting and him standing.

"Tell me all of it. And don't worry that I'll judge you or hold it against you. It's like I said," his voice dropped to a darker tone, his eyes shadowing over to a point where the chill of ice blue churned with the dark gray of a thunderstorm. "We all have our secrets. We all have things that we hope those closest to us can accept and understand."

Alice wondered for a brief moment what his secrets could be, but she lost that train of thought to the very real fear that he would reject her for her issues as violently as her father had rejected her.

Pushing that fear aside, she summoned the bravery to be honest. "I have night terrors, for one. Basically, that means I wake up screaming. Sometimes, I can't remember why I was screaming, why my body was completely caught up in the fear I felt when it stopped and I was awake. And other times, I remember the nightmares. They're awful and I don't understand them, but they happen. Regularly."

Inclining his head once to indicate that he understood, he said, "Screaming doesn't bother me, Alice."

Her brows knit together at the odd statement, but she pushed forward without giving it much thought.

"I also sleep walk, which is self-explanatory, except most people don't really understand what it is like. For me, I go to sleep in one place and wake up in another. Sometimes at a doorway, and other times inside something or underneath it." She laughed, the sound not quite humor. "I've woken up several times in a chest that sat at the foot of my bed. It felt like a coffin when I first opened my eyes and I wondered briefly if my father hadn't followed through on his threat to bury me alive."

Rolling his shoulders back, Max released a soft gust of air from his lungs, his eyes closing and opening slowly before locking back to hers. "Your father threatened you?"

She nodded. "That's an entirely different story." Peeling her eyes away from the anger she could see clearly in his, she said, "For another time."

A few tense seconds passed before he said, "Go on. What else happens when you sleep?"

"Well, you can't wake me during the sleepwalking. I strike out, apparently, and I injured several of my family members before they learned to just guide me gently back to bed. Beyond that, there's the REM behavior disorder – or whatever it is Dr. Chance called it." Her eyes met his again. "Basically, I fight a lot. I've been known to throw things, break things, punch and kick. Nobody would share a bed with me because of it and the worst that's happened is that I wake up with bruises sometimes from where I've struck a bedside table or the headboard. But, if we are to share a bed, I assume that will be something you'll have to watch out for."

His lips twitched on a grin. "If I have to bind you and hold you in place, I will." Reaching out to brush his fingers along the line of her jaw, he added, "For my own protection, of course."

"No," she answered, her head shaking at the distant memories his words had brought about. "My father tried that and all that happened was that I injured myself even worse."

Max stood deathly quiet above her, his body perfectly still, and she looked up to see a mask of anger where an understanding expression had once been.

"Your father tied you up?"

She nodded. "And locked me in a closet, and other things. He said it was for my own safety, and so that he could get some sleep. But it never fixed anything or made it better. I just screamed louder."

His hands tightened over the arms of her chair, the wood creaking like it would break into splinters beneath his hold. With a controlled voice, he asked, "Anything else?"

"The sleep paralysis," she admitted on a frustrated voice. It was difficult to talk about all of her issues and lay them out for another person to see. "I think that is possibly the worst of it. Not for any person witnessing it, in fact, they wouldn't know it was happening. That's my own personal problem to suffer in silence."

Thoughtful silence hovered between them, then, "What is that like? The paralysis?"

A shiver ran across her bones. "It's awful. I wake up – mentally, at least – but I can't move. Can't open my eyes. Can't do anything but lie there. A loud ringing happens in my head and, sometimes, I can feel myself floating. Images flash through my mind. Awful things like demons or monsters. I used to be so scared, but I got used to it through the years. Those faces don't scare me anymore. Not like they used to." Glancing up at him, she explained, "It's the feeling of being completely helpless. Completely immobile and afraid."

Seeking out her hands with his own, he pulled her fingers apart from one another to stop the way she'd been wringing them in her lap. Smoothing her palms over with his own, he spoke gently when he said, "I don't know what it feels like to be helpless, Alice. But I promise you that you're not alone."

The urge to ask him what he meant by those words was at the forefront of her thoughts, but a timer buzzed at the very moment the question was on the tip of her tongue.

THIRTY-ONE

"Dinner was delicious, Max."

Dabbing at her lips with a napkin, Alice placed the white cloth on the table and looked around at the setting.

Her eyes brushed over the beautiful, ceramic plates that were far more expensive than Alice had ever seen. They were a simple pattern, light blue against pristine white. The delicate swirls of color around the perimeter reminded her of a set her grandmother owned; understated, yet elegant, they spoke to a generation of people that was long lost to time. Modern society had moved on from the beauty of the past, however everything about Max, his mannerisms, his clothes, his home and the dishes that sat on the table in front of Alice reminded her of a time long ago.

The sophistication hadn't been lost on her. The fine food and wine, the delicate table cloth and napkins to match. The food had been delectable, and the atmosphere had helped her breathe easier despite the secrets she'd shared just an hour before.

"I should clean up," Max said, the legs of his chair scraping against the floor as he stood to collect the soiled dishes.

"Let me help you," Alice answered, standing up from her own chair to collect a few of the plates and carry them back to the kitchen. Nervousness still a shroud that covered her, she stumbled over her own feet, the dishes spilled from her hands before she could catch her balance.

The plates crashed against the ground, food and shards marring the floor at her feet. Lifting a hand to her mouth, she spun to look at Max where he stood frozen at the table.

"I'm so sorry. I hope – " Her mind raced with the amount of money the plates must have cost. Even worse than that, she wondered if they weren't also a set passed down within the family that she'd now turned to useless and broken pieces. "I'm sorry," she whispered.

A gust of breath blew across Max' lips, his eyes flicking between Alice and the plates that now lay useless and broken. "Luckily, I didn't use the expensive China tonight. I felt bad about serving you on something that wasn't the best I had, but now I'm not as regretful about it as I had been."

"Max, please, I'm sorry. Let me –" Her words spun off her tongue so fast, she had difficulty getting one thought out before another flooded up her throat.

His steps were heavy across the floor as he approached her, one hand balancing several dishes while his other landed on her shoulder. "Don't worry about it, Alice. They meant very little to me." He chuckled and planted a light kiss on her cheek. "There's a dustpan and broom in the pantry closet." Soft laughter still shaking his shoulders, he said, "Come with me, Alice. We need to clean up the mess you've made."

Following him to the closet and back to the dining room where she'd made the mess, she took the broom and dustpan from his hands and bent over to clean the food and shards from the floor.

His voice tender with affection, Max said, "While you manage that, I'll clear what's left of the table. When you're finished, I'll be in the kitchen washing dishes. You should meet me there so you can help."

She nodded her head, unable to speak around the lump of guilt that festered at the base of her throat.

Finishing up, she walked into the kitchen and dumped the mess into the garbage can lined with a white, plastic bag.

Max stood facing the sink, his shoulders moving beneath the black fabric of his shirt, his shoulder length hair a tangled mess where it hung in wild waves. Alice stood and stared at him for several minutes wondering if he knew she loitered behind him watching the way his arms worked back and forth polishing away the remnants of the dinner he'd cooked for their first night together.

Her eyes traced the lines of his shoulders and back, the muscles that lay corded and partially hidden beneath the folds of his shirt. The dark fabric was stretched taut over his shoulder blades before falling to a point where it followed the tight dip towards his hips. Alice found herself intensely attracted to the man that silently washed dishes, and was impressed with the physique that spoke to everything masculine and strong about him.

A kitchen island stood between them with white cabinets and black granite counters. It was a touch of modern against the vintage features of the Queen Anne style house. She wondered when he'd remodeled the place, but knew from the stainless steel appliances that it couldn't have been that long since he had the expensive appliances installed. Her eyes looked at the litany of gadgets that littered the front of the large refrigerator and wondered why any person would need a coffee maker in the freezer door.

"Are you going to stand there all night? Or were you planning on helping me?"

He turned to wink at her, a grin tilting the corner of his lips.

His chin nodded in the direction of the cleaver that he'd left on the kitchen island while preparing the meal. "Pick that up, would you? It needs to be washed as well."

When he glanced at her again, a smirk pulling at the corner of his sculpted lips, she reached over to retrieve the cleaver and walked it around the island to stand next to him at the sink. He plucked the heavy utensil from her fingers and sunk it down into the soapy water before handing her a dishtowel to dry the plate he handed her next.

When they'd settled into a routine of washing, rinsing and drying the dishes and cookware, Alice thought she would laugh at the oddity this change in her life represented. From what moment to the next, she'd been living life alone to find herself standing next to a man who would be her husband, doing something as typical and mundane as washing dishes.

"You know, they have these handy machines now called dishwashers that would make this task a lot easier."

Max glanced at her before pulling another soiled dish from the soapy water. "I prefer to wash them by hand. Dishwashers never get them quite clean enough for my preference."

He didn't bother looking at her, his gaze held steady on the task at hand, the dishes that needed to be cleaned and polished to a shine so that they appeased his need for a clean and tidy house. Glancing at the plate in her hand, Alice admired the reflection that stared back at her, the dead eyes of a woman now brought to life by a man who'd swept in to save her from herself.

He turned to her at that moment, his body dangerously close to hers, his hair brushing over his shoulder as he angled his head in question while watching her with lazy and admiring eyes. Scanning her body, his liquid gaze started at her hips, settling on her breasts as they worked their way up until coming to lock with the nervous anticipation behind her eyes. "Thank you for agreeing to live with me, Alice. Thank you for agreeing to be my wife. You have no idea how much all of this means to me."

He pulled the cleaver from the soapy water, washed it slowly until all traces of the meat he'd used it to cut were absent from the blade and handed it to her to rinse and dry to a perfect polish. The blade was heavy in her hand as she worked the towel over the surface, happiness reflected back at her behind the darker blue color of her gaze.

After finishing the last dish, he watched her as she polished off the beads of hot water and placed it in a rack.

"We've both had a busy day. I think it's time for us to see if we can get some sleep."

A few seconds before and she would have sworn her nerves couldn't get worse, but he'd proven her wrong with two sentences.

Her legs became jelly beneath her, sticky sweat reaching out to grasp onto the fabric of her dress and hug it tightly against her skin. "Bed? Am I...are we..."

He studied her with amusement, the height he had over her making her feel like a small child. With a calculated gaze that was as mysterious and beautiful as an iceberg turned so that its belly breached the surface, his eyes were as alive and dangerous as the ocean that harbored those deadly islands of ice that had sunk so many ships.

"Take the stairs up to the bedroom. Sit down on the edge of the bed. I'll be up in a moment to help you into your night clothes."

Panic set in, her body trembling as she put distance between them, happy to walk away, but nervous about where she was going. Alice wasn't sure if the nightmares would rear their ugly head as she slept beside him, if he wouldn't kick her out the following morning when he discovered all the disorders that plagued her.

However, if it did happen, and if Max were unable to sleep with her beside him, she could offer to sleep in another room, attempt to find a place in the large three story house where her issues with sleep wouldn't become his as well.

Mounting the stairs with a hesitant foot, she climbed them one by one, each time swallowing a knot of panic that kept lodging itself in her throat.

Reaching the top floor, she shook her head of the worries that were whispering in her thoughts.

Her hand grasped the doorway of the bedroom and she paused to take a steadying breath.

Forcing herself inside, she sat on the edge of the bed, her legs heavy where they were pressed together, her mind a wash of concern.

She wanted to run and find another room in the house to call her own, but only because she didn't want to lose this man to the nightmares that had always been her constant companion. Nerves had her fighting herself to not pace the room just to expend some energy. But even given her fears, she was still waiting and anxious to see what *bedtime* in this man's house would bring.

Her hair hung down at the sides of her face where she sat waiting on the soft luxury of Max' bed, a bed so large it took up nearly half of the room. From behind that curtain of her hair, Alice peered anxiously at the man standing in the doorway, his shoulders as wide as the doorframe, his eyes as mysterious and deep as an arctic lake.

For a while he stood watching her, his gaze shrewd in its appraisal, his body tight beneath a black shirt and linen pants. His mannerisms were more fitting for an affluent man that had stepped out of the past into the modern world and he had the swagger that came with the silver spoon life, the hawk-like gaze of a man that could rule any room he happened to deign to enter.

Unsure why he reminded her of a time long gone, she trembled where she sat, attempting in vain to ignore the frantic beat of her heart beneath her ribs, the pulsing nervousness that echoed across her bones with every solitary second he stood deathly still and studied her.

It was the first night they would spend together, the first time they would go further than a breathtaking kiss. It wouldn't be the first time Alice had sex, but she doubted that barely legal man she'd snuck in her window at the college so many years ago was anything compared to the one that now stalked towards her.

Max' steps were measured in his approach, each one closing the distance between them. Her muscles tightened with every step, the shaking of her body becoming more violent with every foot of space between them that was lost.

When he'd come within arm's reach of her - when he paused as if this single moment would be the one that made her writhe in pleasure over a bed of elegant silk - he paused long enough to make her mouth go dry, to add fuel to the already blazing fire of need that burned across her mind. She didn't know what he would do to her – what he could do – but she knew she needed him like she needed air to breathe.

Max didn't touch her. He simply walked away and a gust of breath blew over her lips, the anticipation too much for a woman who was just now learning what it meant to step away from a nightmare life into a dream.

Max disappeared into the shadowed interior of a large closet, lost to Alice's sight as quickly as he'd appeared in the bedroom doorway.

Releasing a shaky breath, Alice's trembling hands wrung in her lap, her heart rate dropping back to a steady rhythm that didn't pound violently through her entire body.

His absence wasn't long. Within a minute, possibly two, he returned from the black shadow of the closet, a flowing garment of pristine white held tightly in his hands.

And like every time he approached, Alice's heart sped back to a dizzying, frantic rhythm, her breath caught in her lungs burning for release. Alice watched his boots move across the floor, finally arching her neck to gaze up at the beautiful face of a man who was as silent as he was still, who wore unbridled lust as a second skin, who gazed back down at her with *desire* behind his sharp, observant eyes.

"I brought you something to wear," he said, the nightgown falling from his hands to puddle on her lap.

"Right here?" She swallowed down her nervousness, her eyes flicking between him and the bathroom, unsure if she should get dressed in front of him, or move to where she could hide behind a closed door.

He inclined his head, taking a few steps back to allow her room to stand.

Barely able to force her muscles to move, she picked up the nightgown from her lap and pushed herself to her feet. She was being ridiculous and she knew it. Everything inside of her wanted to be with this man, he would see her naked eventually, there was no point in being shy now.

Max didn't move, his body so still she would have sworn it was made of steel or stone, hard, impenetrable plaster like that of the statues she'd admired in a museum so many years ago. Not a twitch of his muscles. Not a tick of his jaw. The only part of him that screamed there was life inside his body were the ever-watching, haunting eyes that spoke of wicked secrets, breathless trysts, and passionate desires.

Unable to pull her gaze away from the silent witness in the room, she loosened her grip on the nightgown to place it on the mattress, her hands clenching and releasing as she summoned the bravery to reveal her body to him for the first time.

A shiver ran down Alice's spine, but she kept her attention on Max, allowed her eyes to settle on his eyes before chasing the lines of the mottled scar that ran across his left cheek.

What caused it? She wondered. *What nightmare did he suffer that undoubtedly shaped the beautiful man he was now?*

Letting out a tremulous sigh, she squared her shoulders and told herself to calm down because this was just the beginning of a new and wondrous life.

Lifting up the loose skirt of her dress that was far too modest for a moment such as this, she hooked her thumbs into the elastic waistband of her nylons. Ignoring where they had clung too tight and left a red mark across the flesh of her hips, she slipped them down, the fabric releasing its tight hold as it bunched over her thighs, her knees, and eventually settled loosely at her ankles. Stepping out of them, she kicked her feet free of the material that still carried the warmth of her body.

Max' eyes followed every movement she made, his liquid gaze tracing hot tracks along the length of her legs, silently watching as the stockings went from taut across her skin, to loose and folded at her ankles.

His expression was a blank mask, but the heat behind his stare was sweltering, the small breeze kicked up by the air conditioning system no match against the assault of his illicit inferno. Alice didn't need to ask him what he was thinking, she knew, and she was feeling the same way.

Although his eyes were still the color of dangerous arctic ice, his stare was anything but cold.

When Alice hesitated, her shyness and modesty preventing her from unbuttoning the dress to pull it from her body, a questioning arch to Max' dark brow broke through the impenetrable mask he'd worn, the corner of his lips curling up into a wicked grin.

Their eyes locked, the intensity of the give and take between them so lurid, that Alice felt tingles across her skin, goosebumps of fear erupting over the surface of her entire body.

With nimble fingers she unfastened the buttons down the back collar of her dress, the position pushing her chest out, her breasts tight across the cloth that was the only thing keeping her from his view. Once the buttons were unclasped, she dropped her arms to her sides, matching his stare.

He angled his head in that way that was all his own, his lips betraying his thoughts when they curled even more at the corners.

Daring to give him a smile, she said, "You're not much of a talker, are you?" It was stupid to say, but she needed some relief from the suffocating silence, from the blanket of jittering nerves she felt wrapping her body.

He didn't react but to smile brighter.

She smiled in return.

Another breath to steady herself, and she slipped the dress from her shoulders, allowing it to slide along her body until it puddled around her feet on the floor. She hadn't worn a bra, and despite the lacy underwear that held tight around her hips, she felt completely exposed to his roaming eyes, to the blatant lust that radiated from him at the sight of her breasts now bared to him.

She wasn't sure if it was her desire or the chill in the air that caused her nipples to form tight, painful peaks.

A shudder ran over Max' body. Slight, but still noticeable, it was another outward sign beyond his heated gaze and mysterious smile that gave away anything of what he was feeling.

Forcing her arms to her sides, she felt butterflies in her stomach.

Her body turned to pluck the nightgown from the bed, and with her eyes averted, she felt the heat of his body wash against her back before a large hand fell on her shoulder. No sooner had she gripped her hand over the soft, white cloth than it was ripped from her grasp, tossed to the ground to lie in a puddle on the floor.

The butterflies in her stomach were fluttering so violently it felt like a tempest storm rolling inside her. She craned her neck to look up at him, her body flooded and hot with desire in response to the intensity of his stare.

A slight shake of his head was all he gave her before her body was shoved gently against the mattress, her weight sinking down heavily into the soft luxury of the blankets, while Max stood at the foot of the bed.

Unable to endure the tense silence, Alice laughed softly and teased, "What are you looking at?"

Three words spoken on a gritty, deep voice. "My future wife."

Seconds ticked past, tension building between them until Alice wanted to beg, *please, just take me. I'm yours.*

But Max wouldn't be hurried, wouldn't be denied and wouldn't be forced. He would take his time. Take his fill. Take whatever he deemed worth taking.

His eyes were locked to her body, his stare a palpable burn against her skin. Out of shyness and modesty, she pulled her arms around herself to hide her nudity, but a simple and subtle shake of Max' head stopped her before she could cover herself completely.

She knew she would break beneath him, she'd gift him her soul as easily as her heart and body.

With slow, controlled movements, Max unbuttoned his shirt until it hung open to reveal the strong physique hinted to by the taut pull of the material across his shoulders and chest. Shadows highlighted every curve of his pecs and abs, the V that ran down from his waist to bury itself beneath the waistline of his pants. She was powerless to refuse the advances of a man as beautiful as Max Frost, and even now, with the desire so obvious within him, she was still helpless to resist his seductive charm.

The buckle of his belt clanged like a soft whisper across the room. His pants pulled open, but not pulled away. He stalked toward her with smooth, unhurried movements, allowing the pressure to build with each solitary step he made.

The bed sunk beneath his weight, a prowling tiger whose shoulders moved with a feline grace as he crawled up to hover above her. His heat was a blanket that covered her, his blue eyes the cool, icy promise that sent chills across her sweat dampened skin. Caged against the mattress by strong arms that were as thick as they were rigid, Alice forced herself to close her eyes.

"Look at me when I make love to you."

His thumb and finger gripped her chin and tipped her face up so that when her eyes fell open, she became lost to the emotion in his.

With a voice as delicate as a whisper soft caress, he said, "From this night forward, we will always be together. Never forget that, Alice. I will never let you go."

Her heart sang in response to his words, her body shuddering beneath him ready to take whatever pleasure he would give.

And give he did, his hands exploring every inch of her body before his mouth and tongue traced the same paths.

It took hours for Max to deliver on every unspoken promise he'd made to her with eyes that were filled with desire and hands that were as sensual as they were cruel. He teased her until she was begging for more, finally relieving her just enough so that she felt she would burst apart if he didn't take her completely – making her *his*.

His attention entirely on her, Max pushed Alice into a frenzy of sexual need, pushing and pushing until finally entering her body to become one.

Drenched in delicious sweat, her heart pounding beneath her ribs, Alice fell over a tight precipice into the ecstasy and euphoria of her love for the man that drove her wild with the strength of his hands, the searing intensity of his kiss and the rhythm of a man possessed, taking from her body all it had to give.

They crashed against each other after that first time, but it only took minutes for Max to regain his strength and drag her into the shower to both love her again and help her clean up.

After showering, and before allowing her to crawl back in bed, Max changed the sheets. She found his need to change them odd, but she was too tired to question him about it. By the time her head fell against the pillow, exhaustion rode her so thoroughly that her eyes closed and she slept, her fear of what the night would bring lost in the warm strength of Max' arms.

* * *

The next morning came as ordinary as any morning. Except it wasn't ordinary for one glaring reason that Alice didn't understand until she opened her eyes to find the first rays of morning sunlight trickling past the curtains of a large picture window in the room.

Dust motes glimmered where they hung suspended in a cascade of shimmering beauty, tiny fairies of light that had paused to worship the warmth that was returning to the world after hours of the cold moonlit night. Her eyes followed those small points of reflected light where they danced and swirled within the small air current that worked a path through the room.

She was aware of her surroundings, but not yet awake enough to completely understand it. More importantly, she wasn't pinned to the bed by some unseen specter. She was able to wiggle her fingers and toes, and she didn't open her eyes onto the scene of nightmare that had followed her from sleep into her waking life.

The sleep paralysis she'd suffered so often that it had become a part of her, was absent. There was no ringing in her ears so loud she feared she'd never hear anything beautiful again. There was no weight on her chest that threatened to crush her. Her body was solid and not floating above itself looking down to where she lay comfortably in the arms of a man.

The confusion that came with the absence of a demon that had plagued her for as far back as she could remember was staggering.

Max' arms were a warm weight across her body that prevented her from sitting up, but from what she could see, the pillows she laid her tired head upon the night before were still in place. The sheets were as neat over her body as they had been when Max had tucked her in. There were no obvious points of pain on her arms or legs from where she'd hurt herself fighting some unseen force through the night. She was still in place and hadn't woken to find herself standing in the threshold of a doorway, or lying down in another room.

She'd slept through the night without fighting. Without dreaming. Without panic or fear. And she'd woken peacefully to find the glimmering rays of quiet morning light.

THIRTY-TWO

12:37 p.m.

There wasn't a waiting room any longer. At least not for Alice. No name being called and no doctor standing in a doorway. She woke up to the same couch where she always sat, her bent legs drawn up to her chest, her arms wrapped around her legs as a protective cage.

With her chin resting on the hard plane of her knees, she left behind the memory of what had once been to return her attention to the doctor who sat silently in observation of her now.

As usual, his pen tapped against paper before upending to scribble out some private thought. She could never read the words he wrote, and she wasn't sure she ever wanted to know what parts of her he recorded in her file.

Sure that whatever he thought or recorded was as negative as the feelings she had for herself, she didn't need the confirmation in plain blue ink written in flowing script against the crisp white page of his notebook.

The doctor's head tilted up, his eyes hidden beneath the lenses of his glasses and the shadow of the dimly lit room. "I think you've just found one of the answers you've been seeking during these sessions, Alice." He paused, allowing the silence to become a ticking clock between them.

...*drip*...

"What are your thoughts now that you know your feelings for this man – the love you have for him – wasn't a result of rape or cruelty, but was, in fact, due to a connection that is common among most men and women?"

She didn't need a moment to discover the answer to that particular question. It was already sitting on the tip of her tongue.

"Foolish." Her eyes closed on the word, her mind racing to make sense of everything she'd once been and was still becoming. "I feel stupid and foolish."

Another beat of silence, another tick of the clock.

Another drop of water falling from the faucet to splash against the sink.

"Why do you feel foolish? From what you just told me, Max was as much of a gentleman to you as most men are in this day and age. He offered to care for you. He pulled you from a situation where he felt you weren't safe. He cooked for you and didn't judge you for the issues that have haunted you your entire life.

How can you consider yourself foolish for loving a man who was willing to do all those things for you? A man who treated you with only kindness?"

A bark of laughter shot from her lungs, the sound unnerving and sharp. "He trapped me is what he did. Trapped me and lured me into another type of submission than if he'd simply abducted me and forced me to live in that house with him." A shiver ran across her skin. "I don't know. Maybe believing I had been abducted was easier than facing the hard facts."

Her eyes opened and she locked her stare with the inquisitive eyes of the doctor.

"Being lured is worse than having the choice taken away from me entirely. I *agreed* to stay there with him…" Her voice trailed off on that thought, because, in truth, what she'd done was much worse than simply staying. Unable to bring herself to the point where she could say it aloud, she chose instead to push the conversation along, to remember and understand every detail of what had occurred.

"There's more to it, Doc. That's not the end of the story."

He didn't immediately respond, but when he finally spoke again, his voice was hesitant and grim. "Then you need to tell me the rest, Alice. I don't think I need to remind you that time is running out."

THIRTY-THREE

"Good morning."

A deep voice broke through the giddiness Alice was feeling since the moment she woke. Rolling over to face the man who'd been sleeping so peacefully beside her just seconds before, she smiled. "I hope last night wasn't too stressful for you."

Adding humor to her voice, she'd attempted to phrase the statement as more of a joke than a question about her behavior. Alice very rarely remembered what she did in sleep and she wasn't entirely sure that the night had been as serene as she hoped it had.

"Well," Max answered, a grin pulling at his lips. "You moved around some at first, but it wasn't until you attempted to rip out my throat - the entire time calling me a sadistic monster – that I held you down until you stopped screaming, slapped you around a little bit, and then had sex with you until you fell back into a deep sleep. After that, I wrapped my arms around you and held you in place just in case you were planning a second attack."

Her eyes widened, her heart beating erratically beneath her ribs. "Please tell me you're joking." She knew he had to be joking, but with the life she'd lived, with the things her father had done to her, she couldn't be entirely sure.

A serious expression replaced the once silly grin on his face. "Of course, I'm joking. You slept like a baby the entire night."

Breathing out a relieved sigh, she smiled shyly. "You're sure?"

His eyes met hers, concern rolling behind the light blue. "I can't say for certain, but I assume so because you never woke me up. And I'm a light sleeper, Alice. I would have noticed if you were fighting or screaming."

Relief filled her, a ray of warmth spreading through her chest and head, her muscles relaxing against her bones as she cuddled up against Max. "That's the first time that's ever happened, I think."

He watched her intently, his expression uncertain. "You think?"

Nodding her head, she answered, "I've lived alone for a long time now. And I don't always remember what happened while I was sleeping. Usually I can figure out it wasn't good when I wake up to find the pillows and blankets on the floor, or when I wake up to find myself somewhere else entirely."

Pulling her tighter against his chest, Max allowed silence to settle between them, both of their thoughts kept to themselves as a sense of comfort enveloped them in the morning light.

"We should get moving at some point." His arms pulling away from where they'd held her, Max stood from the bed, the mattress shifting beneath her at the loss of his weight. Alice turned to watch him walk into the bathroom and close the door.

Finally convincing herself that it was time to get up, Alice shimmied to the edge of the bed, her mind still wandering about what she would do for the day when Max opened the bathroom door, a cloud of steam dancing out from behind him.

A white towel was wrapped loosely around his hips as he approached a large bureau. Dropping the towel from around his hips, Max tossed it into a wicker hamper, the firm cheeks of his ass staring back at Alice from beneath broad shoulders, a strong back, and the indented line that ran along the length of his spine. Smooth skin barely contained the steel musculature of his body, and Alice became lost to the way his biceps flexed when he pulled clothes from his bureau.

Dark blue jeans and a simple white t-shirt. It seemed too casual for a man as sophisticated as him.

After getting dressed, Max disappeared into his closet, reappearing with the outfit he'd selected for her to wear.

"I grabbed this for you." He dropped a simple white dress into her lap before turning to walk across the room and out into the hall. From over his shoulder, he said, "Meet me in the kitchen when you're done. I'll start breakfast."

Alice smiled and she couldn't believe her luck for having found a man as considerate as the one who would be her future husband.

She stood up on tired and sore legs to stand before the full-length mirror. Max had chosen a simple dress with buttons up the front, a blue sash as a belt to cinch it at her waist.

Pulling the cloth over her shoulders, she fastened the buttons one by one before tying the sash and looking at reflection in the mirror. The dress was quite beautiful, despite its simplicity, but her hair was a frightful mess of blonde limp tendrils. Reaching up, she braided the mess back to give it the illusion of being styled before huffing out a breath and making her way out of the room and down three flights of stairs.

From the kitchen came loud clanging sounds, pots and pans being pulled from cabinets, the sizzle of bacon heard seconds before the smell hit her nose like an avalanche of temptation. Her stomach rumbled as she stepped barefoot from the wood floors of the entry hall onto the cool stone tile.

"I'm here," she stated softly.

"Take a seat at the center island, Alice. Breakfast will be ready in a minute."

Plates were set down on the counter before her, a different design than the ones she'd dropped the night before. Eggs and bacon, toast and juice, an ordinary meal that made her smile brightly.

"Eat."

"Yes, sir," she laughed, assuming Max' assertiveness was simply a facet of his personality. It hadn't escaped her notice that Max had a tendency to make demands, or even choices, without first asking her what she wanted to eat or wear. She assumed it had more to do with his fastidiousness, the calculated and precise manner in which he ran his own life. He was the type of man who controlled the room around him, but Alice didn't see it as a negative aspect to his personality. Her life, up to that point, had been so far out of control that it felt good to let somebody else take the wheel for a change.

But even with that logic, something bothered her about Max, about the manner in which he'd taken over control so easily.

Picking up her fork, she ignored the whispers inside her head, the nagging reminders that Max reminded her of another man in her life, one she'd run from as soon as the opportunity had been there to escape.

Slipping the tines of the fork into the scrambled eggs, she fed herself slowly, chewing thoughtfully on the food that would sustain her. She enjoyed the salty slide across her tongue, the warmth that traveled down her throat to land on an empty belly. Relief was found in the comfort of the nourishment he'd provided her.

Seemingly satisfied to stand back and watch her eat, Max leaned back against the kitchen counter, a steaming cup of coffee held in his hands, his lips pursed to blow over the surface of the liquid. His face was clean shaven, the dust of shadow gone following the shower he'd taken that morning.

Alice watched him when he wasn't looking, her eyes playing over the sharp lines of his cheekbones and the strong, square jaw that gave him a rugged, but cultured appearance. Despite the scar that marred the left side of his face, he was elegant in his features. With a straight nose that ran above full and sculpted lips, he had eyes that were pale and cold, a sparkling blue that were in stark contrast to obsidian hair and tan skin. An enigma wrapped in beauty, he was as alluring as he was fierce.

A question toyed over her thoughts. Afraid to ask, she worried her bottom lip between her teeth, her curiosity too much for her to keep her silence.

"What happened to you, Max?"

His eyes pinned her in an uneasy stare, studying her over the rim of the cup from which he sipped. His throat worked to swallow down the steaming liquid before he pulled the cup away to place it on the counter. "What do you mean?"

Clearing her throat of the anxiety she felt for bringing the subject up, she summoned everything brave within her to continue forward in the conversation. She knew that, like her, Max had his own share of secrets, he'd made that fact known time and time again. Perhaps the story behind that scar was one of the parts of him he rarely revealed. She wanted to know everything about him: what brought him joy, what he feared, but mostly, what events shaped him into the man he'd become.

"Your scars? How did you get them?"

His glacial stare was a wash of cold contempt across her body, a shiver running down her spine to know she'd stepped in places not traveled but many people. It scared her suddenly to see the expression on his face, the distinct change from a man comfortable in shared silence while she ate to a person she wasn't sure she knew at all.

Silently considering her question, his jaw ticked a slow beat. She wasn't sure whether he'd answer her, and the tension that mounted her shoulders forced the fork from her hands, her pulse an annoying drumbeat that fluttered over the soft point of her neck.

Black lashes framed his hollow eyes, shadows creeping and swirling beneath the blue that didn't give her any clue to the thoughts assaulting him inside.

"My father," he finally said, his voice morose and vacant, "was an exceptionally driven man. I was an only child, his only offspring that survived the journey from my mother's womb to the bedroom where she'd given birth to me. I was the seventh in a line of eight, and the only one who'd taken a breath once the umbilical cord was cut."

Pushing up from the counter upon which he'd previously leaned, he took three steps to stand by the island where Alice sat listening. A sheet of paper sat to his side, a stack of mail neatly organized beside it. Slipping the top sheet from the stack, he slid it to lay between them, his hands working methodically over the blank surface, making folds with sharp creases, before opening it again. Spellbound by the precise motion of his fingers, Alice jumped when he spoke again.

Over the course of several minutes, Max told her a story that shattered her heart. Not much different from her own, but with far more permanent and physical reminders, Max' young life had been plagued by the same domineering father, the same type of abuse and pain that had haunted Alice since the moment she left home.

Lifting his hand, he placed a paper crane on the table in front of her. Its beak pointed at where she sat, its wings perfectly formed at its sides. Small and plain, white with no ornamentation to speak of, the creation was beautiful for its simplicity alone. Reaching out to touch it, she'd almost put a finger against its surface, but pulled back at the last second. There was something sacred about the paper crane, something solemn that kept her from corrupting it with any part of herself.

Her eyes affixed to the inanimate bird, she didn't look up when he spoke again. She couldn't without allowing him to see the tears that rimmed her eyes red. And as she stared at that crane, she listened to him relay the worst part of the story, the physical abuse that caused the scar that now was a prominent feature of his face.

"In retrospect, this scar may have been my only salvation. As soon as he realized the damage he'd done, he no longer expected me to take over the family business. In his eyes, I was as useless as the children buried in the garden on his property, as easily forgotten as those who'd been long dead."

Their eyes locked and Alice shed a tear for the man who stood so open and vulnerable before her.

Max grew quiet and Alice was desperate to fill the silence that fell between them.

"My father was a cruel bastard as well," she offered, "except I wasn't fortunate enough to escape his notice. He tried locking me away in places I couldn't escape from, tried muffling my screams in hopes he could sleep through the night without being jostled awake by his freak of a daughter. But no matter what he did, I was always right there in his sight. Always the dumb child who didn't know how to behave or stay quiet. It wasn't my fault. I was sleeping most of the time. But that didn't matter to him." Her voice trailed off, her mind locked into a memory that she'd prefer to forget.

Max didn't openly react to her statement. His head angled to the side, his hair brushing against his shoulder when his lips pulled up into a playful grin.

"I knew there was something familiar about you, Alice, something very much like me. It's what draws me to you. We're alike, you and I.

Two very different backgrounds, but a shared trait that pulls us together."

Nodding her head in agreement, she swallowed down the knot of memory that was always so thick in her throat.

"My mother didn't know how to handle what my father was doing. She wasn't strong enough to step in between, to stop him from tormenting me about something that wasn't my fault. So, she did the only thing she could do: she kept me out of sight as much as possible when he was home."

Alice looked up from the crane and their eyes met. "She had a garden in the yard around the house, and she forced me to learn all there was to know about caring for the plants that were out there. At first, I hated it. It was always so hot outside. But after a while, I grew to love it." A tear slipped down her cheek. "It's the one thing I miss about that house. I had to leave it behind when I left for school, and since then, I've never returned home."

Tracing his finger along her cheek, he caught the tears that fell. "Never?"

She shook her head, swallowing again so that she could talk clearly around the pain her memories brought to the surface. "Never. My sister, Delilah, calls me often, but I rarely answer the phone."

Slipping his finger beneath her chin, he tilted her face up to look at him. "What does your sister have to do with any of it?"

Alice sighed. "I was jealous of her. Jealous that she didn't have to endure the same *attention* from my father. She was quiet, stayed out of the way. Hell, she still lives at that house with them even though she's a grown woman now. I know she's calling because she wants me to come home and mend my relationship with that man. So, instead of openly telling her it will never happen, that she doesn't understand because she was never made a victim by him, I simply ignore the phone."

Understanding flooded Max' eyes. "Is that who kept calling you on the day we met? At the house where we met?"

Nodding her head, she blinked away a few more tears and pulled away from his touch. "Yes."

Max was thoughtful for a few moments, his eyes studying her face, shrewd appraisal obvious behind the blue of his eyes.

"You're not a victim, you know? Not entirely. The truth is in your eyes, your body language. I'll admit that I took one look at you in that ratty old house and with one glance, I knew you've been fighting your entire life."

Alice laughed, but the sound carried no humor. "You're wrong. I'm not a fighter."

His palms pressed against the black granite of the island, his voice low. "Am I?"

When she didn't answer, Max spoke softly again. "It's the fighter inside you that drew me to you in the first place."

Glancing up at him, Alice's brows knit together in question.

With measured steps, Max rounded the island to stand beside her before he explained, "You've seen darkness, experienced Hell...you've battled nightmares all your life. It's shaped you, molded you and set you apart from the majority. You are human, obviously, but your mind is not the same as the worthless sheep who fill our society. You don't care about the inane. You don't waste idle time discussing bullshit. You, of all people, understand what it is to be haunted by evil."

Drawing her into an embrace, Max rested his chin on the top of her head, his chest vibrating against her as he spoke next. "You have a new family now, Alice. We both do. And we're all the other will ever need. I can't take away the pain of what your father did to you, but I can give you a new haven. A place of your own in this house that you can escape to while I'm busy working or otherwise distracted."

Pulling away from her, he locked his hands around her shoulders, remaining silent until she looked up at him.

"Would you like to see it?"

Sniffling, Alice reached up to brush more tears from her skin. Although reliving the memories had hurt, learning that Max could not only sympathize, but also understand what she went through, helped her feel closer to him than ever.

"Of course," she answered.

Taking her hand, Max led her out of the kitchen, through the dining room and to a door at the back of the house. When he opened it, he allowed her to step outside first, his arms wrapping around her when he finally stepped up behind where she was standing.

Alice looked around the large lot, her eyes skimming over the yard that hadn't been cared for in years. Patches of grass were hidden within weeds as tall as her thighs, but there was potential in the space for any person who cared to take the time to nurture it.

Shaded in part by stately live oaks, their moss swaying in a breeze, the yard had a remote and faraway feel. Alice was delighted to see several areas that had the perfect amount of sunlight for flowers.

"Do you like it?"

She chuckled, "I'm not exactly sure what I'm looking at."

His fist closed over the braid in her hair and he pulled back gently until her neck was arched as far as it would go. Placing a kiss on her forehead, he released her hair so she could look back out over the grounds.

"It could be your new garden, Alice. In fact, because neither you nor I have family or many friends to speak of, we could get married here, and then you can plant whatever you like. You could make it your own."

His suggestion was a surprise to her weary heart, one that washed away all the negativity she was feeling and replaced it with the splendor of *hope*.

"Mine?"

His shoulders shook with silent laughter. "Yours."

Searching the space more carefully now that she understood what he planned for her to do with it, Alice noticed how the ground in certain places had been disturbed, as if an animal had been digging for roots, or creating burrows for its home. Making a mental note that they'd have to hire an exterminator before she planted anything in the ground, she scanned out farther, spotting a black, wrought iron fence that ran the length of the back portion of the yard.

Taking a few steps forward to discover what was on the other side of that fence, Alice stopped when Max' hands tightened over her shoulders.

Turning to glance at him, she asked, "What's behind the fence?"

A shadow fell over Max' eyes, the normally sparkling blue darkening with memories. "My brothers and sisters. And my parents, although they don't have headstones." His voice dropped to a whisper, something grim causing his lips to pull into a thin line. "I'd prefer you not go there, Alice. That's a place I try to forget even exists."

Spinning her in place, he locked his eyes with hers, his hands still tight over her shoulders. "Promise me you'll never go past that gate."

Not understanding why he wouldn't want her in the small family cemetery, she studied his expression and thought it wise not to pry too deeply into a situation that obviously brought him so much pain. "I promise," she answered.

He nodded his head once and led her back into the house. "Then let's get to work planning this wedding."

Laughter bubbled from her lungs. "There's not much to plan, if it's only going to be us."

"That's all there needs to be. Just you and me, and whoever I choose to officiate."

Stopping in place, he looked at her, long and hard, a sticky web of emotions alight behind his eyes that trapped her in that icy gaze.

"We'll have the ceremony tomorrow."

Her breath caught in her lungs. "So soon?"

She felt wobbly suddenly, panicked because it felt like she was caught up in a wind that kept shoving her forward without allowing her to take the time to think anything through. Max was that wind, a man who knew what he wanted, who would have it regardless of the obstacles that stood in his way.

"I think I should sit down," Alice muttered.

After settling her in a wooden chair, Max knelt down in front of her, his hands reaching up to tuck errant strands of hair behind her ear.

His voice was assured when he spoke again. "You have no reason to panic. You should be happy with what I have planned for you. There will be no struggle, no worries or concerns. Life will become magic as it should."

His knuckles barely rubbed against her cheek before he reached up towards her ear. Light flashed against a coin held in his palm, her eyes widening as a slight grin pulled at his lips.

"You had something behind your ear," he teased. "A simple trick, but only the beginning of all you can discover."

Her laughter knocked the tension from her shoulders, sadness settling over her because she knew he'd learned that trick from the books his nanny had given him...and he paid for those tricks for the rest of his young life.

"It's just all happening so fast," she explained. "But I trust you, Max. And I can't wait to be your wife."

THIRTY-FOUR

Standing in the full length mirror in their bedroom, Alice dragged a brush through her hair, her body covered in a silk slip that was the same pristine white of the wedding dress Max had chosen for her to wear. She hadn't had much say in the matter when they went to the small boutique to select the dress, but she wasn't unhappy with his choice. She convinced herself that if the style selected made Max happy, it made her happy as well.

"You're so beautiful. Just as I knew you would be. We'll get you dressed...get you ready for your new life. You'll shine, Alice. It'll be what you always wanted. An escape from the life that has done nothing but hurt you. Even in dreams, you could never escape."

His palms rubbed the length of her bare arms before he released her to retrieve the dress from the closet. Coming back over to her, he helped her step into the expensive material, taking his time to fasten the small buttons that ran the length of her back. She'd protested against the cost of the dress, especially because it would only be the two of them at the wedding, but Max had insisted.

Turning around, Alice looked over the beautiful cut of the black suit he'd chosen to wear, the silver grey vest that matched his tie. With a white shirt underneath, he looked dapper and worthy of the life of ease and leisure he lived.

Taking Alice's hand, Max led her from the bedroom, down the stairs and out into the space that would eventually be her garden. The officiant waited for them beneath the thick boughs of the live oaks, the moss hanging from their branches creating dancing light and shadow over the patch of land where they stood.

The wedding was quick, their vows those that had been used for years by husbands and wives that came together before them. When the officiant left, they remained beneath those stately trees, Max staring down at his new bride with possession behind his eyes.

"We're married, you and I. You are now my wife."

His expression grew serious, his focus severe.

"Until death, Alice. Promise me."

Her eyes shimmering with tears of happiness, she nodded her head.

"Until death," she promised.

THIRTY-FIVE

12:38 p.m.

"It was the beginning of a dream," Alice whispered, her voice breaking as the memories flooded her mind. "At least, I thought it was a dream."

Her head turned to face the doctor, her body balled on the couch with her back pressed against the backrest. Her bent legs were tucked up against her chest, her arms wrapped tightly to hold them in place. Slowly she rocked where she sat, the springs of the couch creaking with the subtle movement.

"But the dream didn't last, I assume. How long were you married before the truth of the man you married started coming to light?"

Her eyes clenched shut to remember the first time Max' anger caused her harm. "A year, maybe a little less. He was always so busy working on the basement. He wanted the entire house finished. He was so particular about those things. Everything had to have its place. Everything had to be in order. Everything had to be perfectly clean. He said it was because he didn't want things to be ugly – not like us."

Leaning forward in his chair, Dr. Chance waited for her to open her eyes. Once he knew he had her full attention, he said, "You're not ugly, Alice. What occurred to you when you were a child didn't make you an ugly person."

A bark of humorless laughter blew over her lips. "Didn't it? If it wasn't for what my father did to me, I might have made different decisions when the truth of Max came to light." Her voice shook over the words, her body beginning to tremble as bits and pieces flooded back, images she could never erase from her mind.

"I was the perfect target, it seems. I'd been conditioned by my father to accept abuse, and Max used that to his advantage. I was tired. I was estranged from my family. I had no friends."

"He took advantage of not only your life, but also the love you had for him. He was a predator, Alice."

"And I was the perfect prey," she answered.

Slapping a tear from her face, she stared at the doctor with bruised and swollen eyes. "I would have thought I'd be stronger than I was. That, perhaps, what my father had done to me would have taught me to run at the first sign of abuse." She shuddered, clenching her eyes shut against the memories. "I don't understand the dreams, Doc. Not the direction they took or the way the memories got jumbled. Why did you keep taking me back to discuss my father? How did you know that he had anything to do with the events of my life with Max?"

Settling back against his seat, the doctor tapped his pen against his notebook before reaching up to reposition his glasses over his nose. "I believe you put yourself in the place of a captive woman because you couldn't face something far more frightening: the fact that you ran away from one abusive man, just to end up in the arms of another. I thought that by remembering the actions of your father, it would open you up to remember what occurred with Max."

She sighed. "Well, it worked. That and reminding me of the damn price I paid for the luxury Max had given me. For the life he'd chosen for me."

Glancing at the clock ticking on the wall, the doctor looked back at her. He didn't need to remind her that time continued marching forward to an unknown end.

"You have to keep going, Alice. We have to piece together this puzzle in time."

Alice shook her head, her arms tightening even more over her legs. "It's not going to save her, Doc. Time has already run out."

Giving her a patient and thoughtful look, the doctor spoke softly when he said, "We've established that the dreams are memories, Alice. Why do you still insist this has something to do with you sister?"

A violent tremor coursed over Alice's body, screams erupting in her mind because she allowed herself to go to that place.

It was the truth that broke her apart completely, the memory she never wanted to face.

"Because it has everything to do with Delilah, Doc. Of that, I'm entirely certain."

THIRTY-SIX

A year had passed since Alice and Max married, and in that year Max had laid down a set of rules that Alice was expected to follow. What he asked of her was nothing surprising or unheard of when it came to the roles played by a married couple, and when Max had first made his demands and listed his expectations, Alice hadn't thought twice about what those demands would one day mean.

It was never more than just the two of them. Neither had to leave the house to work on a daily basis, however Max would often leave for a few days at a time to manage the multiple properties his family had owned and left to him when they died.

In addition, there was still a lucrative family business that provided income to Max, and although he didn't have an active role in any of the companies, he was still an overseer, an owner that had to check in every so often to ensure that the businesses were being managed successfully.

Alice never bothered to ask the details. It never concerned her and she didn't much care for anything that occurred in the outside world. She was happy in the small bubble she'd created for herself, venturing outside of the house only on the nights when Max insisted on taking her to the theater, to dinner or to some other special date he'd arranged.

However, over the course of their short marriage, Max' change in behavior had been subtle. Alice didn't understand the danger she was in until the day came where he could no longer hide the person that he was, the monster that had been hidden inside him all along.

While Max was away on one of his extended trips, Alice had come down with a cold. She'd attempted to work in the garden that she'd planted over the spring and summer months. She didn't have to do much to bring the garden to full bloom and she was thankful for the richness of the soil that fed the plants so abundantly that Alice had to do little more than stick them in the ground. Looking over the garden that had been a pathetic plot of dirt before she selected the plants that were now growing healthy and strong, Alice smiled.

Her head bothered her because of the sweltering heat. She wasn't able to stay outside for much longer than an hour before retreating back inside to drink a cup of tea and lie down for a mid-afternoon nap.

Her disorders hadn't bothered her since the first night she slept in Max' arms, but on the nights he was away, she found herself thrashing, especially now that she was sick.

Having only been able to sleep for an hour, she woke with a start, her body springing forward to find the pillows on the floor and the sheets tangled tightly around her feet. She looked up and jumped in surprise to find Max standing silently at the foot of their bed.

A smile spread across her face to see him after the week he'd been gone, but as her eyes cleared of the blur left from sleep, his expression frightened her and the smile slipped away.

"Max?"

His eyes were a slice of cold steel across her senses, his lips a thin sharp line that pulled up into a sneer.

"Are you enjoying the life I've given you, Alice?" Every word he spoke dripped with sickening venom, the icy chill of his voice crawling up her skin until she'd frozen in place.

Her mouth opened and closed several times before she could find enough strength in her voice to response to the odd question. "Yes."

A single eyebrow arched above his eye, his lips now pulling up into a mocking grin. "While I've been away working my ass off to see to all the bullshit my father left for me to manage, it

356

seems you've taken it as an opportunity to lie around in leisure, to make a mess of the home I've provided you and to shit on every responsibility you've been given."

Not understanding where his anger was coming from, Alice shook her head. "I don't know what you're talking about."

He'd never struck her in the year they'd been married, never lost himself so much to the capricious temper that Alice knew he fought to control. Max was a man of many moods, and before today, when he was taken over by anger, he'd chosen to walk away.

Before today.

But *not* today.

She didn't have time to move before he'd reached out to fist his fingers into her hair. And she barely had time to scream before he'd pulled her from the bed, across the carpeted floor and down three flights of stairs. Pain shot along her body with each step that slammed against her hip or knee, her body being dragged farther despite her pleas for him to release her.

By the time he'd dragged her into the kitchen, she was crying out in agony from the way the hard corners of the stairs had bruised her. The louder she screamed, the harder Max' fist tightened in her hair and the faster he dragged her to whatever place he had in mind.

When they reached the back door leading to the garden, Max dropped her to the ground, standing over her as she sobbed over the tile, silently watching her failed attempts to push herself up from the floor.

Finally managing to find strength in her trembling arms, she forced herself into a seated position, but was grabbed by the hair, once again, her face shoved within inches of the floor.

"Do you see the mess you've made? The mud and filth you've dragged into my house, Alice? I give you a place to live, a place to grow your stupid plants and pretend like you're a good little wife to me, and this is the fucking thanks I receive? What have I told you about your cleanliness, Alice? What have I said?"

It wasn't abnormal for Alice to drag in dirt with her when she returned from the garden, but it was typical for her to clean it immediately when she came inside. However, due to the illness she was fighting, she'd neglected to do so today, and Max' anger at the perceived slight wasn't unexpected.

For months he'd drilled into her his need for a tidy house. Every bit of dust had to be polished from the tables. The floors were to be mopped on a daily basis. Alice had worked herself into exhaustion on several days just to ensure that her husband wouldn't find anything that would spark his frightening ire.

She'd never seen anything wrong with his demands. He provided her a comfortable life; clothing, food, anything she could possibly need. All he'd asked in return was for her to manage the household chores, to leave him without that one responsibility so that he could see to his activities without concern for the state of his home.

He'd never reacted this badly before, not to the point where he'd caused a physical injury, at least.

His voice a threatening growl, he asked, "Who are you, Alice?"

Choking on the violence of her sobs, she forced herself to take a deep breath before answering, "Your wife."

His grin grew feral, her fear deepening until she trembled where he held her face barely above the floor. Leaning over her, his breath was a wash of heat across the skin of her cheek, his lips brushing the shell of her ear when he asked, "And what does a wife do for her husband?"

They'd had this conversation several times since they'd been married – mostly when Alice had been careless or made a mistake - and each time Max found a reason to remind her of the rules he'd set, his anger grew darker.

"I cook. I clean. I greet you when you return from your trips." She choked on the knot of fear in her throat. "I see to your every need."

Her face hit the floor when he slammed her head down, pain shooting down her spine when the toe of his shoe slammed into the center of her back.

Unable to move due to the jagged pain that gripped her in its crippling fury, Alice didn't notice when Max walked away, didn't have a chance to reach up and cover her face before he returned and the tea cup she'd used earlier and had left in the sink to clean was slammed down across her face.

"Clean up your fucking mess. By the time I get back, I expect everything in this house to be exactly as it was before I left on my trip."

His heavy footsteps grew quieter as he walked through the house, Alice jumping in place when she heard the front door open and slam close.

* * *

Max hadn't returned by the time the sun sunk low beneath the horizon and the moon reigned supreme in the night sky. Unable to sleep, Alice sat at the edge of their large bed, her mind racing over the violence she'd suffered at the hands of a man who, until then, had done nothing to physically harm her.

Sure, he'd been temperamental in the past, he'd raised his voice, he'd even grabbed her on occasion, but every time she saw him struggle against his own anger, and eventually, he'd let her go.

After the events of that afternoon, though, Alice wondered if she should leave him – but the thought scared her because it meant she'd be alone.

Her hands played over the small object she gently cradled between them. A symbol of vulnerability and pain, Alice had preserved the tiny white paper crane that Max had created when he told her the story of the scar that followed him from the heartbreaking childhood he'd lived into the emotional mess that became his adult life.

Alice still wasn't sure of all the secrets Max carried, but she knew he struggled from day to day, his anger and wrath a burden that weighed on his shoulders with every step he took, a monster he fought every second of every day.

Whereas his youth had created in him something fierce and volatile, hers had created in her something fearful and timid. Two halves of the same whole, two souls that carried with them the turmoil of a life abused at the hands of the people who should have cared for them the most.

It was the shared story that tied them to each other, the story that connected them so completely that Alice couldn't forget the love she felt for Max despite the abuse she'd suffered at his hands.

In many ways, he never grew from that small boy who only wanted to play like other children, and for that, she could understand him completely. Like him, Alice never matured as she would have if given the balance and care implicit to the seeds of a normal life.

In truth, they weren't much different than the plants Alice nurtured from seedlings into full bloom. With the proper soil and care, those plants were a wondrous beauty, their color and smell a blessing for the world in which they lived. However, if they were damaged in their vulnerable stage, if they were denied the nourishment they required or cut down too many times, they never regained the ability to produce the same fullness of flowers, the same perfect shades of leaves and stems that made them unique amongst the variety of flora that surrounded them.

All Max wanted was a family that loved him. All he needed was a home that spared him the chaos of his earlier life.

That was his reason for the order and cleanliness he demanded, and Alice wondered: If she could provide him the comfort and care he required, would it help diminish the demons that still plagued him?

Standing up from the bed, she walked across the room and placed the paper crane on the bureau that faced their bed, her head turning slightly to listen closely when the sound of the front door downstairs opened and closed.

Max was home, and she hated that she didn't know whether to be happy he returned or fearful for the damage he could cause.

With the house so quiet that even the chirping of the crickets outside sounded like a loud, melodic chorus, Alice could track Max' movements as he made his way up the stairs.

His steps were a warning in themselves. This was a fact Alice was learning, each heavy, booted *thud* a reminder that she was not alone. That he was coming for her.

He'd taken eighteen of those warning steps as he climbed the stairs towards her.

Eighteen beats that counted down her future.

Eighteen beats that cried out in their slow, foreboding tone, *beware the monsters*.

But would it be his monster that walked through their bedroom door that evening? Or would it be the man she loved returning home to rescue her from the loneliness that ensnared her when he wasn't by her side?

His shadow darkened the doorway.

Alice took a deep, steadying breath and turned to see what part of her husband had returned home to her.

What she found shattered her heart, the splintered pieces falling to her feet and her arms reaching out to take the broken man into an embrace that would never quite make him whole.

His face a mask of guilt and remorse, self-loathing, shame and sorrow, Max closed the distance between them in several long legged strides.

They both cried as they held onto each other, both shedding the emotions and pain that left scars in places too deep to be repaired.

Picking her up so that her toes barely brushed over the surface of the carpet, Max walked her back to the bed, sat her gently on the edge and kneeled down before her to rest his forehead against the planes of her trembling knees.

"Forgive me."

Alice's hands moved to run her fingers through his hair. It was an act of the forgiveness he sought, a solemn moment where neither spoke, but the words still passed between them in the silence of the crossroads where they now found themselves standing.

Split apart or come together stronger?

What occurred in this moment would answer the question that had been running endless circles in Alice's head.

He was such a proud man; too proud, too formidable to kneel to any person. But yet here he was, lowering himself to his wife, to a woman who was nothing close to the powerful person he'd somehow become. She was the meek one between them – her fear, her panic, her nightmares that only he could chase away – and yet in her helplessness, she'd become Max' ultimate weakness.

Her hands absently tangled into the thick strands of his dark wavy hair, his hands coming up to rub along her calves, the touch so gentle in comparison to the way he'd handled her just hours before.

Lifting his head, tears shimmered in the icy chill of his blue eyes, regret a shadow that darkened the normally stark features of his beautiful face.

"I can't help myself, sometimes," he explained. "I lose my mind when it comes to you. I try so hard to keep that part of me away from you."

Alice understood every word as if she'd spoken them herself. There was a part of her that he'd chased into the shadows, and if she were to return the kindness – the favor given in love –

could she chase away the darkness that loomed over them both when Max' anger raged?

"I forgive you," she whispered, "I'll always forgive you."

They were too entwined for her to back away now, too closely knitted by the horrors of their youth and the serenity they found when they finally came together.

He was her protector, and she would become his.

It was the price she'd ultimately pay to love a man as damaged as the one that knelt at her feet.

"I know you have your secrets, your places that you haven't shown me for fear of what they could mean...or do. But I made you a promise when I married you, Max, and I'll never break it."

Relief withered his shoulders, his body to relax at her feet. However, there was still that other side of him that lingered just beneath the skin.

Pushing up to his knees, he wrapped his arms around her waist, his lips trailing across her shoulder until he found that soft spot at the base of her neck. Her pulse fluttered against his lips and the violence inside him shifted until his was a shadow that covered her as she fell back helpless against the bed.

She wouldn't stop him from taking what she'd always known was his, and a moan brushed over her lips when his hands explored the curves of her trembling body. The softness wouldn't last, she knew that, but she enjoyed it for the brief moment he could give it to her.

There was fury in the way this man loved her, fury and violence in the way he held her down. One strong hand gripped her wrists to pin them to the mattress above her head, heat flashing in his eyes to look down on her when she was powerless and open to every desire inside him.

The fingers of his other hand traveled up her leg, pulling the white nightgown she wore up to the apex of her thighs, their grip so strong that she could feel the pulse of his heart on the tips. He left bruises on her each time they made love, but those small constellations of marks never deterred her from wanting him again.

Because where this man made her body jump with small pain and torment, he also made it sing.

He knew every small place that drove her crazy, every weakness that pulled a soft moan from the back of her throat. Made for each other, the two danced this sensual torture because they were two halves of a whole.

She needed the sexual violence he gave her. He needed the fear and submission she gave in return.

His hand gripped the nightgown, the cloth tearing as he pulled it away. What was left of the delicate material was dropped to the bed beside them and his mouth found the taut peak of her exposed breast, his teeth biting down until her body arched and begged for more.

Slow.

Precise.

Methodical.

He worked her into a frenzy that drove her mad, until he lost control of his own needs and entered her with one forceful stroke.

The way he filled her was exquisite, the way he moved over her was hypnotic. But it was the way he possessed her that forced her over the edge of breathless anticipation, that left her floating in the euphoria of a love that was as wicked as it was divine.

So full and stretched open, Alice lost her head to this man every time his lips found hers, every time his body pushed forward, taking and claiming, spilling into her with a final push that had her screaming his name as tears rolled down her bruised cheek.

She loved him too much to walk away.

So she would pay the price to forgive him. She would pay with her heart, her body and her very soul because it was the only thing that would keep him strong.

THIRTY-SEVEN

12:39 p.m.

Gray walls.

Black table.

Plastic, fake red roses.

Everything in place.

"Alice? ... Ms. Beaumont? ... Alice Beaumont ..."

"Yes, Doctor."

Five steps across the room, three steps over the soft, patterned carpet. Four cushions. A white throw draped loosely over the armrest.

Alice took a seat, her body so tired that she fell back against the cushions of the couch, her vacant eyes staring at the man who was seated across from her, his expression filled with dread and concern.

"You're regressing, Alice. Distancing yourself from everything you've fought to uncover."

His pen tapped against his paper. The clock ticked from the wall. Water dripped from the faucet in the bathroom that was hidden behind the dark wood of a partially open door.

"I don't want to go there, Doc. It's too awful, too frightening to believe it could be real. It's the beginning of the end and I don't want to remember it." She shivered, her arms wrapping around her abdomen, her head jerking to the side with a painful tic.

"I'm sorry, but you have no choice. Everything is riding on you now, Alice. The truth, no matter how awful, will be lost if you don't push ahead."

She knew he was right, but it didn't make the task any easier. Preferring to hide in the shelter of insanity, Alice longed for the confusion and lies that had prevented her from reaching this point for so long.

"I'm not regressing, Doc. I can promise you that. What I'm doing is stalling the inevitable. Delaying the end because I'm not sure I'll survive it."

Shifting in his seat, the doctor pinned her in the seriousness of his stare. "It's your choice whether you survive. It's always been your choice."

A tremulous breath shook through her, her mind racing as her body struggled to remain still. "He was a monster. I told you that."

Nodding his head, the doctor spoke softly, "Yes. You've said that many times before."

She grinned, the expression strained with the negativity she was feeling. "But, did I tell you that I was the worst monster of all?"

His face a wash of confusion and surprise, the doctor spoke slowly, pronouncing his words with such care that she knew he was walking on thin ice.

"That's not possible, Alice."

Her smile brightened, insanity alight in her eyes. "I'm sorry, Doc. I'm sorry to disappoint you. But it is possible. What I did is unforgivable. And if I had to do it again, I'm afraid to admit I would."

Dr. Chance settled against his chair, his pen poised, his eyes opened wide.

"Take me there, Alice. On your own terms, take me there. I'm here to listen."

THIRTY-EIGHT

Months went by following the day that Max unleashed his violence on Alice. And in those months, they shared a peaceful unity, a power play between husband and wife that had been decided by her submission to every demand he made.

Alice believed that the effort she put into being the perfect wife had paid off, that it had somehow prevented the violent side of Max from coming forward, from using its sharp teeth to shred the tranquility between them.

She'd deluded herself to ignore the stirrings of rage that Max often fought against. She'd ignored the fits of aggression that surfaced every time some small misunderstanding occurred.

Her husband was a ticking bomb, it seemed, and what Alice would learn next was that there was no foolproof way to bury his secrets or silence the demons inside him.

Getting dressed late that morning, Alice chose a dress Max had purchased for her in a cheery color of yellow. Not normally a style or color she would wear, she shrugged the dress over her shoulders and stared at herself in the full-length mirror.

Canary yellow cotton covered her body, a simple dress that was fitted in the chest and waist, blossoming at the hips to flow over her legs. The material was tucked at the waist in such a way as to make the skirt appear full, as if crinoline pushed the skirt out, not fully belled, but close.

The demure neckline was adorned by a scalloped white collar, a set of pearls circling her neck tight enough to choke her.

On her feet were a pair of modest white pumps, the heels only an inch off the ground, her legs covered by nude nylons.

From behind her, Max approached, his eyes surveying her clothed body, approval and satisfaction obvious behind the deep blue color. His feet were heavy against the ground, his chest pressed up against Alice's back as his gaze met hers in the mirror.

Rubbing his large hands over her shoulders and down her arms, he leaned in to brush his lips across the shell of her ear, those same lips moving softly over her skin as he whispered.

"You look beautiful, Alice. So much more appropriate than what you were wearing before."

She shuddered beneath the heat of his breath. "I had on my gardening clothes before," she teased, humor a subtle note in her tone.

A soft kiss against her cheek, his chest vibrating with soft laughter against her back. "Ah, so that's how you sullied yourself. You're such a dirty woman, Alice."

Her laughter was in harmony with his, the morning enjoyable and bright, until the threat of storm clouds rolled in.

Max squeezed her shoulders and kissed her again before stepping away to cross the room towards the door.

Calling to him, Alice asked, "What are your plans for today?"

It was a simple question, one she'd asked a handful of times before, but for a reason unknown to her, Max' expression darkened at the innocent inquiry.

"I'll be in the basement. You should find something to do for a few hours because I'll be down there for the rest of the day."

A sigh blew over her lips, she wondered why he spent so much time in such a filthy place. Although she'd never been down there to see it for herself, Max had warned her time and time again about the weak spots in the stairs and floors, about the dim lighting and hazards that could trip her and cause her to fall. She worried about him on the days he spent hours working in those conditions.

"Try not to hurt yourself down there," she replied, intentionally keeping her tone pleasant despite her concerns.

Inclining his head once in response, Max made his way down the stairs.

Alice went about her day as she normally would. Everything in the house was already immaculate and clean, but she found chores anyway, sometimes dusting a table that didn't need it or polishing a vase that already shimmered clean in the light that flowed in from the stained glass windows.

While in the kitchen, Alice stood by the island with a rag in hand, stepping up on her tiptoes to rub the cloth in circles over the granite. It had already been cleaned after they'd eaten their breakfasts that morning, but with nothing better to do with her time, she decided to wash it again.

Struggling to reach across the counter, she pushed up higher on her toes, her arm extended out as far as it would go when her body was caged against the granite, two large hands slamming down on the black surface as a heavy weight pressed against her back.

She yipped in surprise, her breaths coming out in panting gasps just as a soft mouth pressed down against her ear.

"Did I scare you?"

The weight pressed against her more and the bones of her hips ground against the edges of the hard counter.

"Yes," she breathed out, instantly recognizing the voice of her husband. The masculine notes of his cologne wafted beneath her nose and she relaxed beneath him. "And you're hurting me as well."

Mistaking her husband for being playful, she attempted to wriggle out from beneath him, but his body slammed down on her harder, pain shooting along her bones that were now jammed against the hard granite edge.

"Max..."

His hand wrapped over her mouth, his fingers digging into her cheeks so hard that the inside of her mouth cut against her teeth.

"Shut up, you stupid, little bitch. I'm not here to listen to your whiny voice."

Her eyes rounded in surprise, instinct taking over that made her struggle against him harder. He laughed when she attempted to push back at him, the sound dark and disturbing as his other hand ran up the back of her leg, closed over the waistband of her nylons and tore the tight fabric away.

Alice couldn't speak, couldn't complain or tell him to stop. Her only option was to relax beneath him in hopes he'd remove some of the weight.

However, instead of easing up on her body, he pressed against her more. Alice struggled again when relaxing didn't work, but the more she fought against him, the harder his breathing became. The bastard was enjoying the pain and fear he was forcing through her, his finger slipping beneath the silk of her panties to slip inside her body.

His lips traced the line of her jaw until his teeth caught the lobe of her ear. Biting down hard enough to make her cry out against his palm, his chest vibrated with laughter as he shoved her against the granite even more, her pain now radiating over the width of her hips.

Tears sprang from her eyes as he pumped his finger inside her, his movements becoming faster and more erratic as he forced her off the ground. Using his knees, Max knocked her off balance and spread her legs apart. Alice teetered on the edge of the counter, her eyes clenched shut in anger and pain when Max laughed one more time and told her, "I suggest you hold the fuck on."

Her hands gripped at the opposite edge of the counter, her biceps struggling to find the strength to pull her up farther where her hips wouldn't grind against the granite edge. But Max had her pinned too tightly, and only pulled his weight away one quick time to flip the skirt of her dress up over her back, so he could force himself inside.

She wasn't ready for him, and the way he thrust inside her burned from the sudden intrusion within her skin. More tears spilled from the rims of her eyes, the relentless pounding of his body against hers driving sharp bursts of pain across her hips.

Her body was ground against the edge of the counter, her fingernails digging into the opposite side as she held herself in place. What he did to her in this moment wasn't love, he was taking without asking her if she would give.

Over and over he pounded, his breath coming out in heavy bursts across her cheek. Releasing her mouth, he gripped his fist into her hair and pulled her head up until her neck was arched at a painful angle, his relentless pounding never easing despite her pleas for him to stop.

He wasn't listening. He didn't care. All that mattered was his own selfish need to dominate her in every way.

The more she begged, the harder he thrust inside her, his actions that of a man thoroughly possessed.

Fighting against him was useless, and soon Alice's voice quieted down, her body accepting the pounding until that one final push so deep inside, she knew that he was done.

He didn't release her gently, instead just backed away and dropped her into a broken puddle over the ground.

The tears wouldn't stop falling as he stood watching over her, her throat torn on the inside because of the way she'd screamed and begged. And when the only sound left in the room was Alice sobbing, Max simply walked away.

THIRTY-NINE

Sitting outside among the flowers that were now in full bloom, Alice surveyed her garden, her hands idly digging at the ground where she'd planned to settle new seedlings into the earth. However, she couldn't bring herself to focus on the task as her eyes studied the rings of bruises that marred her thin wrists. These bruises weren't the first she'd received from her husband, and they weren't as dark and angry as the ones that had darkened the skin of her hips for several weeks after the way he'd attacked her against the island counter.

With every new day, Max had become more distant – more violent – but not in anger. Alice hadn't done anything to deserve his wrath, hadn't misstepped or forgotten a chore that he'd insisted she manage within the house.

Several times, she'd asked him what was causing the worsening shifts in his moods, and each time she'd been blown off when he refused to answer.

How many times had he fallen to his knees begging forgiveness for his actions? And how many times had she fulfilled the promise she'd made to him on the day she agreed to be his wife?

She'd lost count over the months that followed that first attack.

Blowing out a resigned breath, her eyes tracked the fence line that led to the family cemetery. She'd seen Max out there every so often, usually when the sun was just settling down over the horizon, casting its last brilliant rays over the land. She'd watched him from an upstairs window noticing how it was never the graves with headstones where he stood. Recalling the conversation they had on the day before they were married, Alice remembered his claims that his parents were buried along with his siblings, their graves left unmarked as if nobody had cared they'd ever existed.

Anger tore through her at the thought of what his parents had done to him, at how the cruel hand with which they'd raised him had left scars both physical and emotional. She was glad they were dead, but unhappy about it as well. At least, if they were still alive today, she could unload some of the pain and frustration their son had created inside her when she gave them a piece of her mind.

After several more minutes during which she couldn't bring herself to finish up the task she'd intended to complete, Alice gathered her tools into her basket and decided to give up for the day. Walking into the house, she cleaned up the dirt she'd tracked in before running upstairs to wash her hands and change into clean clothing.

Max had been spending more and more time in the basement, and even though he'd all but forbidden her to go down there, she couldn't help her growing curiosity.

She stared at her reflection in the mirror, at the bruises that already marred her body and shrugged.

What's a couple more?

Settling on the decision to investigate the place where her husband disappeared to often, Alice left the confines of their bedroom and crept down the stairs.

Slowly she toed her way through the kitchen and dining room, taking a deep breath as she entered the small parlor that led to the basement door. She knew better than to intrude on his private space, but wondered if what was contained inside wouldn't answer all the questions that Max had always refused to abide.

A shiver ran over her spine, but she ignored the fear she felt and her hand reached to open the door.

Hit by a wave of a musty scent, Alice flinched when the door creaked open. Max hadn't been lying about the lack of light, but the dim flicker she saw drew her down that first step, her curiosity growing more intense when the first hint of sound met her ears.

"Scream all you want. Nobody will hear you. Although, I prefer that you stop."

It was Max' voice she heard, but the sound was wrong and she realized it couldn't have been him that had spoken.

Another step down, the board creaking beneath her foot, she paused to listen to the voice that was distant and flat.

A scream erupted next, feminine and terrified, but it didn't have the volume Alice would have expected if a woman were down there hidden in the depths of the dusky shadows.

"Are you done? Or will you continue going until you pass out?"

Definitely Max' voice, amusement and humor evident in his eerily calm tone.

"Who -"

"Stop talking."

"Please," A woman begged, *"let me go. I won't -"*

Max laughed, the sound soft before he answered, *"You know, it's always the same - in real life as well as in entertainment. It never ceases to amaze me how the same lines are used in movies: Please let me go. I won't tell. I'll keep this a secret. They never change the script, and even when it actually happens, people follow the same typical path. What do the victims expect to happen when they beg? That they'll be let go? That the person who took them will respond: oh sure, here let me loosen those ties, and would you also like my name to take to the police? Perhaps a copy of my driver's license would be helpful?'"*

Max paused, a resigned sigh filling the dark room. *"I'm sorry, beautiful, but that won't be happening this time. Save your breath."*

Alice tipped her head to the side, as if the angle would help her understand what she was hearing. The play of light flickered from around the corner, and if she could just take one more step, she'd be able to see what caused the sound.

The risk at that point far outweighed the threat of her husband's anger, so Alice took that one last step.

The board beneath her foot broke and she fell forward to crash against the dusty floor.

* * *

It was disorienting, the ephemeral glow of fractured light, filthy windows lining the top of a room, her exposed skin practically frozen against a floor as cold as ice. Blinking open her eyes, Alice watched the barren walls morph and bend around her, the ability to focus on any one thing stolen by her confusion.

Where am I? Alice thought, her head pounding and her body thrumming with pain. Pushing herself up, she looked around the darkened room trying to remember where she was and how she'd arrived there.

Damp and dirty, the room was unfamiliar. A destitute place with crumbling plaster walls and a sickening stench of mildew and filth. Everything was out of focus, not one object settling within its own perimeter lines.

"Hello, wife."

Max' voice, and from the sound of it, he wasn't happy. A shiver ran over her spine at the pure menace in his tone.

Ignoring the terror that crippled her, she attempted to speak calmly to soothe the beast that she knew had risen to the surface of her husband. "I can't see you, Max. Where are you? At least show your face."

No response, no noise, nothing.

He stepped into view after a minute, but only so much that Alice could see his silhouette, a dark shadow in contrast to broken and dirt filtered light.

"Why did you come down here? Especially since I've warned you so many times before. Dark places are dangerous for women like you."

He paused, his voice dropping to a bare whisper. "Or don't you know that already?"

Her head fell back against the wall where her body was leaning. She winced in pain at that soft contact. "I wanted to know what you do down here all day," she explained.

Max laughed, the tone cruel and ill-humored.

"Is that what you want? To know your monster?"

Seeing her husband, knowing he was real and not an illusion cast by a frightened and disorganized mind didn't help Alice in the slightest.

Unable to peel her eyes from the form of his body, she watched silently as he sat down in a chair she hadn't noticed before, the wood feet scraping against the cold, concrete floor.

"Where do we go from here, Alice? Now that you've stumbled upon a place where you were never invited?"

Shaking her head, she regretted the movement instantly. Her tongue ran over the film on her teeth, her voice laced with the pain she was feeling. "I don't know, Max. That depends on what I heard when I was coming down here."

Silence for several moments, and then, "Would you like something to drink?"

Calm, collected, even kind, the voice broke through the sticky film of darkness across Alice's senses.

She laughed at the odd question, her throat as gritty as coarse sandpaper. "Depends on what you're offering."

Her laughter took Max by surprise, if his silence was any true indication of his reaction.

"Water," he answered after a span of silent seconds. There was no inflection in his voice, no anger or loss of control in response to Alice's behavior.

Nodding her head in acceptance of the water proved difficult. Alice was sluggish and uncoordinated. But the jostled movement had been enough.

Chair legs scraped against the floor, the rhythmic thud of shoes against the ground announcing Max' approach. The joints in his knees clicked when he knelt down in front of her, betraying the length of time he'd been sitting motionless in the chair.

With a face masked in shadow thick enough to conceal his features, he held a plastic bottle of water between them.

Alice's efforts of accepting the bottle were thwarted by a weakness in her arms, a remnant of injury she'd sustained by falling down the stairs. It wouldn't surprise her if she was suffering from a concussion, if the pain she felt at the back of her head were any indication of how hard she'd fallen.

"Why are we still in the basement, Max?"

It took him a few minutes to finally answer the question.

"You walked through a door, Alice."

Settling himself on the concrete at her feet, he studied her silently before adding, "and now you're here."

After uncapping the bottle, he grabbed her chin, sliding his thumb along her bottom lip before pulling her mouth open. The lip of the bottle met her mouth, tilting up to pour cool water over her tongue as he said, "Swallow."

Cool liquid slid down her throat, a soothing balm against the burning flesh, and she swallowed fervently, greedily, until only a few drops were left.

Pulling it from her lips, Max recapped it and tossed it to the side, the plastic ricocheting off a wall that only existed in Alice's peripheral vision.

Her head fell back against the wall, a thick blanket of silence sliding between them until his smooth, deep voice broke it apart completely.

"I have something I'm going to show you." He paused, looking Alice over with a critical eye.

"After that fall, I don't think you can walk. I'm going to carry you."

"How far did I fall?"

It wasn't until her words echoed back to her from the walls of the dark, desolate room that she knew she'd spoken them aloud.

"Far enough." A grunt escaped his lips, his strong body lifting her from the floor. Heat was thick across his skin, uncomfortably so.

As he carried her through the space, Alice couldn't make out much of the objects that were down there. A flashing light caught her sight, a door that was closed and an electric panel to its side. Beyond that, she could see the empty black square of what resembled a television. And next to that, a shelf with rows and rows of DVDs.

Max' steps were labored over the cement floor, his thick leather boots creaking with every small movement of his ankle; the sounds amplified by the pervasive moments of silence that came between.

Reaching the second level, Alice clenched her eyes shut against the onslaught of bright, white light that bathed the room. She opened her mouth to question him about what he'd been doing in the basement, but speech failed her, the words thick on the tip of her tongue.

As if sensing her struggle to fill the deafening silence, Max spoke, relieving her of that small part of her anxiety.

"I'll give you time to regain your strength. We have a lot to discuss."

Kneeling down, Max dropped her weight on the cushions, keeping his eyes on her as she settled against the couch.

He stepped away after climbing back to his feet and crossed through into another room, disappearing from sight.

When he returned, he had a plastic case in his hand. Alice recognized it as a DVD, but there was no cover photo or anything to indicate if it was a movie or something else entirely.

Sitting on the coffee table in front of her, Max set the case aside and looked down on her with a sullen and dark expression.

"Before I show you this, before I let you in this far, I want you to know that I'm not a monster, Alice. Not entirely."

Dread shot through her, memories of the strange conversation she'd overhead while climbing down the stairs. "Who's in the basement, Max? Who was that woman I heard?"

He stared at her for a few tense moments before answering, "She's not in the basement anymore." There was no inflection in his voice. It was a placid tone with no hint of emotion.

Alice breathed out, a shudder running over his skin as her head turned to glance around the room. "Then where is she?"

He grinned, the expression more menacing than friendly. "She's in the garden."

Shaking her head, Alice attempted to clear the fog of pain that muddied her thoughts. "Who is she, Max? Why was she in our house and why did she go outside?"

He laughed, his eyes growing colder and darker than she'd seen before. Reaching over, he brushed his palm along her cheek. "Don't worry, my love. She's been there for a long time."

Fighting the urge to cry, Alice jerked her face away from his hand, her brows knitting together in anger. "You're not making sense, Max. Just tell me who the woman was. Why was she in our basement?"

Refusing to answer her, Max silently watched as the confusion overwhelmed her. Ideas raced through her mind, questions on whether Max had been unfaithful to her, if he'd somehow been sneaking women into the basement so he could cheat. She shook her head at the ridiculousness of that idea, but then her thoughts focused on the trips he often took.

Were they really so he could oversee his business?

Her voice broken and shaking, she spoke with panic obvious in every word. "Damn it, Max! What are you trying to tell me? I don't understand."

Practically shrieking the final words, the pitch of her voice had been a crescendo driven by the emotions that were a vicious deluge inside her.

"Just watch."

Stepping over to a television tucked into the corner of the room, Max inserted the silver disk into a player. The television turned on.

A closed circuit camera view of a small, well lit room revealed a woman sitting on a bed, her head concealed by the hood that covered it.

Alice's breath caught at the sight of the chains that hung above the bed where the woman sat, the glint of light against metal striking fear into her heart and mind. Curled over herself, the woman's shoulders shook on a sob, but the sound didn't carry through the speakers of the television.

Pink paint covered the walls above white chair rails that ran the room. Posters with kittens and rainbows were hung on each wall, a day bed pushed off to the side with a gold frame and white, frilly bed sheets. The carpet was pink shag that matched the paint, and dolls were scattered throughout the room on shelves and perched to appear lifelike on a large, overstuffed chair.

Alice felt sick staring at the contrast of the innocence of youth against the sinister truth of that poor woman's captivity. Studying her every expression, Max stood off to the side of the television, his shrewd gaze fixed on Alice.

"What am I looking at?" she murmured, asking the question of Max as much as herself.

The disbelief inside her kept her from recognizing what she saw. Horror and denial kept her from considering that the video had anything to do with Max.

However, when a tall man stepped into the picture, when her eyes focused on the wavy, shoulder length hair, the scarred olive skin and eyes the color of an artic sea, she froze in place, terrified of what she'd see.

The man in the video wasn't in a hurry. He stared down at the woman, angling his head as if in question. Alice knew that behavior well, it was a habit of the man she loved. His mouth moved as he spoke to the woman, but the volume wasn't high enough for Alice to hear what he said.

The woman opened her mouth to scream, and Max struck out with his hand, clipping the girl upside the head before lunging forward to buckle her hands into the shackles above the bed.

"Open your eyes, Alice. You need to see this."

Max' voice was soft when he called out the fact that she'd clenched her eyes shut against the secret her husband had been hiding.

Barely dressed, the woman had no defense against Max's strength. Her mouth opened on another silent scream, Max hurting her in ways that left Alice crying angry tears. He forced himself on the woman, violating every part of her despite the blood that dripped down her legs, despite the shade of red her face had turned because he was choking off her airway with his hand.

"Turn it off," Alice begged, her words barely discernable.

"You should watch it, Alice."

Screaming at him with a strength that came from some place deep inside of her, she demanded, "I said turn it off!"

The picture went black.

Max stared at her with cold calculation in his dead eyes.

"Do you understand now?"

FORTY

12:40 p.m.

"I can't do this, Doc." Her eyes clenched shut, the rims burning from the salt in her hot tears. Alice trembled where she sat, her body thrumming with the terror that crept along her bones, slithered up her spine and trapped her within the crushing weight of memory.

"I can't," she whispered, her voice pleading for some relief from the horrifying truth of her life from the man who studied her.

It spoke to the professionalism of the doctor that, even in the face of such a traumatic and gut-wrenching confession, he was able to preserve a gentle expression, sympathy and bits of horror obvious behind his eyes. His voice remained studious, his body relaxed in order to provide a safe place for his patient to come to terms with the nightmares that haunted her.

"I wish I could give you the permission you're seeking to stop the story here, Alice. But to do so would be a mistake. I'd handicap you emotionally and mentally if I told you that you didn't have to see this through to the end."

Shaking her head, Alice couldn't dispel the racing thoughts and memories, the horrifying truth of the decisions she'd made when she discovered the secrets her husband had been hiding.

A tap of a pen against a notebook, and the doctor's tender voice filled the silence between them.

"I can imagine how hard it would be to learn how vicious and cruel Max truly was. Judging by the violence committed against you, however, I'm not surprised."

"It wasn't his fault," Alice interrupted, a harsh bite to her tone that took the doctor by surprise. She glanced up at him, her eyes bruised and practically swollen shut from the amount of tears she'd shed. "He was sick, Doc. Sick. I don't know another way to describe it. There was *something* inside him that needed release and the only way he could find that release was to do those things. But it wasn't his fault. If anything, it was the fault of that son of a bitch who raised him. The father that beat him and told him he would never be good enough. The mother that turned a blind eye to the abuse."

A thought occurred to the doctor. Toying the pen between his fingers, he cleared his throat and ensured his voice remained kind and calm. "Did you ever discover what happened to his parents? How they came to be buried on the property without a marker to designate where they were interred?"

Giving him a sharp nod of her head, Alice answered, "He eventually told me the truth. After everything came out in the open, there wasn't a point to him hiding the rest of the story. His parents were the first people he…he killed."

A sob broke free of her lungs, her entire body visibly shaking with the sound.

"He had no choice. The things they did to him." She barked out a humorless laugh. "God, and I thought my father was bad. He was a walk in the park compared to what Max went through."

"It drew you more closely together," the doctor surmised. "Cemented the bond – the love – you two felt for each other."

Nodding her head again, Alice sniffled loudly, but didn't voice a response to the doctor's statement. Pulling a tissue from the box on the table beside him, Dr. Chance leaned forward to hand it to the woman who was falling apart before his very eyes.

She accepted the tissue, blowing her nose before calming down enough to continue speaking.

"I loved him deeply," she admitted. "And for a long time after his secrets came out, I considered the love I had for him. Studied it, pulled it apart and analyzed it, because, logically, it didn't make sense."

"Emotions rarely do," the doctor noted.

She grinned, the expression sorrowful, regretful. "You know, during all that time, I kept coming back to the same question: How could two people who lived similar childhoods, who experienced abuse and torment in their formative years, turn out in such opposition to each other?"

Glancing up at the doctor, Alice connected with him by the way she locked her stare to his. "My father made me the perfect victim. I was scared, alone, and reclusive to the extent that it made me the perfect target for a person who wanted to make me disappear. Max, on the other hand, became a monster, a predator, a person so twisted by the abuse he suffered at the hands of his parents that a part of him snapped and took control of the man he would have become if he'd been raised in a loving home."

The doctor's clothes made a soft noise as he settled back against his seat. "You don't know that, Alice."

"Actually," she argued, "I do. I saw that man when I first met and fell in love with him. And I saw him again when the monster inside him was allowed to come out and relieve the pressure of the darkness that had built up over the year we'd been married. Once he was given the chance to bleed that evil from himself, the man I married returned to me."

Startled by the admission she was making between the lines, Dr. Chance leaned forward. "What do you mean, Alice?"

Her expression darkened, her mouth pulling down into a frown that was frozen in bitter guilt. "The room I saw on that tape was behind the doorway I noticed in the basement. The keypad to the side of the door was the lock that allowed that door to open or to close. The DVDs were recordings of all the women who'd been trapped down there."

Emotion overwhelming her, Alice took a shuddering breath and continued. "For the first year that we were married, he hadn't brought a woman into the house. Hadn't killed or done any other horrible things. That's what I meant when I said the pressure built up inside him. It was leaking out, Doc. Through the abuse against me, his mood swings and his cruelty, it was like water leaking out of a crack in a glass, slowly seeping until the crack got bigger."

Interrupting her thoughts, the doctor suggested, "So, the abuse against you was worsening over time because he couldn't channel it elsewhere."

Nodding in agreement, Alice swallowed down the emotions that were taking control of her body. "He spent a lot of time in the basement watching those recordings, hoping that just by seeing the violence, it would somehow relieve some of the pressure."

She winced, but then widened her eyes as tears poured down her cheeks. "Watching the recordings only made him worse. He didn't want to hurt me. For some reason that I've never figured out, he wanted to protect me."

Alice grew quiet, giving Dr. Chance the opportunity to interject. "Perhaps when he learned that you suffered a similar type of abuse in your childhood, he felt a kinship to you. When he saw you'd become weaker as a result of it, he felt a duty to stand strong where you could not."

"Maybe," Alice replied. "Or maybe by protecting me, he was in some way protecting the abused child that he had been at one time. I was a symbol of that weak little boy he hadn't been strong enough to protect because he was a child."

Her head ticked to the side, her movements becoming more erratic as they closed in on the confession she was attempting to voice.

"Whatever the reason, he truly did love me, and he hated himself each time he hurt me or caused me to cry. He wanted to change, Doc. He just didn't know how."

Several seconds passed in thick silence, the weight of Alice's memories suffocating them both.

His voice calm and unhurried, the doctor asked, "How many women did he kill before you met him, Alice? Do you know?"

She nodded. "Around thirteen. Their bodies were buried in the yard that eventually became my garden."

A keening sound filled the room, Alice's pain so severe that it was leaching out of her in audible, heartbreaking sounds. "I got married with those bodies in the ground beneath me." Her eyes met his. "I loved that plot of land because it fed the plants so well. How fucked up is that, Doc? Those women were rotting and I was excited because I didn't have to use fertilizers to keep those plants alive."

Hands clenched into fists, Alice slammed them down onto the cushions beside her, her face twisting into a mask of anger and shame, her body moving so suddenly and without coordination that the doctor sat forward in case he needed to keep her from harming herself.

"Alice, I don't want to have to restrain you…"

"There's nothing to restrain," she yelled. Taking several minutes to calm herself, Alice relaxed back against the couch, blinking her eyes rapidly to expel the tears that wouldn't stop welling in her eyes.

Only when she'd grown quiet again, did the doctor speak.

"You had no way of knowing."

A bark of angry sound blew over her lips. "Yeah, but that doesn't excuse me turning a blind eye when he started killing women again. It doesn't excuse the fact that I enjoyed that he was killing again because, when he was with me, he was the man I fell in love with again."

"Alice –"

"No, Doc. Don't say anything. I need to say this and I need you to just listen and understand what I'm trying to tell you."

With a serious expression on her face - her eyes wide, her mouth pulled into a thin line and her brow furrowed with the anger and self-loathing that she was feeling - Alice finished the confession that proved just how horrible she had been.

"For once in my life, I was the pampered person. Growing up, I was the freak, the one who was hurt, the one who was hated and the one that nobody cared whether she lived or died."

She paused, her throat working to clear away the thickness of guilt that clogged it.

"For once, I wasn't that girl anymore. And it was because of those women. And instead of hating my husband for what he was doing to those women, I enjoyed it. I didn't watch. I didn't listen. I didn't participate. But I didn't stop him either. Not at first."

"How many, Alice? How many women died while you lived in that house?"

"Four," she answered, "and although I knew it was wrong, although I tortured myself by watching the news reports and their families begging for their safe return, I said nothing. I had my husband back. He was kind to me and he was loving. I wasn't the abused freak anymore, and for that, I turned a blind eye."

Refusing to react in a way any normal person would react to what she'd revealed, the doctor schooled his expression, forcing practiced kindness into his voice when he asked, "When did that change? What happened that you're here now instead of still living that life with Max?"

"It changed on the day that a storm blew a tree over in the garden. Max was on one of his trips and I was alone in the house when the roots that had risen above the surface pulled up the crushed skull of one of the women Max had killed."

Pausing long enough for those words to sink in, Alice visibly shivered, her eyes clenching shut, her teeth grinding together before she opened her mouth to say, "And that's when I made the biggest mistake of all. I decided to leave."

FORTY-ONE

Sitting in the aftermath of a fierce storm that blew over the rural town where Alice and Max lived, Alice surveyed the garden that was now torn apart by the high winds and pounding rains that had saturated the land. Most of the larger oaks that provided shade over the expanse of their yard had withstood the winds and rain, their roots securely anchored in place. Some had lost branches, while one smaller tree in particular, a laurel oak known for its shallow root spread, had tipped from the winds, the large trunk now crushing the rose bushes and hydrangeas that Alice had planted only a handful of months before.

When she'd first stepped outside, her heart had broken to see the disarray of the garden, the plants that had lost limbs and blooms, that would die from the amount of rain dumped by the storm.

Max was away on a business trip and Alice wondered how much of the area she could clean herself without calling in people to assist. Knowing what she knew of the horrors contained inside the house and on the grounds,

Alice hoped that Max could handle removing the fallen tree.

Stepping around the chaos of downed branches and debris, she wound her way through the mess to stare at the root ball of the laurel oak that had fallen.

At first, she assumed her eyes had been playing tricks, her mind not registering the grim horror of what the fallen tree had pulled up and out of the ground. Dropping to her knees when realization firmly took hold, Alice stared in open-mouthed terror at the crushed and broken skull, the empty eyes that stared out at her, hollow and accusing that, through Alice's silence, she had allowed so many women to die.

Pulled apart by the love she felt for Max and the pervasive understanding that what she allowed him to do in the dirty underbelly of the house was pure evil, Alice shattered to look at the stark evidence of the broken lives and shattered families Max, and now Alice, had left in their wake.

Alice felt frozen in place, her eyes unblinking as the screams of the four women who'd died while she lived in the house haunted her thoughts. She doubted the skull she stared at now had been one of those women. The bodies wouldn't have had enough time to decompose so completely, and the placement of burial would have been impossible given the roots of the tree. However, that knowledge wasn't enough to appease the overwhelming ache of guilt and remorse that gripped her between skeletal fingers.

She loved him, and since the time she'd acquiesced to his needs and ignored the acts he committed in the basement, she'd been unable to shake the strong feelings she had for Max. Several times she'd considered asking him to stop, but memories of the abuse he'd committed against her would always shoot to the surface of her thoughts.

It was selfish of her to do nothing, selfish of her to remain silent about the death that surrounded her simply because, for once, she wasn't the person enduring the abuse.

But it wasn't just herself that Alice fought to protect. Max was so kind when his demons were given their outlet, so generous to *her,* that she focused on the side of him that was soft rather than condemning that part of him she wanted to believe didn't exist. She made excuses for him and for herself, she justified their actions as just a means to an end when it came to living with the memory of the cruelty they'd both suffered as kids.

But she couldn't ignore it any longer, couldn't find it within her to continue making excuses and telling lies, not with the vacant eyes of death staring back at her, the grim reminder that innocent people had suffered and more lives would be lost.

Picking herself up from the ground, Alice found her way back into their three story home. She managed to pull herself up the stairs and into the bedroom where they'd slept and made love. Unable to cry because she'd run out of tears over the time they'd spent together, Alice went into the bathroom to wash away the muck and mud on her skin that she'd dragged in from the flooded garden.

She'd been conditioned to be clean. Any speck of dust, or smear of mud, that marred her skin had to be removed, wiped away so quickly that the errant dirt couldn't remind her of the ugliness that enshrouded the house – the ugliness inside her husband and herself.

It hadn't occurred to her at first, the reason for Max' incessant need for the house to remain clean, to remain pristine. But now that she shared the same ugliness inside, now that she knew the secrets that lingered on the fringes of what society considered normal or good, she understood his need to wash away the remnants of truth that sullied the home that was as much a nightmare as it was a dream.

The bath water turned a light shade of brown as she lowered herself down in the confines of its warmth. Her hands played idly over the surface creating ripples that washed across her body, that twisted and obscured the parts of her that were as scarred as Max.

And in the stillness that permeated the silent space of her thoughts, in a moment where her weakness and apathy had been brought out of shadow into light, Alice struggled with a decision she didn't want to make.

Finishing her bath, she took her time drying her body and finding a clean set of comfortable clothes. She descended the stairs and wound her way through the halls into the kitchen, preparing a warm cup of tea before making her way into the small parlor that sat outside the basement door.

The screams were silent while Max was away, but they still managed to echo inside her thoughts.

There was only one way she could silence them, and the understanding tore her apart.

She loved him. She would never speak of the things she knew he did in the grim, musty darkness of the basement. But she couldn't remain in the house and endure the slaughter either.

The thought of turning Max in was a crushing weight she couldn't carry. It was the prison of his childhood home that created that dark monster inside him. He didn't deserve to die in a prison of another kind.

She would remain silent. She would carry his secrets to her grave because that was the price of the life he'd given her. But she would also break a promise that she made to him on a bright, sunlit day where they stood over the buried bodies of his past.

Picking up her phone, she dialed a number she knew from heart only because it had flashed on her screen so many times. She'd never answered the phone because she couldn't face the horrible memories the voice on the other end would elicit.

"Alice?"

The phone hadn't been given a chance to ring more than once before it was answered, and for the first time in months, Alice cried.

"Delilah. I need help." Her voice trembled over the words, her strength continuing to wane as she faced a future that didn't include Max by her side.

"Of course, Alice. Anything." Her sister's voice trembled just as much. "Oh, God, I've been so worried about you. Why haven't you answered my calls? Where are you?"

The conversation moved awkwardly along, and by the end Alice had given her sister the address where she lived so that Delilah could pick her up.

Ending the call, Alice sobbed, her heart releasing all the anguish and pain that had been trapped inside it for so long.

When her tears had stopped falling, and when she found the strength to move from the couch that had cradled her since she broke down, Alice moved through the house, climbed those eighteen steps, and packed a bag of her things.

She was going home.

And in doing so, she was running from the arms of one abusive man back to embrace of another.

* * *

After the sun had set and the moon reigned high in the sky, Alice sat alone in the front living room, her pack settled by her feet, her eyes staring out at a doorway that hadn't been darkened by her sister's shadow.

Delilah never came as she'd promised, and while it saddened Alice to feel abandoned by her family once again, it didn't surprise her in the slightest.

More than likely, Delilah had mentioned where she was going to their father, and he had prevented her from leaving because he didn't want Alice back in their home.

Releasing a resigned sigh, Alice faced the grim reality that she would never leave the life Max had given her behind.

It was for the best, she presumed. She deserved the limbo where she now found herself stuck.

If nothing else, Delilah's failure to arrive had been both a final kick to Alice's gut, and a relief that removed the weight of remorse from her withered shoulders.

Her father didn't want her. Her family didn't need her. And she wouldn't have to leave the one person in the entire world that needed her the most.

From one prison to the next.

From one tortured life into another where her silent suffering provided her the physical comfort of home.

Picking up her bag, she stumbled her way through the house and up the stairs. Putting away her things, she dragged herself to bed.

Sleep wasn't easy that night, and when she woke up screaming she remembered why she would have never been able to live without Max by her side.

* * *

Max returned home later that evening, his expression sharp and accusing, his eyes much colder than they had been when he left. Alice assumed his meetings hadn't gone well, and resulted in an itch he needed to scratch.

While they ate an early breakfast, Alice casually inquired about the meetings, not wanting to pester him too much while he was in one of his moods. However, Max was quieter than normal. He wasn't forthcoming, and the sticky silence that floated between them wasn't doing any good for Alice's lack of appetite.

"You haven't touched your food."

The tines of Max' fork scraped across his plate.

Barely able to stomach the smell of the food, much less take a bite, Alice considered the fact that she was a trapped woman, held captive to a man because of the love she had for him and the failure she'd faced when she'd attempted to escape. Unsure that she'd ever find happiness in a life where women died so that she wouldn't suffer the abuse of a monster, she looked up into the face of her husband. Based on his certainty that she would eventually accept the life he was creating for her, she had no choice but to believe it as well.

"I'm not hungry," she admitted, her voice so soft it was barely audible to her own ears.

Max' fork fell to his plate. The small sound was jarring in the quiet room, Alice's eyes drawn up to see the silent anger in the gaze of her husband.

"You'll eat when I tell you to."

The light blonde of her eyelashes fluttered over her vision. "But if I'm not -"

She couldn't finish the thought, not with the way his hand clenched over her face, her cheeks painful against her teeth, her eyes as wide as the beautiful saucers that sat on the table.

She'd wondered why he'd chosen to sit on the chair next to her rather than at the head of the table. She didn't have to wonder any longer. He remained in reach of her in case the opportunity arose where he would have to correct her behavior.

The monster had returned, and it was in need of an outlet where it could sharpen its lethal claws.

Leaning in, his expression - the flared nostrils and sharp cut of his cheekbones - was a barely controlled threat of rage. However, his eyes remained lazy, the light blue color hazed over as he studied the terror that ran in small quakes across her body. She'd never understood that emotion could be a physical thing, but her silence didn't disguise her fear, not with the prickles that ran across her skin or the blood that rushed to her cheeks as tears wept from her unblinking eyes.

"When I tell you to eat, you eat. You won't be allowed to wither away in this house. You won't destroy the body that now belongs to me. I won't let you."

If he'd screamed the words, they would have been less menacing than the cold way in which he'd spoken them in that moment. Like the blade of a sharply honed knife, they sliced across her senses, opening her up in places she'd rather remain hidden from the world.

She knew then that this is what the monsters could do when they got you alone. They tore you to pieces slowly, methodically, because they had all the time in the world. If only she'd known what to do when you woke up in the monster's arms. She'd never had the chance to run or refuse. She'd been seduced into loving him without knowing the threat was there. And now she was stripped from the world. Alone. Terrified. At the mercy of a man that had captivated her when she hadn't been aware.

With one hand, he held her, his fingers clamped down on her cheeks until her lips were pressed open from the strength of his grip. Picking a piece of food from her plate, he slipped it between her lips, the spices he'd used to cook it a burst of flavor inside her mouth. Releasing his grip on her face, he sat back, studying her as the small bit of meat sat lingering against her tongue.

"Chew, Alice."

Hating herself for fighting against that small spark of rebellion within her, she did as she was told. Swallowing down the bite took effort, and when it finally slid past the knot in her throat, it fell like a boulder into her stomach, writhing in the churning acid of her fear.

When she didn't move to take another bite, her fork lying useless against the delicate pattern of the plate, he lifted a questioning brow. "Should I continue to feed you myself? Or do you think you can manage without being forced?"

A veiled threat, a tender question. The dichotomy of one against the other was staggering. She didn't want to eat, didn't think it was possible to force another crumb past the throat that restrained her silent scream. But what choice did she have?

Only the one he gave her.

Fifteen minutes passed, Max' eyes set and focused on the small woman as she picked at the breakfast on her plate. He studied every movement she made, the food she selected, the manner in which she chewed slowly and thoroughly to ensure she didn't choke on the nutrients he'd prepared for her body.

Had it been up to her, she would have starved that body until there was nothing left but skin and bone. It was the only escape she could imagine from a life torn between love and the bitter truth of death.

"Thank you," he whispered, his hand coming across the plate to rest on her own. The fork dropped from her fingers, her head bowed so that only the scraps of food left on the plate were visible to her tear filled eyes.

Forcing the words over her lips that she knew would silence the monster, Alice asked a question that cut her deeply because of the life that would be lost as a result.

"Have you..." She paused, barely able to speak the horrid thoughts rushing through her head. "Have you found another woman, Max? You're scaring me right now."

"I have," was his curt response.

Nodding her head, Alice pushed what was left of her food around on her plate. "That's good." It was all she could manage in response.

After finishing their meals and washing the dishes by hand, Max and Alice climbed the stairs to their bedroom and made love in the first rays of dawn before falling asleep for an early morning nap.

FORTY-TWO

When Alice woke two hours later, Max was noticeably absent from the bed. Alarmed at first at the lack of his warmth against her body, she understood where he had gone when she heard the commotion occurring outside their bedroom window.

Dragging her body out from beneath the security of her blankets, she padded across the carpeted floor to glance out into the garden below.

Max stood shirtless and sweating beneath the boughs of the stately oaks, his head turning slowly as he surveyed the damage the storm had left behind. He'd made quick work of most of the downed tree that had fallen upon the rose bushes and pulled up the skull, and all that remained was the trunk that lay heavy against the ground.

She watched him for several minutes, admiring the way his body moved as he hauled heavy branches and used an ax to chop the small trunk into pieces light enough to be dragged away. When he finished that task, he tossed the skull that the roots had uncovered back into the hole where the tree had once stood before reburying the bleak evidence of that past crime.

Alice considered joining him in the garden, but decided against it for the time being. Unsure of whether he'd finished with the new woman he'd acquired, she wasn't certain that the monster had been satisfied enough again to sleep.

After showering and getting dressed, she made her way into the kitchen to make a cup of tea. Carrying the mug with her, a swirl of steam dancing behind her as she moved between the kitchen and the family room, she settled down on the comfortable couch and turned on the television.

It was self-abuse in the worst possible way, a habit she'd started when Max brought his first victim into the house. Usually it took a day or two before the first rumblings of a missing woman would begin to filter through the news. Alice didn't know why she suffered through the endless tears and pleading voices, the happy pictures the family provided to the media that showed the smiles of the woman before they were lost to the monster. However, despite the knowledge that those images would be permanently seared onto her brain, she flicked the channels in search of the identity of the lost soul trapped in a cheerful room in the basement of her house.

...body...Beaumont...missing woman...

Alice spilled her tea when she shot up to the edge of the couch, her feet hitting the floor before she fell from that edge to her knees.

In the practiced voice of the news broadcaster, Alice heard words that her mind couldn't comprehend.

...Delilah Beaumont was reported missing earlier this morning after failing to return home. Although Ms. Beaumont is a legal adult, the Sedgefield authorities declined waiting the standard forty-eight hours to begin a massive search in hopes of finding her alive. We've reached out to the police regarding the matter and the urgency given to this particular missing persons case and were told that, due to the questionable mental stability of Ms. Beaumont, she is considered a danger to herself...

Alice sat in frozen silence, her face a mask of unabashed panic. Even after the announcer had moved on from the morbid news broadcast regarding the disappearance of her sister, and was now introducing another person to discuss the mundane details of the weather, Alice remained frozen in place, her eyes unseeing as she stared at the television screen. The easy change in topic and the cheerful quality to the anchor's voice sickened Alice because it took away from the reverence that should have been paid to the news that a woman was missing.

Feeling him enter the room although he'd never made a sound, Alice finally blinked when she realized that Max was standing at the doorway behind her.

Her trembling hand reached out to steady her body where she sat, her heart shattering to splintered pieces inside her.

"What are you watching, Alice? I thought we talked about this."

"You have my sister," she accused, the words flat and without emotion.

Several silent seconds ticked between them before Max' voice filled the space. "You were going to leave me, Alice."

Heartache bled through his words, his fear that he'd lost the only woman he'd ever loved.

Alice crumbled over, her forehead pressed against the cool wood of the coffee table. Tears streamed down her cheeks, falling in heated drops upon the surface of the wood. Fear ensnared her, reality crumbling apart in front of her eyes.

"Where are you keeping her?" she finally asked.

He didn't answer immediately, and he never moved away from the doorway from where he studied her every move.

"She didn't suffer, Alice. I didn't..." His voice trailed off, shame an acrid note to his words. "She's dead, Alice. She's dead because I refuse to let you go."

Anger bursting inside her with such vehemence that it shot her to her feet, Alice spun on her shaky feet to stare at the expressionless face of her husband.

Satisfied with having gained her full attention, Max closed the distance between them with measured and controlled steps.

"How could you even think of leaving me, Alice? Haven't I loved you enough? Provided for you enough?"

His hands reached out to grab her and Alice stepped back to avoid his touch, her leg tripping over the coffee table before she crashed down on top of it, her weight splitting the wood before she fell to the ground.

Max lunged to pick her up, but she crawled away, ignoring the pain that sliced across her body in electric shocks.

"Don't touch me," she warned, her voice low and dangerous. "Don't you ever touch me, Max."

His eyes narrowed with the rage her behavior was creating inside him, but instead of continuing towards her, he stared down at her with betrayal set behind his stare.

He said nothing as he stood watching her, and Alice was the first to cut through the suffocating silence.

"How? How did you even find her?"

He grinned, the expression a slice of steel across her bruised and battered senses. "You led her right to me. Like a beautiful gift wrapped in a pretty pink bow. I came home early last night and what do I see stuck on the winding path through the woods? Another car driven by a woman that had no business being on my property."

Alice's eyes rounded, her head shaking in disbelief.

He smiled brighter to see the panic written clearly across her face. "She deserved what she got, Alice. You should have heard the things she said about you. But I didn't kill her like the others. I wouldn't do that to you, my love. I knew you would never forgive me for doing something as terrible as that."

He was insane. She'd known that since the moment he'd hurt her for the first time. But the realization had never been as immediate as it was to her right then.

Forcing herself to speak calmly in an effort to temper the rage she could clearly see building up inside him, Alice asked, "Didn't you think I'd be upset that you killed her at all?"

Max didn't answer her, and instead he looked away. Several seconds passed before he explained, "I thought you'd understand, Alice. I thought you'd appreciate the fact that I silenced one of the people who caused you so much pain. I dug a hole for her, a plot next to my parents in the family cemetery. She doesn't deserve to remain in your garden. Her body would only destroy the sanctity of your space."

Stepping away, he stopped before he'd crossed through the doorway into another room. Turning his head to talk to her from over his shoulder, he said, "I'll finish burying her before her body starts to rot, and when I come back inside, we'll fix this. I won't let that bitch break us apart."

It was the final straw, the unforgivable event that finally broke through Alice's carefully constructed web of denial. Reality slammed into her like a runaway train, the realization that with one phone call – one single bad decision – she'd handed over her sister to the Devil himself.

Something snapped inside Alice, a cord pulled taut that had once held all her delicate and fragile pieces in place. And with that snap came the stark and blinding truth that the only kindness Alice could ever provide the man she loved was to end him and finally put the monster down.

She waited in place for Max to climb down into the musty depths of the dark and damp basement, for the door to close behind him so that she could move quickly without fear of being heard. Dashing into the kitchen she saw the cleaver on the black granite counter, its silver blade gleaming beneath the pendant lights that swung softly above it.

Her fingers gripped around the wooden handle, the metal sliding against stone as she pulled it away and held it down at her side. Tears streamed over her cheeks at the thought of what she had to do, at the harrowing reality that she'd been left with no other choice than to end the nightmare of her life.

Shock was a balm that numbed her sorrow, and with furtive steps, she crept forward until she stood by the basement door.

Unsure if she could go through with the quick decision she'd made, she grit her teeth as she shifted her weight between her feet. She loved this man, more than anyone she'd loved before, but he was so utterly broken, so incapable of repair, that she couldn't see a way to mend the damage. Like a wounded animal, injured and in pain, Max had no hope of a bright and beautiful future, no chance to survive a normal life in a world that had done nothing but hurt him.

Alice knew that pain, and she couldn't allow him to continue leaving bodies in his wake, couldn't stand silent any longer as he stripped innocent futures away from people who had done nothing to him besides having had the bad luck of walking in his path.

Certainty became her strength to end him. Her love became the mortar holding together the wall she'd constructed around her heart in order to follow through with a decision that would end the dark cruelty of a man too shattered to exist in this world.

Raising the cleaver above her head, she cried her angry tears and waited silently for the basement door to open.

A flash of surprise and betrayal behind blue eyes, her arms coming down in a sweeping chop that landed the cleaver at the junction of his shoulder and neck. Her heart crumbled beneath her ribs, her soul tearing apart in one painful rip as his body sunk to the floor at her feet and she heard her sister's body fall down the steps into the basement below.

He didn't die from the first strike she'd made, his eyes opened wide as he watched her drop to the floor beside him.

With a gentle hand, she wiped the splatter of blood from his cheek, her body shaking with a keening sob as she bent down to kiss him one last time.

Whispering so that her voice was a soft caress against his mind, she begged his forgiveness for the choice she'd made. "I love you for eternity, my dear husband." Her voice cracked and shattered, her eyes blurred from the tears that wouldn't stop. "I love you."

Kissing her fingers and pressing them to his lips, she gripped the handle of the cleaver with the other hand and pulled it from his body. "Until death, Max," she promised.

One strike, and his gorgeous face was split apart.

Two strikes, and his skull was crushed on one side.

Three strikes, and his shoulder was separated where it met his neck.

Four strikes, and the hollow of his neck was gouged open.

Five strikes, and the blade of the cleaver was buried into his chest.

With five vicious blows, Alice silenced the monster inside her husband and freed the man trapped inside the body of pervasive darkness. Alice watched the blood running off her hands in rivulets of crimson red, and prayed that the good part of the man she'd known could escape to find the light.

* * *

The time following Max' death was a blur. She remembered bits and pieces: the bloody trail left behind him, the difficulty she'd faced to drag his weight through the house. By the time her thoughts were clear enough to follow the sequence of events that occurred around her, Alice found herself kneeling at a shallow grave, the land open and cradling the body of her beloved husband.

Bending down to run her hand over the freshly turned soil, she felt a tear slip down her cheek. She said her goodbyes with whispers that were stolen from her lips by a peaceful wind that blew through the canopies of oak trees and carried the sweet scent of roses as it floated by.

She had no idea how long she'd stayed there, but the sun was high in the sky. Sweat slipped down her face to land in a muddy puddle on her white dress, a dress now splashed and stained by the blood of the man she'd loved.

Alice didn't regret the decision she'd been forced to make, didn't cry for the loss of the monster Max had been. Instead, she cried for the man he might have been if fate had been kinder to the child.

Balancing herself by grabbing the handle of a shovel, Alice stood up from the soil and walked past the unmarked graves of the people who'd failed Max, her hand slamming the iron gate closed when she left the small cemetery behind.

Unhurried, she wound her way along the trail through the garden and entered the house to look upon the filth that had been left behind.

He would have hated this mess, she thought. *Would have hated the ugliness and scars the sweep of blood had left along the tiles.*

Fighting the urge to clean up the mess, she grabbed her cell phone from the island counter and forced herself up eighteen steps into a bedroom that was pristine white. Her muddy, red footprints marked her trail across the carpet as she made her way into the bathroom.

She stared at herself in the mirror, the cell phone held in her hand as she lamented the choices she'd been forced to make.

Setting the phone on the toilet by the tub, Alice sat on the rim and reached over to turn on the water.

And at 12:30 p.m., on a Thursday afternoon, with the birds singing outside and a grave left open to the rain that would eventually fall, Alice lowered her body into a warm bath, her pale skin turning red in response to the heat of the water as she washed away what remained of the nightmare her life had become.

FORTY-THREE

12:41 p.m.

The tap of a pen.
The tick of a clock.
Water dripping from a leaky faucet.

It was all that could fill the space between Alice and her doctor, her confession finally at its end and leaving them both in shocked silence.

Unable to handle the harsh reality of what she had done, Alice spoke first, her voice an intrusion into the peaceful stillness in the room.

"I think I did the right thing. Don't you?" With pleading eyes, she stared at her doctor, whispers of accusation a symphony in her head while she waited for him to respond.

The doctor studied her for a brief period of time, concern and appraisal obvious in his calculating eyes. "I think you did what you believed you had to do. What other choice did you have?"

She nodded her head, tears slipping over cheeks that were chapped from the amount of times she'd cried. "I loved him more than anything, Doc. Destroying him destroyed me in the process. But he hurt so many women."

A beat of silence between them, the sound of water dripping in the sink.

"Why didn't you call the police, Alice? Why did you take the matter into your own hands?" He paused, his pen no longer tapping over the notebook in his lap. "How will you live with what you've done?"

Blinking away the liquid that blurred her vision, Alice shook her head. "He would have been locked up, Doc. Imprisoned and most likely killed. He didn't deserve that, not after what his parents had done to him. I know what it feels like to be locked away. My father..." A sob tore through her chest, her eyes clenching shut at the memories assaulting her mind. "I know what that feels like, and I wasn't going to do it to him. It was better this way. Better that the man I loved was freed from the monster. Perhaps in another life he can find the happiness he deserved."

A tick of the clock drew the doctor's attention, his head turning slightly to stare up at the timepiece on the wall. "Your time is almost up, Alice. You still have a few more minutes to do what needs to be done."

Her face turned up towards the ceiling, Alice opened her eyes and stared at the perfect

432

blankness of the white paint. Her body trembled in place on the couch, her heart beat slowing in rhythm until it was only a whisper of a pulse inside her chest.

"Is there anything else you should remember, Alice? Anything at all?"

She looked at Dr. Chance, a sad smile pulling at her lips. "I've remembered everything I need to remember, Doc. There is nothing that can make this better. Nothing so important that it will change what has already occurred."

Nodding in understand, Dr. Chance said, "It's time, Alice."

Standing up, the doctor offered his hand and Alice reached up to accept the assistance. Pulled to her feet, she stood on shaky legs, her free arm wrapping around her abdomen, a false sense of security in the way she held herself together.

"Let's go in the bathroom and get you cleaned up."

As they stepped towards the door, Alice asked the doctor a question that had bothered her from the first moment she'd first walked through his door.

"Was it all for nothing, Doc? Max is dead. Delilah is dead. I didn't save anybody." Her voice trailed off, her steps over the carpet feeble and uncoordinated.

Still holding her hand, Dr. Chance squeezed her fingers between his, a weak attempt at consolation.

"I can't answer that question, but what I do know is that your sister is still very much lost. You need to call somebody, Alice. You need to tell them where your sister's body can be found."

He stopped them both in their tracks, turning to her so he could lightly grip her shoulders and stare down at the small woman who has been his most difficult patient.

"Wasn't that what you wanted in the beginning? To save her?"

Nodding her head, Alice swallowed, not sure if she was ready to take those final steps. Finding the strength, Alice pulled away from the doctor and said, "I should go."

Giving her a solemn smile, the doctor backed away. But before Alice could take another step, he reached out to touch her arm and draw her attention to him.

"Why me, Alice? Why did you come to me with all of this?"

She smiled, the expression sorrowful, yet serene. "You were the person I looked to when I was young and got scared, Doc. You were the only person who understood and cared to help

434

me make sense of my nightmares. You always were the voice of reason inside my head."

The doctor nodded in understanding and released her arm, taking a few more steps back so that she could walk away.

When Alice turned to enter the bathroom, the scene around her changed. No longer an office with gray walls, white doors, a dark wood desk, and a white and beige striped couch, the room where she now stood was the bedroom that she and Max had shared. The transition was instantaneous, but that's usually how all dreams worked.

Beneath her feet was pristine white carpet, the space in front of the bathroom door a mucky grey with pink staining the edges.

Taking a deep breath, Alice stepped forward to open the door and saw herself sitting in the bath, the water that flooded the floor and tub both stained pink with blood. The faucet dripped with sorrowful drops, and Alice's arms were positioned at the rim of the large basin with long angry gauges that split the skin from wrist to elbow.

* * *

One last gasp as her eyes flew open, one last chance to make things right. Alice struggled to reach for the cell phone that sat on the lid of the toilet, her fingers fumbling over the small device until she wrapped her fist around it.

Pulling the phone to her ear, she dialed nine-one-one. All she had left was the strength to say her name and address and to tell the authorities where her sister's body could be found.

The phone dropped from her hand into the water before Alice took her final breath, her head slipping beneath the surface with her unseeing eyes opened wide.

EPILOGUE

Addendum to Report of Psychological Assessment
Confidential Material

Date of Addendum: July 29, 2016

Dates of Treatment: January 1998 through September 2007

Patient Name: Alice Marie Beaumont

Chronological Age: 26 years, 5 months

Parents: Lydia and Jack Beaumont

Siblings: Delilah Beaumont (1 year older); Jack Beaumont, Jr. (2 years younger)

History:

    In brief history, Alice Beaumont was a patient treated in my office between January 1998 and September 2007. Her range of age during treatment was roughly eight years old through seventeen years old, at which time she was institutionalized and released from my active care.

Initially, Alice Beaumont's mother, Lydia Beaumont, presented with her daughter with complaints of severe nightmares, sleepwalking, and other type sleep disorders. Lydia Beaumont mentioned the discovery of Jane Greely's body – a missing persons turned murder case in the area that was prolific in the media – as a possible trigger for Alice's first nightmares. Following the discovery of Ms. Greely's body, Alice became obsessed with the 'monsters', as she called them, in the world.

Through counseling, and a regimen of medications, Alice improved over her course of treatment with me. Several key issues I noted during counseling included Alice's father's frustration with her ongoing disorders, and what he believed was a worsening in the severity of the disorders. I suspected abuse towards Alice on the part of the father, however, there were never any physical indications of abuse, and the family would not admit to any abuse occurring. Alice would only admit that her father became 'frustrated' and would lash out verbally.

Over the course of her teen years, Alice would often become non-compliant with her medications. As a result, her sleep disorders increased in severity, and Alice also developed waking delusions. When I questioned her regarding the new development, she'd claimed that although her body woke up in the morning, her waking mind was always dreaming. Due to her non-compliance with her medications, Alice eventually reached a point where admission into a treatment facility was required.

As a courtesy, the psychiatric facility that treated Ms. Beaumont following her release from my care provided me with intermittent case status updates. Review of those documents indicates that Ms. Beaumont suffered from several sleep disorders, which then led to delusional thoughts and erratic behavior. When first admitted into the facility, Ms. Beaumont made comments, and acted in a manner that led her physicians and caregivers to note that she believed she was a college student studying for a degree in neurology. At first, the staff allowed Ms. Beaumont to read texts on neurology while under their care, but they were quick to remove the books from her room when they realized the severity of the delusions Ms. Beaumont was suffering. Her caregivers assumed the medical environment where she was being treated for her particular disorders is also what contributed to the delusions.

Through therapy and a strict pharmaceutical treatment regimen, Ms. Beaumont improved and was eventually discharged from the facility in 2011, when she was 21 years old.

Narrative:

On July 28, 2016, Lydia Beaumont met with me in my office to discuss the events in Alice's Beaumont's life, as well as seeking counseling for her eldest daughter, Delilah Beaumont. As my specialty is primarily pediatric therapy, I declined to treat Delilah Beaumont for reported depressive episodes, however, I referred Ms. Beaumont to an associate who can better handle her care.

During the meeting with both women, I was provided with information that disturbed me regarding events that occurred in Alice Beaumont's life following her discharge from the institution in 2011.

Per Lydia Beaumont's recollection and report, Alice Beaumont never returned home to live with her parents and family following her discharge from the institution. She sporadically kept in touch with her family up until meeting a man by the name of Maximilian Frost, whom Alice married. Alice moved into Mr. Frost's home and subsequently refused contact with her family. Her parents and both siblings had attempted to contact her on numerous occasions following her marriage to Mr. Frost, however, Alice failed to answer their calls or return emails or other types of correspondence.

From what little information they were able to obtain from Alice prior to her marriage to Mr. Frost, Alice had attempted supporting herself with several failed careers, which they believe may have contributed to Alice's interest and subsequent marriage to Mr. Frost. Per their information, Mr. Frost was a wealthy man who owned several businesses in the state.

The family had little information to give me regarding the events of Alice's life during her marriage to Mr. Frost, however on Wednesday, June 8, 2016, Alice contacted Delilah Beaumont and requested that Delilah drive to the house where Mr. Frost and she lived. Alice was not forthcoming regarding the reasons she wished for Delilah to pick her up, and stated she would explain once they were away from the property she shared with Mr. Frost.

Delilah Beaumont reported to me that the Frost property was located in a rural area of the county on several acres, the house itself surrounded by woods. The driveway leading to the house was approximately a quarter mile long and due to a storm that had recently flooded the region, Ms. Beaumont's car ran off the narrow road and became stuck in mud. Ms. Beaumont attempted to call for help, however her cellular reception was weak. Several hours later, while on his return home from a business trip, Mr. Frost encountered Delilah where she'd become stuck off the shoulder of the driveway. Mr. Frost was unable to help free her car and offered her a ride to the house. They had the opportunity to discuss concerns Mr. Frost had regarding Alice's ongoing difficulties and behaviors.

According to the information Delilah obtained from Mr. Frost, his marriage to Alice had been enjoyable for the first several months they'd been married. He commented that her sleep disorders were practically non-existent during that time, however after several small marital disputes, the disorders returned. He attempted to help Alice manage the problems she was experiencing, however he claimed the disorders became significantly worse which led to delusional thinking and erratic behavior. He specified his belief that Alice was unable to differentiate between her dreams and reality. Mr. Frost admitted to several incidents of physical altercations as a result of Alice's hostile behavior. He claimed the altercations were a result of his insistence on seeing to Alice's hygienic and health needs. When in a delusional state, Mr. Frost had to force Alice to bathe, eat, get dressed and clean up after herself.

According to Mr. Frost, Alice had become fixated on a small family cemetery that existed on the property. He revealed to Delilah that the cemetery had actually been larger at one time, however, following the death of his parents, Mr.

Frost had most of the headstones removed to make space for a back deck he had intentions of building. He installed a fence that divided the space for the deck and the grave plots for his immediate family, seven siblings and his parents. Due to Alice's morbid fixation with the cemetery, Mr. Frost had requested she never venture past the gate. Once married, Mr. Frost abandoned his plans to build the deck he'd intended, and instead made the space available for Alice to plant a garden. He never advised Alice that the space immediately adjacent to the house had been an extension of the cemetery at one time.

Additionally, Mr. Frost addressed his concerns with Delilah about specific fantasies and fixations Alice had regarding abducted women. Per the information he gave to Delilah, Alice would often watch crime shows and news broadcasts specifically seeking stories regarding women who'd gone missing around their county. Mr. Frost attempted to prevent Alice from watching those reports because, as he claimed, she would become aggressive, and on several occasions, he had to use physical force to keep her from harming him or herself. Mr. Frost explained that after watching the crime shows or news reports, Alice believed she was the victim portrayed, or she would blame Max for the disappearance of local women.

Upon arriving to the house, Mr. Frost requested that Delilah remain in the car so that he could go inside and determine Alice's mental state. He explained that if Alice was off balance, Delilah's sudden appearance could present a potential problem. He further explained that Alice blamed abuse by her family for many of the problems she was experiencing.

When Mr. Frost returned to the car, he advised that Alice was, in fact, having an episode and he felt it best that Delilah remain out of sight until the following morning. According to Mr. Frost, a tree had fallen in the garden as a result of the storm and had revealed a skeleton from one of the grave plots beneath the ground. Alice had discovered the skeleton earlier that day, and Mr. Frost believed it was a catalyst for the episode she was experiencing when he returned home. Delilah agreed to remain out of sight until the following morning and Mr. Frost was able to get her settled into an efficiency apartment space he was renovating in the basement of the home.

The following morning, Delilah heard screaming upstairs, but chose not to investigate until such time as Mr. Frost requested her to come up to see Alice. Within a half hour, Mr. Frost retrieved Delilah from the apartment and was walking her up the stairs to see her sister.

Alice attacked Mr. Frost, taking both he and Delilah by surprise.

Delilah was unable to provide additional details regarding the events immediately following the attack because she was knocked off balance and fell down the stairs. Due to trauma to the head, Delilah lost consciousness. She additionally severed her spinal column as a result of the fall, and is now confined to a wheelchair due to paralysis of her legs.

Lydia Beaumont was able to provide me with police reports regarding the incident. According to the reports, Alice Beaumont called the emergency line and was able to give them her name, her address, and additionally request an officer to appear on scene due to several murders in her home. The police arrived on scene at approximately 1:29 p.m. on Thursday, June 9, 2016. When they entered the house, they located Delilah Beaumont at the base of the stairs in the basement, and immediately rendered care.

A bloody trail led from the basement door out into the garden area of the home. Following the tracks, the police located Maximilian Frost's body in a shallow grave in the small family plot that lay beyond the iron fence. Per the medical examination, Mr. Frost died from trauma to the head, neck, shoulders and chest with a cleaver.

Police then discovered Alice Beaumont's body in the third floor bathroom that was set off from the master bedroom. Water had overflowed from the tub and soaked the carpet in the bedroom in the vicinity of the bathroom door.

Alice Beaumont was deceased at the time the police arrived. Per the medical examination, Ms. Beaumont died from self-inflicted wounds to her wrists and subsequent blood loss. Additionally, there were varied bruises on her body, both recent and old, that the Medical Examiner opined were common injuries associated with domestic violence.

Police investigated the scene per the claims made by Alice as to murders that had allegedly occurred on the property. No evidence was found indicating any such events had occurred, excluding the death of Maximilian Frost. However, evidence was discovered that indicated someone had been bound in varied locations in the home. Police suspected Alice had been the person bound per the ligature marks evident on her ankles and wrists.

Pursuant to the timing of the phone call Alice made to the police, the time of her death was listed as 12:41 p.m.

It was my opinion, based solely on the information presented to me by Lydia and Delilah Beaumont, that Alice had become non-compliant with her medications during her marriage to Mr. Frost. Lydia Beaumont further admitted that in Alice's childhood, her father had been abusive due to his frustration with Alice's disorders. The abuse by her father typically triggered a worsening of the severity of the disorders. We theorized that the physical altercations between Max and Alice might have had the same effect.

Prior to leaving the meeting, Delilah pointed out that, had her sister not called the police, Delilah would have most likely died, as well, due to her injuries and her inability to call for help. She was tearful when making that point, and she claimed that her sister's last act in this world was finding the strength to make the call and save Delilah's life.

This concludes the addendum regarding Alice Marie Beaumont. It saddens me to have discovered such a tragic and untimely end for a patient I'd enjoyed treating when she was a child.

Dr. Harold C. Chance, M.D., Ph.D.

THE END

If you are interested in reading additional books by Lily White or would like to know when new books are being released, Lily White can be found on:

Facebook and

Twitter

Join the Mailing List!!!

If you are interested in receiving email updates regarding additional books by Lily White or would like to know when new books are announced or being released, join the mailing list via Lilywhitebooks.com.

Join the Facebook Fan Group!!!

If you are interested in receiving exclusive previews for upcoming novels, or to participate in giveaways, join the fan group for Lily White Books via Lilywhitebooks.com.